Never
Going Back

Never
Going Back

Antonia
Banyard

thistledown press

Thistledown Press Ltd.
633 Main Street
Saskatoon, Saskatchewan, S7H 0J8
www.thistledownpress.com

Library and Archives Canada Cataloguing in Publication

Banyard, Antonia
Never going back / Antonia Banyard.

ISBN 978-1-897235-69-0
I. Title.

PS8603.A64N49 2010   C813'.6   C2010-900915-0

Cover photograph (detail): barbara miller/istockphoto.com
Author photograph: Jacob Dulisse
Cover and book design by Jackie Forrie
Printed and bound in Canada

Canada Council   Conseil des Arts
for the Arts   du Canada

SASKATCHEWAN
ARTS BOARD

Canadian   Patrimoine
Heritage   canadien

Thistledown Press gratefully acknowledges the financial assistance of the Canada Council for the Arts, the Saskatchewan Arts Board, and the Government of Canada through the Book Publishing Industry Development Program for its publishing program.

Never
Going Back

To my friends from home, who are both crazier and more sane than anything I could imagine.

Vancouver, British Columbia
July, 1999

SIOBHAN

WHEN SHE GETS BACK FROM NELSON, Siobhan will talk to the landlord about the bedroom window that's impossible to open. Lately she has woken with a strange pressure against her chest as if she might suffocate. The room needs more air or maybe it's that this new apartment is too small after all. What had once felt cozy now feels cramped and the romance of a historic attic hideaway evaporates about half way up the stairs.

"Tell me again why you're going?" Michael calls from the kitchen. The words are burred with irritation.

Siobhan purses her lips. "*Michael*," she says, peeved, and crams rolled up T-shirts around her camera case.

The thud of his runners on the wooden floor comes closer. She glances up to see him lean into the doorjamb. He sips the smoothie in his hand and fixes his pale blue eyes on her. "Well?"

"Like I said, Evan's mum . . . " she begins and when he frowns she sighs heavily. "My friend from high school, Evan. His mum Hannah wants to put on a memorial for Kristy. I told you about Kristy, remember?" Michael purposely forgets everything she tells him about home. "She's Evan's cousin. She lived with them all through high school. She's the one who died just after grad." She takes a deep breath. Maybe the car crash *had* been an accident. "Hannah thought that after ten years . . . " Even now, it bothers her that there'd never been a funeral for them to attend. Well, there had been *something*, but Evan, the idiot, hadn't bothered to tell anyone about it. Her throat tightens, which surprises her. God, it's been ten whole years, why's she feeling choked up now? "Hannah wants to do an anniversary thing."

The trip back to the Kootenays will give her an excuse to see Mandy before the baby's born, at least. Mandy might like to have someone around. After all, her boyfriend disappeared to Nepal months ago so she's on her own. Lance, the hermit of the bunch, might even join them. Last she heard, he still lives in Nelson, too.

She doesn't mention to Michael the letter that arrived two weeks ago, the day after Hannah had called. As she bends to pick up a pair of pants, the letter crinkles in her back pocket. She turns away from him and fingers it nervously. Despite a premonition about what the message inside will be, she can't bring herself to open it. She just knows that something — maybe the letter itself — is pulling her back to Nelson, whether she wants to go or not.

Her friend Lea had offered to drive Siobhan and Evan the long way to Nelson. She should be happy for the chance to spend time with her. They used to be best friends. She and Lea and Mandy did *everything* together. Now she lives on the other side of Vancouver. They get together for coffee sometimes, but it's not the same. As for Evan, well, she runs into him on the streets of Nelson every Christmas holiday and they exchange pleasantries. That's about it. You'd never know they'd been inseparable.

Michael persists. "But this trip is so . . . unnecessary. Can't you send a sympathy card or something? I was hoping we could arrange our trip back east this weekend."

"I thought we couldn't afford it." She yanks open a drawer, only to stare at the rolls of socks. "I can't explain, Michael, I've just got to go." They'd never talked much about Kristy's death. It had happened the summer after they'd all finished high school. There they'd been, on the verge of real life, so how could one of them die? But September came and they scattered, each in their own direction, and before she knew it, their tight-knit group was over. She picks up two bunches of socks and squeezes them together absentmindedly. It still struck her as unbelievable that Kristy was dead, that she wasn't somewhere packing her bags too, about to join them for a party. Kristy had been such a party girl. Siobhan tosses the socks back. What is she *thinking*? It's far too hot for socks.

"If she'd died of cancer or something, you wouldn't be trekking all the way across the province ten years later, would you?" Michael says.

"But it wasn't cancer."

"You're going out of obligation, aren't you?" He reaches out to grab her sleeve, then pulls her into a hug and mumbles into her hair, "You're such a good Catholic girl." He likes to tease her about this. For some reason, Michael thinks that growing up Catholic is funny and quaint, like black and white TV. "Too good."

"If I were a good Catholic," she mumbles into his chest, "I wouldn't be going. Suicides don't go to heaven, remember?" Her nose presses into his shoulder so she turns her head sideways and wills herself to relax against him.

"Well," he says as he releases her. "If you insist on going, you'd better hurry. You're late."

"Really? It's still early . . . " She squints at the clock by the bed. "Oh, you're right." Michael doesn't wear a watch, but his instinct is rarely more than fifteen minutes off. What would she do without him? She zips up her pack and follows him down the stairs to the front porch. He's on his way to jog along the sea wall in Stanley Park. Once she asked him why he didn't just jog around the park, which is a ten-minute walk away. "And jump over dog shit?" he'd replied. Michael is a pavement kind of guy, a city guy. That's one of the reasons he's never gone back to Nelson with her, never met her family. "Eight hours in the car?" he'd said in disbelief. So she'd never even suggested it.

With a quick hug, kiss and a directive, "Well, drive safely, at least," he trots down the porch stairs to the car and flips out his keys as he goes. He is efficient with his movements, always certain. Briefly, she wishes that he had paused, looked into her eyes a moment and asked her what she was thinking, but the car pulls out and he moves briskly into his day and she is left on the front porch.

After his car disappears, her shoulders ease down. Her pack slides down her leg to rest by her foot. She can almost feel her joints settle into their sockets. Now that she's alone, she can hear the morning: the swish of traffic, the twitter of songbirds punctuated by a crow's rusty-hinge croak.

She lifts the bangs off her forehead and glances up and down the street. Lea should be here by now, but Siobhan can't see her car anywhere. Lea *always* has to be late.

While she waits, she retrieves the envelope from her back pocket. She'd recognized the handwriting instantly. Now, the sight of it adds to the mixture of guilt and irritability that has dogged her since she woke. With a deep breath, she rips it open with the old skeleton key that hangs from a chain around her neck. The painting on the front of the card is of an angel holding the limp body of Christ, a dark and detailed image, moody as a Caravaggio painting. The message inside is simple, a typed notice of Albert Hiller's death, aged fifty-four years. Oh shit. There are no details, no how or where, but she can guess. The handwriting on the envelope is Mr. Hiller's, but inside, the date of death is written in another hand. His heart condiditon must have been serious enough that her old English teacher prepared his own death notice in advance. The final unknowable details had been left for someone else to fill in. The thought sends a shiver over her shoulders. It's as if he wanted to leave his affairs in order, to be considerate at last. She shoves the envelope back into her pocket. No one needs to see it, certainly not her friends. They would never forgive her. Some things are too complicated to explain, like the fact that for years she wrote to Mr. Hiller while he was in prison.

On impulse, she opens her wallet and fishes out a piece of paper from the stack of business and membership cards. The typing paper is thin and she unfolds it carefully so that it doesn't rip. She hasn't looked at it since she first read it, years ago, on the bus, and then she'd carelessly shoved it in her wallet to get off at her stop and forgotten about it. It had been mailed from Stave Lake Correctional Institute. "Thank you for your last letter," it says. "It still surprises me that so many former 'friends' no longer write, after all I've done for the community. But I can count on you. I'm pleased to hear of your definite plans for study. Photography will suit your fine artistic sense and will enable you to record the truth, rather than resort to the fabrications all too common in journalism. I am confident that you will meet Jesus on his way to Calvary and, like the two disciples, will walk with Him. You're a good girl. Yours, Albert Hiller."

In his eyes, she really had been a good girl. When she was little, she'd told an aunt that when she grew up, she wanted to be good. Her brother laughed and laughed when he overheard. He would follow her around the house and mimic her declaration in a little-girl voice. In the same way that Mandy wanted to be popular and Lea smart, she wanted to be good. Not obedient, she was far too ambitious for that. She wanted to be the edgy kind of good, the go-against-everyone-and-everything Joan of Arc kind. She wanted the supernatural goodness of martyrs who did the unexpected, who disregarded convention for the higher cause.

She'd been willing to work hard to be good. In Mr. Hiller's catechism class, this meant crossing her ankles and listening with a rapt expression on her face. It hadn't been hard — his enthusiasm was infectious. On her own, she'd read biographies of saints from the school library. In them, everyone shunned the saintly one except for the one faithful believer. That would be her, she vowed. Then later, in the Catholic youth group, which Mr. Hiller led, she eagerly helped to organize events.

But good was a slippery fish to hang on to. Goodness had a blurry edge to it. What if she didn't see it, and it slipped by without her knowing? She got so that she was ready to believe good was everywhere.

She is suddenly disgusted with herself for hanging onto the old letter and crumples it up. Her hand reaches out over the porch to toss it away. But the hand hesitates, withdraws, slowly uncrumples the paper and smoothes it down the familiar creases. Maybe later. She tucks it back into her wallet.

Just then a horn honks. She looks up and waves. With her pack over one shoulder, she crosses the street. Lea climbs out of the car and bops her head from side to side in an imitation of her old teenage mannerism. "Bonny-baby!" she squeals. When they were thirteen, Lea started calling her "si-bon" (and a thousand variations) instead of "sha-vahn" because she knew it irritated the hell out of Siobhan. Still does. But this is what they do when they're around each other, act like teenagers. God forbid they should grow *old*.

Lea wears an expensive crêpe sundress though they will sit in a hot car all day. Makeup covers her freckles and brings out her deep-set eyes. The last hint of wave has been blow-dried out of her thick brown hair. She throws her arms out. "Aren't you so excited!"

They give each other a one-armed hug, and Siobhan's throat catches against her friend's shoulder. "Excited?" she says. "Well . . . " Not really.

As they push her pack into the trunk, Lea groans. "Gawd, this weighs a tonne. What's in here?"

"My camera, extra lenses."

"Jeez, I hope Evan travels light."

"For sure, he's a guy."

"What, are you kidding? He'll have his blow dryer, bottles of hair gel and three changes of cool clothing for each day."

Siobhan scowls, irritated. "I think he's past that stage. Where are we picking him up, anyway?"

"The mall in Coquitlam. Didn't he tell you?"

Siobhan props her painted toenails against the dashboard and eases the seat back so that she's semi-reclining. "Haven't had a chance to call him. Did you?"

"Of course." Lea grips the steering wheel and leans forward with her whole body. "I'm all prepared, just in case Mandy has her baby while we're there. Wouldn't that be so exciting?"

"Well," Siobhan says and chews on her lip. "It would be different." Outside the window, the stores that line Grandview slip by before they merge onto the freeway.

"The baby's due on the twenty-seventh. I mean, she could be in labour right now! Criminy, what if there are complications?" Lea is the only person she knows who says "criminy" without being ironic. She stops talking suddenly and takes a deep breath. As she drives, her eyes flick back and forth from Siobhan's face to the road ahead. "So, do you think we should do something for the anniversary ceremony? A kind of tribute from the friends?"

Siobhan catches her breath. She leans forward impatiently to wind down the window. "The midwife can worry about complications. It's not like we'd know what to do." With her face averted, she leans into the wind.

Lea purses her lips, then shrugs and turns back to the traffic. "I just thought . . . "

Siobhan pulls her head in. She puffs her cheeks out then lets the air out in a whoosh. The timing of this trip couldn't be worse. Maybe she shouldn't have agreed to go. She needs to get an estimate to a client by the end of the week, and print up shots from a three-day food shoot. It's no problem for Lea. She's a teacher and gets the summers off. Evan's in one of those high-tech sales jobs where he's expected to work around the clock, so how will he manage?

He waits them for them in a café, the business pages spread out across the table. Siobhan still finds it hard to believe that he lives in suburbia, surrounded by 7-Elevens and strip malls. To her, he is still a back roads kid from the hippie strip in Bonnington. He and Lance were the weirdest kids she'd ever met. They were best friends. As they walk towards his table, the jarring contrast between the kid she remembers and the man across the room makes her so uncomfortable her teeth hurt.

Evan is not especially tall, but he carries himself as if he is, with his shoulders back and hands on hips. His once shaggy, bleached hair is now its natural glossy raven black, cut close to the shape of his head. The smooth angles of his face are broken by a neat moustache and a clutch of black hair on his chin. He pushes the newspaper aside and stands up. "Hey," he says and lifts his chin in their direction.

Lea stops him in his tracks with a hug and squeals his name. What can Siobhan do but the same? As she wraps her arms around him, she takes in a deep breath of roasted coffee and soap. "Hey yourself," she says. "Mr. Fancy Facial Hair," and pokes him in the ribs.

"Piss off," he replies. "It suits me."

"Sure." She reaches out for one of his silver-grey overnight bags while Lea reaches for the other. The bag bangs against her shin as she tries to squeeze between the tables. Evan packs up his laptop then trails behind, muttering to himself. Once outside, he stops to check all his pockets. "Wait a sec, I want to try Lance one more time before we leave the city." He flips out a thin silver phone and dials with his thumb. "Letting him know when we're arriving," he mumbles, the phone pressed between his shoulder and ear. He taps his foot on the pavement while the phone rings, then hangs up in irritation. "That guy's unreachable. It's outrageous. Downright irresponsible."

"Has it ever occurred to you," Siobhan says, "that he's got more important things to do than answer the phone?"

"Like what?" He holds his arms out as if to challenge her.

"Come on you two," Lea says. She hates an argument.

Evan agrees to sit in the back seat and claims he'll sleep the whole way anyway. He climbs in and promptly closes his eyes.

"So, Ev, what's your news?" Lea gamely tries, but he doesn't answer. She catches Siobhan's eye and they both shrug. Siobhan shifts her seat forward and tries to get comfortable, She stares absentmindedly out the window, at the big box stores that line the highway. "Lea," she says finally. "Do you think you'll ever buy a house in Vancouver?"

"Maybe a condo," she replies. "If I'm lucky."

"Michael figures we'll be able to afford something in three years," she says, with a mixture of pride and doubt. The week before, he'd roughed out a five-year plan for them. Despite his confidence, she finds the idea of owning anything that large incomprehensible. And just a little terrifying. Michael, however, is convinced — and very convincing. Hadn't he convinced her they needed to move in together? Sure, they'd been going out for two years, but Siobhan still can't understand the rush. They could have waited until . . . well, later. "He's got me following a budget now."

"Wow," Lea says. "That's impressive."

Siobhan chuckles, but the smugness soon dissipates. On-ramps and off-ramps shift the sea of traffic back and forth. This part of the suburbs stretches on and on. New subdivisions climb high up the mountain slopes. She wonders what it would be like to live in one of those new, cookie-cutter houses but she just can't imagine it. Finally, they are sucked onto the Port Mann Bridge and cars press in on them from both sides.

"Let me know when you want me to drive," Evan mumbles from the back seat. His eyes are closed but his thumbs tap against each other nervously.

"Keep an eye out for the turnoff, Bon-bon. I missed it once."

"I'll warn you," Evan says. "But we're nowhere near it yet."

Lea turns on the radio, fiddles with the dial, then switches it off. "Sorry, nervous habit. There's no reception past Hope anyway."

"What's to be nervous about? Mandy's the one who should be nervous."

"No, I mean about driving."

"Let me, then," Evan says, insistently this time.

"Don't distract her." She never realised what a jumpy driver Lea is.

"There's a pullout just past Hope when we first get onto the number three." Evan leans his head back, his eyes still closed.

"Just lay off, would you? Let her concentrate."

They are silent for a few minutes until Lea purposefully says, "So. Evan." She looks at him in the rear-view mirror, but his eyes are still closed. "We were talking about doing a kind of tribute from the friends at this ceremony for Kristy. What do you think?"

Siobhan glances back to see his eyes open suddenly. He shifts in his seat with a grunt. "Man, it's tight back here," he mumbles.

"Evan?" Lea ventures as she tries to catch his eye in the rear-view. His head disappears as he bends down to rearrange the clutter at his feet. When she sees Siobhan glaring at her, she hisses, "I was just *asking*," before she clamps her lips together.

"Well, he doesn't want to talk about it, Okay?" Siobhan whispers. "Could we just stick to other topics?"

"So, what's with the tie-dyed T-shirt, Siobhan?" Evan says after he straightens. "You've been living in East Van too long?"

She exhales with a short, sharp laugh. "Ha. You've lived away from the Kootenays too long." She hasn't seen him for years but already they are tetchy as teenagers, just like they used to be. In high school, they had bickered like siblings, but now it feels strangely comfortable. With Michael, she's much more polite. He would not be amused. Not that there's any comparison between Evan and Michael, of course. Evan's just a friend.

"Let's put on some music," Lea says brightly.

Siobhan rummages through the glove compartment and holds a tape in the air, victorious. "Aha!" she says. "A Mandy classic!" As a teenager, Mandy spent hours recording mixed tapes, which she presented to the lucky few like precious gems. Siobhan slides it into the player. The paper insert is stiff with acrylic paint — spirals, stars, and wee faces, Mandy's miniature work of art.

"Agh!" Evan exclaims. "I can't stand Tears for Fears. Turn it off!"

"Oh, come *on*." Lea's jaw drops. She turns to Siobhan and mouths a silent "Impossible!"

Siobhan sighs and ejects the tape. "Killjoy," she mutters, loud enough for him to hear. She rescues another mixed tape from under piles of insurance papers and tissues. This one is a rare Lance mix, the case decorated with stylized Greek letters, quantum equations, and depictions of sound waves. She pops it in.

"Ah," Evan sighs. With his hands behind his head, he settles back.

Lea's perfect mouth pulls down into a frown. She's silent a few minutes, then blurts out, "This Pink Floyd stuff is *so* depressing. I endured enough of it in high school."

"Why do you have it then?" Evan asks.

"Lance made it," Lea replies, as if the reason is obvious.

Siobhan's finger hovers over the eject button. "Well?"

Lea grimaces. "We'll have to entertain ourselves with scintillating conversation I guess."

The silence thickens like a cloud of dust. Siobhan leans against the headrest and pretends to sleep. Against the back of her eyelids she sees the dream from last night, a recurring one. There she is, in the cloakroom of her grade seven classroom. She's late and rushes to get back to her seat when she realizes she is stark naked. Everyone turns around and stares at her and she is so horrified it wakes her up, even now . . . and she's twenty-seven years old. That's what every day of high school felt like. Being the only one naked and you can't figure out how you got there and you don't know what to do about it and everyone is staring at you.

She thinks about this when she should be at work, deadlines pressing in on all sides. High school is a state of mind. Not a building, not a stage of life, but a worldview. Some people never grow out of it. High school is a religion, the most prevalent 'ism' around. Forget consumerism, or Zen Buddhism, or environmentalism. High school holds more power over the masses. It has the ceremonies, the rites of passage, the music, the trance-like states, even the ritual substances. She tried to explain this to Michael once, but he didn't get it. The bands she and her friends worshipped were the high priests and priestesses. It was just unfortunate for her that she grew up in a small town where everyone else attended the Church of Van Halen and AC/DC.

Then around grade ten, a small group of them broke away, became the musical protestants. Back then, listening to Brit pop was enough reason to get your head kicked in. They were the Chapel of Alternative Pop, they felt *radical*. They clung together, too terrified to do anything on their own. She can remember all of them lay on the floor at the end of one house party, and listened to an album with the speakers pointed to the little cluster of their heads. They didn't speak for the entire album. When they finally sat up, she felt such peace, as if they had shared some great communion. It was the most religious experience she had ever had. She knew she'd never grow distant from the people who'd shared it with her. Then Evan had ruined the mood by asking her whether she thought some girl liked him or not. He was pathetic back then. A relentless hunter.

EVAN

EVAN SHIFTS IN HIS SEAT. THIS drive to Nelson is really a pain in the ass. Literally. It can take anywhere from seven to twelve hours. He does some quick calculations on his palm pilot. They'll make it in nine. Shit. Going to Nelson requires *commitment*. What a drag.

If his car had not broken down at the worst time possible, he would not be on this road. But here he is, crammed into the back seat of Lea's chipmunk-tiny Toyota, knees up by his ears, listening to their endless yammer. He'll just have to chill and take in what he can of the scenery that flashes by the window. At least on this stretch of the country there is variety. The craggy-topped Coast Mountains rear up on either side of the Fraser Valley farmland. The wide-open fields stink of manure. Then they will drive through the Okanagan where the hills are covered in tufted brush, before they reach the dense conifer forests of the Kootenays.

He scans the subdivisions that spread up the mountains like hair on a man's back. Though his mother brought him up to hate materialism, he really wouldn't mind one of those big fat houses with a two-car garage. Some day. He had enough of being a back-to-the-lander as a kid.

Right now, unfortunately, he can only look out the window and dream of comfort. For a second there, it looked as if he would have a sweet week, but then the shit hit the fan. Or rather, the transmission blew. He'd been driving down the Sea to Sky Highway to join his buddy, Ross, and a few friends for three days of mountain climbing. They had planned to meet in Squamish, where they would climb that granite monolith, the Chief, then spend the evening sampling microbrewed beer. That's Evan's kind of day.

If he scrunches his eyes tight and ignores his aching legs, he can still feel how beautiful that drive up the coast had felt. His engine had purred like a kitten, he had an espresso in hand, and enough credit to buy beers for everyone in the whole damn town of Squamish.

He likes Ross and his buddies because they're so straightforward. They call a spade a spade and don't suspect you really mean a spatula. A spade isn't a phallic symbol of patriarchy, it does not refer to the capitalist hierarchy, it doesn't remind them of the spade-you-hit-me-with-in-grade-nine-and-I'm-still-offended. Because that's what it can be like with some people. Old friends for instance. For some people, a spade is never just a spade.

Evan opens one eye to a slit. In the front seat, Siobhan rakes her fingers through her fine hair and lifts it off her neck. Lea reaches over to disentangle Siobhan's earring. Siobhan starts and knocks Lea's hand away, then mutters, "Oh, sorry."

"No, I'm sorry," Lea says. "I just meant . . . "

Evan rolls his eyes, then shuts them tight. Old friends! With Ross and his buddies, life is simple. They even look straightforward: short hair, solid-colour T-shirts, quick-dry Goretex pants. He likes that. They haven't slept with each other's sisters and no one tells stories about the other guy's embarrassing teenage days. They don't look at him and immediately think of his cousin, Kristy. They don't give him that pitying look that tells him they're thinking about what happened to her.

That was the other great thing about his plans to go climbing — while it lasted. Their mountain climbing plans meant that he didn't have time for a trip back to the Kootenays to indulge his mother's morbid request. For fuck's sake, can he think of anything worse? Life is meant to be lived. To him that means having a good time. Does his mother seriously think he wants to wade through old shit again? It was bad enough at the time. First, he had to live with his cousin — his freakin' *cousin* — all the way through high school. He can still remember that day, just before the start of grade eight, when his mother told him Kristy would move in. That sinking feeling. And then . . . then there was the car crash and those awful months afterwards. He left that all behind when he left home and he wants it to remain that way.

But then his transmission died. He'd managed to pull the car over to the side of the road but couldn't get it going again. It just wouldn't shift out of neutral. Of course, the batteries of his cell phone were dead, too. By the time he had hitched back to North Vancouver, Ross and his buddies were long gone and Evan was in his white-walled apartment with nothing to do. Then the phone rang. *Right on, Ross!* he'd thought and snatched it up.

"Evan? Is that you?" It was Lea. "Hey, do you want to carpool up to Nelson? You're coming, right?"

Yeah, well.

In Keremeos, Lea pulls over to a fruit stand, the orchards just visible behind. She eyes the strip of market stalls that line the highway, then insists the peaches at this place are better than any of the other ones. Sage-coloured mountains rise from the edges of the fields. One hot dry summer when they were teenagers, Evan and Lance hiked along one of those crags and camped under ponderosa pines. He doesn't call Lance daily anymore, but he still tries to keep in touch, which, with Lance, is a challenge.

He was relieved when he'd heard that Lance broke up with his woman a few months ago, even though his friend was obviously bummed. When she and Lance bought the house together, Evan had felt let down. With Lance single again, they are all freer. Now they can still hang out, just the two of them. Evan won't have to make small talk with some stranger who has suddenly become a bigger part of Lance's life than he ever was.

He likes to keep his options open and can't understand why his friends won't do the same. They're too young to close doors. Now that Mandy is going to be a mother, they will all have fewer possibilities. Even Siobhan seems to be settled down, in a rut with some guy. Evan expected more from her. Don't they realize the danger of this? Now when they hang out, there will be nothing to talk about. Everything will already be decided. They will be paired up and mortgaged down — stuck.

Lea still insists on driving, as if it were a chore she could not possibly ask of anyone else. He wishes she'd just give up and hand over the keys.

"How many days did you get off work?" Siobhan twists around to catch his eye. She has dark-blonde bangs that hang in her eyes and a deep dimple on one cheek, giving her a wicked, impish look.

"I make my own schedule." In his line of work, promoting wireless technology, the hours are flexible, theoretically at least, as long as the job gets done. He closes his eyes. If he keeps them closed, he doesn't feel so carsick.

They stop in Greenwood for a bathroom break. Evan tries Lance on the cell phone one more time, but they are out of reception range. Cursing, he jams the cell into his back pocket and paces in circles around the car, then glances at his watch. When Lea and Siobhan walk out of the Copper Eagle with cinnamon buns, he sees his opportunity. "Here, keys. I'll drive while you two eat."

Lea climbs into the passenger seat. "Sure, whatever. I'm not picky." Oh, sure. She's the pickiest person he knows, the biggest control freak.

Once behind the steering wheel, he eases the seat back, adjusts the rear-view mirror and stretches his arm along the seat. With a practiced swipe along his T-shirt, he polishes his Ray-Bans. He tried cheap brands but the lenses were murky and clouded his vision. They never really cut out the glare of the sun. And besides, they looked . . . *cheap*. As he slips them on, he feels ready at last.

Lea turns in her seat to face Siobhan. "Did you call Mandy before you left?"

"No, why?" Siobhan sticks her feet on the back of Lea's headrest. Her toenails are painted bright blue. Long, finger-like toes. She should cover those up.

"To make sure she's okay. What if she's in labour already?"

"If she's in labour," Siobhan says to Lea, "there's nothing we can do about it."

"Well, of course we could, we'd hurry."

After rolling her eyes, Siobhan says, "I heard she's got a new guy already," feigning nonchalance.

"Yeah. Mick, I think his name is," Lea says. None of them has met Mick, but Evan wonders what he's like — this guy who has fallen for their pregnant friend.

"Hmmm." Siobhan pops the last sticky piece of bun into her mouth, then licks each finger. The movement catches his eye. She has slender, tapered fingers. Beautiful, really. "Drive faster, Evan."

"No, don't." Lea puts a bracing hand on his forearm. "Just be careful. There are so many accidents on this road."

Siobhan's head falls against the back of the seat. "Lea," she says wearily. "Would you just . . . "

He tunes out the rest of the conversation, which breaks up like a bad cell phone connection.

LANCE: QUANTUM CHAOS

THE PHONE RINGS, BUT LANCE TAKES no notice. He measures the distance across the top of the plastic-covered hole in the wall to make sure that the window he bought, months ago now, will match. As he works, he wonders about the possible consequences of installing a window. If he changes the conditions of his house, will he create some unknown effect on the other side of the world? A butterfly flapping its wings and all that, causing tsunamis in Japan? Stranger things have happened. Everything's interconnected. If only he had something better than this measuring tape to describe the physical world around him. If only he had some kind of framing device. But all he has to guide him is his own mind and principles of physics, like quantum chaos.

Principles, however, aren't going to install a window. So with the crude instrument of a tape measure, he calculates the amount of lumber he will need for the frame. This primitive method of measuring space is his only tool for communication — a blunt instrument, to be sure. But that's what life is: an exercise in bludgeoning the inexpressible void with blunt instruments.

The telephone, he thinks grumpily, merely amplifies miscommunication. It widens the already cavernous gap between word and meaning. He lets it ring and wonders, one more time, why he has the thing. Telecommunications are nothing more than systems for creating chaos.

Ever since he started thinking of such things, Lancelot Marley Jensen has not believed in systems. The Canadian political system, the school system, the system of checks and balances in economic theory, the sewer, the circulatory. Life is filled with too much randomness to fit neatly into any system. And everyone else is crazy for trying. Even as a child, Lance knew this. His parents certainly act as if they do too, but everyone else — especially in the city — insists that systems make sense. People follow them, like hound dogs tracking a scent, confident that a duck awaits them somewhere out there in the swamp. No wonder they are all so fucked up.

Lance, at least, can embrace the inevitable, omnipotent order of chaos. The randomness of people and events and feelings that fly at him from all sides. It is all chaos, and the best thing to do is just flow with it, float in its erratic current.

Lance understands this because he is an outsider, not part of the system. A bystander, really. An alien. He'd realized this when he was twelve or so, not long after his mother, Stella, had to stop teaching him at home. He believed in his alien-ness for the longest time because it made perfect sense. Stella was teaching him about the weather but Lance pushed for more about glaciers. He needed to know the name of everything. He wanted a field trip to the Kokanee Glacier, he wanted to buy Kokanee beer. She closed the book with a sigh. "All that's up there is a lump of ice," she said, but he wouldn't give up. "It's no use," she said, then called over her shoulder, "Frank!" That's when she and Frank had decided to send him to school.

Once he was enrolled, it became obvious that he wasn't like everyone else, and everyone else was not like him. It was not simply that he was still small for his age, nor that his hair hung past his shoulders. Going to school, playing with kids, answering questions in class were systems that Lance had no hope of understanding. "It's 1984. We don't wear velour anymore," his teacher told him that first day in September, and looked down at him. She was a bony woman in a skirt that had zippers that lead off into nowhere. "Even in the Kootenays," she added. But she was wrong, and Lance knew this better than she did. He wondered what was behind those zippers, what was hidden.

Very quickly, he discovered that school was made up of meaningless systems and schedules. School meant forms that had to be filled for no good reason, complicated procedures for simple tasks, hallway passes for taking a piss. At first, he didn't say anything. But when the social studies teacher assigned a chapter on child labour in Victorian England, he had to say *something*. What did Victorian England have to do with him? He needed physics, algebra, astronomy, not *this*. After the other students had filed out of the room, he stood in front of the teacher's desk and said, "Yeah. Uh, I won't be reading this after all. Do you want the book back?"

The teacher looked up, folded her hands on the desk. "And you're . . . ?" She glanced at the roll call.

"Lance." He held out his hand but she ignored it.

"You're the home-schooled kid, aren't you?" He nodded. "Listen, Lance. This is high school. It's not like home. You'll read this and you'll understand it for next class."

She spoke in a tone used for babies, but he heard a threat as well. No one had ever talked to him like that before. "I don't see how this could be useful to me. And it's not interesting."

She laughed and shook her head, then turned back to her papers. "You're something else."

In math class, he sat in a chair in the back row. As he waited for the teacher to start, he stared off into space, until something kicked his foot. It was a running shoe. He looked up to see a guy with dirty blond hair cut like a shaggy mop.

"I sit here, loser," the guy said. He was long and thin all over and wore a red bandana tied around the skinny pipe of his thigh. Two guys stood behind him. They also wore leg bandanas.

Lance looked around. His desk was no different than any other in the room and, besides, he was comfortable. "Here's an empty seat, you can sit beside me if you like."

The guy's lip curled and he drew his eyebrows together. "What the — " but the bell cut him off. He fell into the seat, his long legs sprawled across the aisle. His two friends choked on laughter and the guy scowled.

"Jason Lashinski?" The teacher looked up from her class list and glanced around the room. The bandana guy lifted a limp finger in response. "So pleased you could join us," she drawled and checked off his name.

From that moment on, unexplainable phenomena occurred: boys Lance had never met shoved his shoulder and called to him as they passed. *Hippie freak*, they said and from the way they said it, he understood this was the worst thing to be.

All that autumn he carried himself as if his skin was not his own. He walked on the balls of his feet; his limbs were made of glass. This human shell felt alien to him and so his real self must be alien to humans. He stumbled along on feet that were not really his, and his fingers fumbled with pencils and volleyballs.

He had to be from another planet, dropped here as an earthly experiment before the mother ship had moved on.

Lance read everything he could about aliens — comic books, magazines, true stories of sightings — until he was convinced. The night sky was such a comfort, he could pick out constellations faster than his father. What else could explain this aptitude, except that the sky was his real home? He figured his parents had been zapped by the alien ship so that they could know just enough to raise him, but their understanding only went so far. He was on his own.

He remembers one winter night he and his parents took a sauna. Frank had just finished converting the old Russian banya, so they wanted to celebrate. It still smelled of the fermenting apples that had been stored there in previous years, but the bundles of pine needles that they threw on the old stove would mask that eventually.

Stella was giddy and Frank jubilant, cocky about his self-taught carpentry skills and the dream of their own sauna finally realized. They were *living the life now*, he kept saying as he splashed a ladle of water over his back. It was one of those traditional Russian ladles, the kind the Doukhobors around here carved to sell in the local museums. For Frank, it was some kind of cosmic pun to use it for sauna water, an elbow poke to the previous owners of the property.

The previous owners were a Doukhobor couple and their seven grown children, who had moved up to Ootischenia years before. Their old wooden house was falling over when the Jensens bought the property, with black tar paper fading on the walls and mildew clouding the windows. After the heavy snows of that first winter, it finally collapsed. By then the construction of their new space was almost done, after many fits and starts. Frank or Stella had found a helping hand from every neighbour or acquaintance, anyone who knew how to hold a hammer.

They built spaces, not rooms — a modular house — spaces contained yet connected. Frank's space was open and barren to allow all the possibilities of life to enter. The bathroom bisected his module. Stella's contained low-lying, plush furniture around a yoga mat, with the kitchen at one end. Lance's space straddled the area between them, chaotic and cluttered, but ordered according to his own internal logic, with the TV squeezed into a corner. Then there were the hallway-like connecting spaces that gave a person time to adjust.

They each needed their own space, Stella explained to him when he had first realized other people did not live such neat and ordered lives. She and Frank had stayed together all these years, she said, because they always stayed a little apart. It was a koan, an unsolvable riddle she had spent many years rolling over in her mind like a pebble in a swift-flowing stream. We are essentially alone in this world, she said, and only intersect at certain points. At first Lance did not understand, but eventually he could see the beauty of it: sets, subsets and their areas of intersection.

Frank and Stella loved to describe the old Doukhobor house to customers in their shop. They had never intended on living in the original house, Stella was quick to add, it was *full of bad energy*. Their spaces were new, open, free of past associations. But, in another cosmic pun, they never finished the outside walls. They only got as far as the tar paper. Frank called it a sign of respect for the values of the Doukhobors, who denounced material wealth and pride. *When in Rome,* he said.

That evening they toasted the sauna. Toasted, drank, smoked up, and generally celebrated it. Stella had confiscated the water pistol, but Lance was allowed a spray bottle. He shot it at the wood stove when Stella's back was turned, and the stove vapourized in a cloud of steam and returned to the mother ship. Frank winked a bleary eye and scratched his belly.

His parents finally declared it time for bed. They banked the fire and trudged through the snow, Frank's hand snaking under the folds of Stella's tightly wrapped towel, her giggles thin in the crisp night air. Lance could see the steam rise from their shoulders like smoke, wispy haloes that disappeared into the black sky. He slipped back into the warm room, and continued his war on the stove. But eventually the drips from his hair grew colder than glacier water and chilled his already cool skin. He rubbed himself down with a towel, then perched his bare bum on the icy bench to tug on his socks. He jumped into his new white Sorel boots, wrapped a towel around his waist and opened the door, gauging the distance to his space. He wondered whether he'd need his jacket or not.

He'd just decided the jacket was necessary when he saw *it*. Felt it, really. A shadow passed over the bright moon so quickly it was almost as if *it* hadn't happened. But it had, right over Lance's head, just behind the sauna. He jumped onto the path to look behind the building, but saw only the last ghostly wisps trailing out of the smoke stack, the bright moon.

But there *it* was again, a shadow that moved through the darkness, a prickle up his spine, and he *knew*. It was the mother ship, coming back for him. The aliens had finally realized the experiment was a failure and had returned to take him home. He whipped around and stumbled in the direction of the fleeting shadow. His boots stuck in the snow, sucked at his feet with every step he took. He waved his arms frantically and screamed, "I'm here, I'm *here!*" until he tripped, and fell against the side of the barn.

"No! Don't leave me!" he cried as he picked himself up and brushed clumps of snow off his bare arm. He peered hard into the darkness until he couldn't see anything anymore. Clouds swirled over the sky, and partially obscured the moon.

He didn't even know he was crying until Stella wrapped a jacket around his shivering form and his wet face fell against her shoulder. And then Frank was there, and lifted him clean out of the Sorels as if he were still a small child. His feet dangled in the cold air as Frank carried him. The empty boots looked as lonely and abandoned — as alien — as he felt.

The next day he started building the snow cave, just like Charlie FeelGood had shown him. Charlie was Stella's former lover, but still came by for long visits. He was a musician but like all of Stella's friends, knew how to live in the bush for weeks on end. Lance found a high drift behind the sauna and dug, packed, and smoothed the walls with his mitts. When the mother ship came back, he'd be ready. If he waited outside, he could hear or see it better.

From the outside, the snow cave didn't look like much, but inside it was almost warm, with every sound swallowed by the walls of almost-nothingness. Snow is not just frozen water, it gathers traces of everything it falls through. He could see the dust of the atmosphere if he stared hard enough.

The days were short at that time of year and darkness came by four o'clock. He wanted to be out all night, to stay awake and be close to the sky. He lit five candles, then returned to Stella's space for supplies: a sleeping bag, a wheel of hard tack, chocolate and peanuts. It was pitch black outside but, through the walls of the cave, the candlelight was visible, a feeble, blue, unearthly glow.

But the mother ship never came. Even now, Lance is still earthbound, fumbling around with tape measures and blunt instruments. Installing a window so he can view life on earth.

SIOBHAN

SOMEWHERE AROUND GRAND FORKS, AN HOUR and a half outside of Nelson, Siobhan takes over the driving from Evan while he programs her number and Lea's into his phone. Does he really believe he will phone them?

"So, how's work?" Lea asks, poking her head between the front seats.

"Oh, fine." In fact, she had just sent off an application for travel funding to go to the Arctic. (It's hard to imagine the Arctic even exists, with the sun beating down on the car.) The trip up north, if it happens, is to photodocument icebergs. It's the first non-commercial photography she has contemplated since she graduated from art college. If Michael knew she'd applied, he'd tell her she's being impractical and he'd be right. She applied on a whim, out of a childish fascination with icebergs. They float around so silently, way up there above the Arctic Circle. She loves how they seem so innocuous — just lumps of frozen water — yet are so powerful and dangerous. But the trip will likely never happen. She'll never get a grant. Mentally, she shrugs it off.

"And how's Michael?" Lea continues.

"Fine." She smiles at her friend. "Just fine." She doesn't want to talk about him right now.

Lea falls asleep in the back seat for the last leg of the trip. "Brake before the corners, accelerate as you pull out," Evan says. Siobhan gives him a dirty look but tries it anyway. He pays attention to things like driving skills. She's never had ambitions that way.

"Why do I feel so old when I think of Mandy being a mother?" he asks suddenly.

She shrugs and steals a glance at him. His expression is genuinely disturbed. Though she's known him for so long, now he looks like a stranger to her. But when he says, "You think we can convince her she made the wrong decision?" she detects a flicker of the old Evan cross his face. He's very slick now, very urban, but now and then she catches a glimpse of the hippie kid — in his slow, deep laugh, or that unwillingness to look anyone directly in the eye. Always tentative, sliding his gaze away. Animal shy.

She smiles. "I think we're too late now."

"I'm not going to have anything to say to her anymore. Having a kid ruins everything. They're always crying when you're trying to have a decent conversation. You can't take them out to bars. You can't have any fun when they're around."

"Mandy's having the baby, not you."

"But still. It will make her boring. Listen, it's making me boring already. We'll have nothing to look forward to except bargains on diapers or mortgage rates. All of us."

"Maybe mortgage rates *are* really exciting," she says and hopes to convince herself. She glances in his direction. Her camera is packed away in the trunk, but her mind's eye snaps off compositions: Evan's profile backlit by the sunshine that streams through the car window; the curve of Lea's eyelashes against her cheek, visible in the rear-view mirror. Not that she's ever had the courage to photograph her friends. Nothing more than snapshots.

He slides his sandals off and sticks his feet out the window. His shoulders ease down and the wind ruffles his black hair. She knows that under that new and tiresome trendiness of his, the real Evan still lurks. The Evan with a slower pace, an easier attitude. Michael calls that attitude slack and lazy, but maybe because he doesn't understand what it's like in the Kootenays.

Admittedly, in their last years of high school, they had all taken it to an extreme. Always late, always casual. Siobhan perfected the heel-dragging, loose-jawed Kootenay kid shuffle. In those days, her crowd was so laid back, they were lying down. Their only ambition was to out-slack each other. Now she can admit how ridiculous they'd been, but still, she smiles to see Evan's feet hanging out the window. Michael would never think to do such a thing.

They pass the traditional brick breadbox-style Doukhobor houses near Castlegar, less than an hour away from Nelson. The Doukhobors must have been the original hippies, living in communes and walking around naked before the hippie generation was even born. Since the late 1800s, anyone who wanted to live in their own new way ended up in this part of the country. So often when Siobhan meets people, they exclaim, "Oh, I've always wanted to live in Nelson!" Or they lived there once and remember the time fondly. But most people leave eventually. Laid off, no prospects, the commune collapsed. Nelson is the small town people move to for the lifestyle. It is to BC what BC is to Canada. It's not a backwater town so much as an eddy in the stream, where a person can float in their own slow circle while the world rushes by. Most Nelsonites don't care if they miss out on the goings-on in the big city. Such things mean nothing to them anyway.

Besides, Nelson is where people go to get away from somewhere else. The area has always been a home for wanderers: English remittance men, Doukhobor dissidents, opportunistic loggers or silver-miners, American draft dodgers, and members of alternative societies. These days, Nelson is a strange stew of personalities: relaxed and uneasy at the same time. A small town with big city touches. Laid back, but politically charged. The slackers made you forget about the tireless few who kept it all running. Unlike most people, however, Siobhan didn't move there as an adult. She wasn't smug at having found the ultimate haven. Nelson was her starting place.

"Is your mum picking you up at the highway junction?" she asks.

"No," Evan replies. "Could you drive me to the house?"

EVAN WALKS INTO HIS MOTHER'S HOUSE to find his mother at the kitchen table, drinking tea.

Problem is, his father Gerald sits beside her.

"What's *he* doing here?" Evan says as his bags drop to the floor.

Gerald stands, walks towards him saying, "Ev," and grasps his shoulder in an awkward hug. Evan shakes him off.

"So, what's going on?"

"Well, I suppose we'll just tell you now," says his mother.

"Yeah, you will."

"We'd hoped to wait a bit." She looks at him and hesitates.

Gerald clears his throat. "Relax, buddy. Your mother and I have thought this through and — "

Evan holds up a hand. *Your mother and I?* That's the kind of phrase a *couple* uses. An uneasy shiver creeps up his spine. "This isn't the first time, is it?"

"If you're asking whether your father and I — "

He winces. Why do they keep on talking like that?

" — well, we have been reconnecting lately."

Evan closes his eyes. Could "reconnecting" be a euphemism for some carnal act? Or is his mother just speaking in counsellor-talk again?

"Well . . . " Gerald's voice fills him with the usual mix of conflicting emotions. "This is what we'd like to talk to you about, Evan."

In the last few years, Evan has come to a kind of truce with Gerald. He is finally at the stage where he doesn't feel like arguing with him every second. Maybe they don't have a particularly close relationship, maybe it's even cool, but at least he can handle it, at least it's predictable. A visit with Gerald no longer messes him up for days afterwards. But *this* situation with his mum, this is *not on*. The last time he saw his parents in the same room together he was five years old and Gerald was leaving with one of his students to live in Venice. Moving the last of his stuff out of the house. After that, the only communication between his parents had been the necessary phone calls to discuss things about Evan — money, shuffling him off for the occasional visit. That was it. As far as he knew.

He opens his eyes and takes in his mother's dusty collection of Guatemalan fertility dolls on the kitchen windowsill, and decides that he will just not give a shit. He waves a hand in their direction, says, "Whatever," and walks to his room. It's their business.

His room is not much bigger than a closet. Over the years it has come to look more and more like one. Boxes, piled up against the wall, lurch to one side. "What's all this shit?"

His mother's voice comes from just behind him. "This shit belonged to your cousin, remember?"

"Oh." Kristy. For the past ten years, her stuff has been tucked away in the closet or under the bed, where he can't see it. Now it's half unpacked, spread out over every available surface in the room. He feels the familiar queasiness at the thought of her. It's not as if he'd forgotten her because she is always on his mind at some level. But he prefers not to think about her.

Coming home makes that almost impossible, especially this time. Maybe, if he'd paid more attention in high school instead of just being irritated by her, he would have noticed what was going on. He could have stopped everything from happening. He could have . . . ? What could he have done? Nothing, that's what. He throws the suitcase down on the floor and pulls out his clothes. "So why are you unpacking her stuff?" The closet is full of Kristy's clothes, which he pushes, carefully, to one side.

"I think it's time to sort through it, maybe give some of it away," she says as she picks up a jean jacket and begins to fold it. "Sally shipped the urn up here," she says. "We talked about it a lot and she finally agreed that it would be better for Kristy to be with family, not some public cemetery in Fernie." She wrinkles her nose.

Evan looks at her in surprise. "So, where is it?"

"Under your bed," she says.

"Shit, Mum, could you move it out to the shed or something while I'm here?" He shivers.

"Well, *all right*. But that's not the point. The point is, Kristy's *home* now. Will you say something at our ceremony, Ev? Do it properly this time?" She waits for an answer, but he remains impassive. She turns back to the jacket and, with a gentle hand, strokes the angry row of safety pins that Kristy had fastened to the front. "It's time to let her rest in peace, and she'll be here on the property at last. Especially with *him* gone . . . "

"Who?" he asks.

"Hiller. He's just been given a decent burial." She sighs angrily, then presses her face into the jacket to breathe in deeply. "It doesn't even smell like her anymore," she murmurs. "Just the thought of him gets me riled. He was so obviously guilty, yet people still went to his funeral." She shakes her head. "What were they thinking? Even if he'd made some confession to God on his deathbed, does that just erase what he did?"

"The world's messed, Mum. Get used to it." The sound of water running through the pipes reminds him that Gerald is in the house. *Messed*, he thinks.

He tucks the now-empty suitcase under the bed. "Look, I don't give a shit about him. I'm having a shower, okay?"

"Say hello like a human being first."

He pulls her in tight, the skin of her shoulders softly slack under his hands. The familiar smell of patchouli fills his nostrils. She gives him a squeeze, then pushes him away. "Go. You're excused."

He continues to the bathroom. She's giving him time to "process things," he can tell. He wonders how much he'll get.

In the shower he can't stop thinking. There he is, back in grade eight, when Kristy first moved in. When Aunt Sally got together with "Uncle" Rick (Dick-head Extraordinaire), it had all gone downhill for Kristy. Rick had never liked her, and Aunt Sally was so absorbed with her new lover, she had no time for her daughter. So Kristy moved in with them, and Evan was told she'd sleep in his bedroom so that she could have space to herself. He slept in the spare room, which did not even have a door, only a curtain.

On his first day of high school, he couldn't sit at the back of the bus with his best friend Lance, as he'd hoped. Instead, he was stuck in the front seat, next to his cousin. She stared out the window and started whistling. She did that kind of thing just to embarrass him, to draw attention to herself. Then, in a high, thin voice, she started to sing. Something she'd made up probably, not even a real song. She was always too loud, too awkward, too tall, the kind of girl who laughed in all the wrong places, then didn't get the joke. She'd always been in a world of her own, couldn't read the cues that were so obvious to everyone else. She grabbed his hand tightly. "You're my best friend, you know," she said and smiled, showing the big gap between her front teeth.

"Am not," he mumbled, pulling his hand out of her grip. But he knew it was true. He was the only friend she had in the world.

"Thanks for coming with me." She kept smiling but turned to the window, singing louder. Living half way between Nelson and South Slocan, they could have gone to the small high school at the Slocan Valley junction, but his mother wanted him to accompany Kristy to the Nelson school. Kristy had struggled at the school in Fernie, so was now enrolled in the class for difficult kids. It wasn't that she was stupid, she was just having a hard time getting it together. It wasn't easy having a mother like Sally, his mother had explained. In this strange new place, she needed to see a familiar face, she said. They were the same age, after all, and got on well.

Kill me now, he thought as he slithered down in his seat.

For a kid from Bonnington — hippie country — high school was where he learned that he was all wrong. This made him a target. His clothes, for instance, were all wrong. The tie-dye, the purple, the cords and plush velour slacks were suddenly disastrously wrong. He wore black jeans, black T-shirts, and tried to lie low. But Kristy was no good at lying low. Her wide mouth open, gap between the teeth flashing, she shouted every word. He would only talk to her when no one could see them. At lunch, he looked the other way. But she was indomitable and grinned widely when they passed in the hallway, shouting his name in delight, like she'd never had a friend before. Maybe she hadn't.

As he lay in bed each night, he cursed his mother. He faced the wall, a hand between his legs, headphones in his ears, and listened to a tape. Pink Floyd was his favourite. He stared at the leafless trees that swayed meaninglessly outside the window. If he ever got tired of Pink Floyd, he hung out with Lance, who was a hippie kid just like him.

"Kristy's driving me," he would say, and Lance would nod, knowing exactly what he meant. That's why he liked Lance, because they didn't have to say anything to understand each other. They lay on the cushions in Lance's space and listened to the music without saying a word.

On the bus, one Friday afternoon, Kristy grabbed his hand and squeezed it until his fingers went numb. "I made the basketball team!" she whispered loudly, her face bursting with excitement. She held onto him as if her life depended on it, as if she'd float away if he didn't anchor her down. But he was in no mood just to sit there and be an anchor. Kids stared and pointed. As he pulled away, he hissed, "Kristy, *stop*. Quit it." But her grip was lethal, locked as a steel trap. A grin was fixed on her face, her dark eyes glittered. With a mighty heave, he freed his hand, but at the same moment, she leaned forward — maybe to share something more — and his elbow whacked her in the head. He felt bone hit bone, the soft plushness of her eye as it gave. He heard teeth clink together.

She hardly peeped. They glared at each other, her hand over one eye, the other eye gathering tears. Then she turned away and hid behind the thick, brown curtain of her hair. His elbow throbbed and he rubbed it, eyes to the floor. It was not his fault, he screamed in his head. Neither said anything for the rest of the ride.

It wasn't that he didn't like her. Outside of school, he liked her pretty well, for a cousin. For a girl. When they were kids, the two of them had always run off to play. She would do anything, unlike most girls. She had no fear. You couldn't say that about most of his cousins. She hardly ever cried, or whimpered, or complained of being cold. She was a trooper. Hanging out with her was almost as good as hanging out with Lance.

But school was different. They weren't crashing through the bush anymore. At school, everything mattered so much. Anything you said or did would be remembered by the entire student population and used against you. Which was why lying low was so important. Was that too much to ask?

Yes. For Kristy, it was. That day, Evan had offended her so she had to be obvious about her wounded state. When they got home, she walked through the kitchen — arms wrapped over her head, moaning in a low, but audible, voice — to the room that had once been his but was now hers. She locked the door.

"What happened, Evan?" his mother asked. He shrugged, pretending interest in his homework. She followed Kristy and was let in. For the next couple of hours, he listened to their voices rise and fall, cry and laugh. Finally, he was so hungry he made hummus sandwiches with endive and alfalfa sprouts — one for each of them, to show that he was not a total jerk. He just wanted to make it through grade eight alive and if Kristy would make his life a little easier, he'd be happy to talk to her now and then.

Much later, his mother emerged, red-eyed but smiling, and took a sandwich in to Kristy. Then she came back and sat at the table.

Kristy was staying with them because no one was there for her at home, his mother explained. Here she had the two of them. He was very lucky, she said, and should learn to share now and then. "She was just happy about making the basketball team," his mother said, her voice heavy with disappointment. "She wanted to share that with you. You should support her. She's only ever been criticized. You're so lucky." His eyes roamed over the unfinished wood that lined the kitchen walls, cobwebs in the high corners, cardboard boxes of onions and potatoes, broken blender, stack of second-hand books, and Kristy's discarded maroon sweater. "You're very lucky," she said once again and wiped the last of the dishes dry.

Only now does he know how lucky he was. If only he had protected Kristy. If only he had *understood*.

Lance: Entanglement

Lance hangs up the tea towel and puts the last dish back in the overhead cupboard. In his kitchen a row of glass and plastic containers that contain several healthy and essential nutrients line the counter. Every morning he drinks or chews these nutrients one by one and then heads off to work. In the afternoons he slices vegetables into very thin strips and eats them lightly cooked and barely warm. This method maximizes the absorption of nutrients. Working in a natural foods grocery co-op means that the subject of food is ubiquitous but also strangely absorbing. He knows more about the politics, biology and economics of food than he had ever thought possible. It fascinates him. It bores him equally. He works in a food store, comes home to eat food, and this gives him the energy to work in the food store, one more day.

He leavens the flat texture of this life by reading books on the laws of the physical universe. *The Elegant Universe*, *Black Holes and Time Warps*, *The Life of the Cosmos*. And, of course there is the house. Sometimes he simply sits on a cushion in the gutted room of the ground floor and stares at the four walls that surround him, all exposed beam, tangled rainbow-coloured wiring and pink clouds of insulation. These walls define the edges of his world, but tonight he needs to push those edges out a little bit. Frame an opening. A window that will look out onto the facing mountain and the thin west arm of Kootenay Lake. The lake is so deep, some say its bottom cannot be measured. It will be his view. Not that he can see it yet, because the space-that-would-be-window is covered in two layers of translucent plastic, old plastic that he'd once used to build a greenhouse. The pieces are taped together, the wide tape emblazoned with the manufacturer's logo, a kind of stained-glass window for a contractor. These are the first words he reads every morning are Tuck Tape.

With a dull pencil, he writes down the figures for what he will need when he goes to the building supply store, but this act gives him no sense of accomplishment, no feeling of forward motion. He doubts he'll even have the energy to buy the lumber after all. Because the whole purpose of this window was so that he and his love — Linda — could stand together and contemplate the perfection of the lake. But where is Linda now?

In one sense, she works in a government office in Victoria. In one sense she is a woman with neatly-cropped hair who wears navy skirts, nylons over freshly shaven legs, and makeup. She is the perfect model of a fully-functioning modern woman. But what does that Linda have to do with the woman who used to read Starhawk out loud while sitting on the toilet, who smoked joints under a canopy of bed sheets, who used her menstrual blood to fertilize the plants, who had not once, in the five years they were together, not once snipped so much as one hair on her body? What sense is there to be made of such a creature? Are these two women, in fact, the same?

And if, merely on the physical plane, This-Thing-Called-Linda can be one thing and yet definitely not that thing, what of her words? Linda had talked almost non-stop for five years, and her every word was uttered with a sincerity that could only be interpreted — at the time — as heartfelt. Even less tangible, even less measurable, what of the understanding, the connection, they shared? Had he got it all wrong? Were, in fact, the last five years of his life a dream? Did those years even happen?

Lance only has to fall into bed to know that those years did happen. Too often, he barely has enough energy to walk through the dusty expanse of the house and fall straight into bed. Sand, wood shavings and nubbles of gyprock plaster rub between the sheets, like sand in a desert. And each night as he tries to surrender to sleep, he glimpses, out of the corner of his half-closed eyes, the pink and purple ball on his bedside table. It's filled with sand, cornstarch, whatever. Linda gave the to him, "to relax and, like, massage your hand". Now the ball reminds him too much of his own sadly underused organs, so much so that he can hardly bear to touch it. But neither can he throw it out.

As he rolls up the tape measure, he knows that all he needs is someone to fill the void. Failing that (for he is a practical man), he will settle for the solidity of this house. So while part of him curses the limitations of a measuring tape, of inches and feet, another part of him clings to the paper in his hand and the figures marked there, simply for being something he can cling to. Hang in there buddy, these figures promise, if you stick with us, we will become a ledge you can grab onto.

But installing a window requires lumber. Lumber must be bought. Which is a problem. Reluctantly, Lance climbs into his van and backs out of his driveway.

If Lance believed in things like one "reality," then the "real" reason he feels so unenthused about going to the building supply store is that Jason Lashinski works there. And Jason Lashinski — grad '89 — had, before graduating from L.V.

Rogers Senior Secondary, beaten up Lance Jensen — also grad '89 — three times. Now Lance has to buy lumber from the man. Jason has married, produced two children, let his ruddy face swell with age and comfortable living. On the surface, he is an amiable, average guy, a small town, small business employee. But Lance is wary of him and has difficulty meeting his eye.

He thinks of this throughout his shifts at the Kootenay Country Co-op, as he stocks the produce section and sorts the incoming boxes. He remembers each of the three run-ins with Jason, occasions he won't ever forget. What had prompted Jason that time in the mall's parking lot? Or the night when Lance walked out of the 7-Eleven? Or, for that matter, that afternoon behind the high school? He can't say for sure, can't even guess. Lance had worn Fleuvogs. Maybe that was it. They looked like shit-kicker shoes, but it was he who had the shit kicked out of him, not Jason.

Now, from the distance of ten years, the randomness of the attacks almost makes sense. He can almost think about them objectively. There are, after all, many things in life that are uniformly random. And though he places boxes of tea — chai, yerba maté, and rooibos in the most neat and orderly rows, this act is a futile resistance against the inevitable spiral towards chaos. Chaos is the norm, order is not.

These days, Jason's grin is wide but ragged, because someone, sometime — not Lance — chipped his front tooth in a hockey game. There are days when Lance stands at the checkout till and is overpowered by the urge to ram a two-by-four right through that gap until it emerges out the other side. But he never does.

What holds Lance back is a fear that he and Jason are entangled. If two or three particles are entangled, they are mysteriously linked together no matter where they exist in space, far apart or near. Whatever happens to one instantly happens to the other. Lance suspects this phenomenon also applies to humans, to large groups even. And he wants to know with whom he's entangled. There's always the possibility that physical beating is enough to induce entanglement. Lance's fate is connected to Jason's, he's convinced of it. So today, he pays for his lumber quietly and doesn't make any trouble.

He throws the wood into the back of his old VW van and slips his wallet into his jeans' pocket. As always, he murmurs a word of thanks to his old friend, Mandy. If it hadn't been for her, he would never have been able to buy the house. His parents actually handed him the money, but it was largely because of Mandy that they had it in the first place. It was not much, but after ten years of interest, had grown to a substantial amount, enough for his half of the down payment. He slams the doors closed and looks around to shake free of the memory.

At one of Mandy's house parties when they were in grade ten, she had found him out back, smoking up. "I have a friend who needs your help," she'd said. At the time, he was still hopelessly crazy about her and would have done anything she asked. She had a friend, she explained, who needed to feel better and his parents could help.

At first he'd refused. If his parents ever had a bumper crop of weed, they were happy to share the wealth. Their land, after all, was a sacred garden where they grew their sacrament. But selling to a stranger? They'd never agree to that. Then Mandy gave him this sweetly imploring look and his heart stopped for a second, then started again double time. "Um, yeah, sure," he'd said. Then, when she pressed a warm hand against his chest, it took a few seconds for him to realize there was a twenty between their two bodies.

That's how it had started, innocently enough. How was he to know who her friend was? He never would have known, but one day Mandy let it slip, overcome by the delicious melodrama. "My friend is so sad," she said. "She said she, like, wants to hurt herself sometimes. I mean, she's got a *lot* of pressure on her." He felt slightly uneasy about accepting the money she handed over every week and gave it to his parents as quickly as he could, as if the bills burned his fingers. They never questioned him and he never questioned Mandy — he did *not* want to know — but she told him anyway, in a breathless rush. *Kristy*. At the time, they just thought Kristy was going through the usual teen traumas and needed something to blur the edges. Besides, who wasn't smoking up in this town? Mandy had more friends — the popular kids — who also needed "help." The weekly exchanges passed through so many hands, Lance lost track of where the money came from originally. There was even something empowering about being part of the underground economy. The underground, after all, kept Nelson afloat.

Then, when Linda wanted to buy a house with Lance, the money resurfaced. One day his mother, Stella, pressed an envelope into his hands and said, "You should have it. It's yours." Tears hovered in her eyes. The hugeness of what he was contemplating — buying a house! Living with Linda! — had him all jittery and distracted. He didn't think about where the money came from, just that he was overwhelmingly grateful to his parents. Frank engulfed them in a three-way hug. Lance had felt the gravity between them, the pull that kept them together as a family: three points in a fixed constellation.

That was back when he and Linda were still together, of course, when the world had looked so bright, so different, and he wasn't interested in sorting out what had happened all those years earlier.

SIOBHAN

SIOBHAN'S MOTHER STANDS IN THE DOORWAY to greet her as Lea drops her off. "Sweet Girl," her mother says. "It's late. What took you so long?"

"Nothing," Siobhan replies with an obligatory hug. "It's only seven, Mum."

"But still. Let Dad help you with those."

"I've got them." She struggles with her backpack, wondering why she never cares when Michael carries her heavy things, but hates it when her father insists. Perhaps *because* he insists. As she climbs the carpeted stairs to her bedroom, Siobhan knows she doesn't want to be here — in this house, in this town. She thought she would look forward to the change of scene, but now she isn't so sure. Before she can figure out why, her mother comes in. "You probably haven't heard the news yet, being down there in the city. About Mr. Hiller?"

"I've heard, Mum." Unconsciously, she fingers the envelope that she stuck in her back pocket just before Lea picked her up. She'd almost forgotten about it.

"How did you hear?" Her mother is momentarily confused.

"I can't remember . . ." she lies. "Someone told me. I think I ran into someone who, you know, kept track of him." His sister and her small group of supporters still believe he was charged unfairly, that those who laid charges made everything up. She doesn't like to think about it, so busies herself with unpacking the few clothes she's brought. "I don't know, it doesn't matter."

"This must be strange for you dear. He certainly was . . . *important* to you. You must be feeling . . . "

"I'm not feeling anything, Mum." She keeps her eyes lowered and zips up her backpack. "Do I have time to call Mandy before dinner?"

"Of course." Her mother sighs. "Poor Mandy, on her own at a time like this."

Siobhan rolls her eyes, then hands her mother the box of green peppers she'd bought in Keremeos. "Here's a little something for you, Mum," she says. She'd bought them for how they looked more than anything. She's always had a fondness for their glossy curves, for the photograph she could take of them.

One of her favourite photographers, Edward Weston, built his fame on photos of peppers and cabbages as sensual as naked bodies, or naked bodies as abstract as cloud patterns. At one time, she'd idolized him, and obsessively read his journals for a clue to how her own mind might work. The pages revealed the intense engagement and technical detachment that preceded each photo, for example, like the tear rolling down his lover's cheek after a terrible argument. He was notorious for his bohemian life, and for sleeping with his female models after a passionate session of photographing them.

He'd left his wife and three sons to pursue photography in Mexico with his mistress, a move that one critic called courageous. That word, "courageous," was what soured her adoration for Weston and his work. Artists are brilliant assholes, it said. She didn't want to be an artist if that were the case. What if you were an asshole your whole life, but in the end, had no brilliance? You'd never know until it was too late — friends betrayed, love turned against you.

Right around then, she'd switched to commercial photography, left the artier stuff behind. She couldn't love a Weston photo unreservedly after that. Now she's ashamed that she ever admired him, maybe because she could relate to him too much.

But when her mother takes the box of peppers, she is merely concerned with practicalities. "They'll spoil before we're back from Marriage Encounter," she says. In the morning her parents leave for one of those church-organized retreats for older couples. "That's very sweet of you dear, but . . . "

"Oh, don't worry about it." She takes the box back, then brushes past her mother and down the stairs. On the way to the phone, she walks into the living room to find her father sitting on his recliner, a hand hovering over the remote control.

"Oh, I thought I heard you pull up," he says, and looks up over his half glasses. Since the sawmill closed down and he lost his job as a foreman, her father has developed a passion for shows like *The Nature of Things*. He's never made the connection between his former logging days and newfound interest in conservation.

"Yeah, thanks for coming out to say hi."

"I leave those things to your mother. What's with the get up?" He gestures to her clothes.

She doesn't pay him any attention, and surveys the room instead. It looks old. The carpet was the latest style when they'd put it in but is now worn along the familiar routes. The furnishings look heavy, all dark, lacquered wood with the pile on the cushions flattened. Browns, oranges, and dark greens dominate the room.

Her father picks up his favourite magazine and flips to an ear-marked page. "There's something here you should see. They're making TVs with computers in them now. You should keep on top of these things." He has it fixed in his head that she is a technology buff, perhaps because she was the first person to explain the internet to him. Now with the zealousness of a convert, he knows more about any new gadget than she does. "You can check your e-mail and watch a sit-com on the same screen. At the same time. Isn't that amazing?" He says this in a reverential tone.

"And?"

"You can send an e-mail! While you're watching the tube!" He stares at her, incredulous. How could she not be grateful for progress, or at least enthusiastic? With a practised motion he pushes down on the lever of the chair so that his body propels forward. "Here," he says irritably and hands her the magazine. She glances at it briefly, then passes it back with a shrug. He settles back and lifts the footrest once more. A dreamy look comes over his face. "Isn't it amazing, what we can come up with?"

"Dad, how did Mum convince you to go to this Marriage Encounter thing anyway?" Siobhan can't believe her parents are going, that they've made such an uncharacteristic move. They are usually so matter-of-fact about their marriage. It's just *there* like her father's old chair is just there. Useful, but not worth contemplating.

"Huh?" He waves her away with the remote as if the thin black box can control her movements. "Outta my way," he says.

"It's been a slice, Dad, as usual." She bends down to kiss him on the forehead but misses. With an irritated grunt, he swerves to keep the television in sight.

"We'll catch up over dinner," he says as he turns up the volume and adjusts his hearing aid. "We ran into the Guiotto's youngest the other day, he works at the bank. I think you should meet him. He's . . . responsible."

Responsible means Catholic, but her parents haven't got too close to many Catholic men her age and can't possibly know what they are really like. Her father has never approved of Michael because he's not Catholic. Their disapproval is one of the reasons she's made sure he's never met them. Besides, when you're the youngest of five kids, you appreciate a bit of privacy now and then.

Dinner has been waiting for her arrival. She joins her mother and peels plastic wrap off platters which have been neatly arranged on the dining room table. Mashed potatoes, thick slices of roast beef and a salad. When she was growing up, they always ate in the kitchen. Now, when Siobhan or her sisters or brothers come home to visit, her mother serves them in the dining room, as if they are guests. Siobhan sits straight-backed in her chair while her father says grace.

As he serves, he asks Siobhan how she's doing. Or rather, how her business is doing. He can't quite get the word "photography" out of his mouth, so he simply refers to it as "your business." The idea of photography as a career makes him uneasy. It's the kind of thing that should only be a hobby. She can't blame him. She's as uncertain of her future as he is. For years, she has only been able to mumble about prospects, spec work, or how to build her portfolio, wondering all the while when she'll be able to quit her waitressing job.

But today she tells him about the new marketing campaign, about target markets and the anticipated increase in contracts.

Silently, Siobhan thanks Michael for giving her something tangible to report. Her father nods in satisfaction as he cuts his meat. Her mother pats her hand with a smile then turns to her husband and says, "Do you think we should pack our rain jackets?"

"The weather report said temperatures in the high twenties," her father replies with authority. He loves the weather channel.

"Oh phhht," Her mother dismisses him with an indulgent wave of the hand. "How often is the weather report right?"

Her parents have always been supportive of Siobhan in a vague way. The particulars, however, are not that interesting. They just want to know that she's settling down nicely.

Every time she comes home Siobhan goes through the same ritual. Her mother makes up the bottom bunk in her old room, tidies anything that might be out of order, and places one or two books on the night stand in the hopes that she will read them. The books have titles like *Wise Investing for Women* or *Living the Christian Life in the Twenty-First Century*. This time it is *The Artistic Approach to Web Design*. The web is obviously The Future. They've always hoped she would get into a field with a Future. If she has to be artistic, at least she could be one of those computer artists. Something that makes money. They are only concerned for her well-being, after all.

Siobhan strips the sheet off the bottom bunk and makes up the top one. She unlocks the cupboard, pulls out her favourite cover, a raggedy quilt made by her grandmother, and settles it over the top bunk. She slides the book under the bed so she won't have to see it every morning.

She reaches into the back of the cupboard and pulls out a figurine and puts it on the night stand. It's a cheap replica of one of Bernini's sculptures, *The Ecstasy of St Teresa*, made in cream-coloured plastic and clumsily painted, with the seam of the mould visible down each side. Teresa lies in a swoon, her eyes closed, while an angel stands over her with an arrow in his raised hand. There is a slightly creepy aspect to the figurine, perhaps because the blue paint of the angel's eyes is off-centre, which gives him a lazily deranged expression. But it had been a gift from Mr. Hiller, an award in catechism class. His wife had bought it from a street vendor in Italy, he'd told her, but a few years after she disappeared (no one knew she'd left him until years later), he decided to give it away. In the eyes of the church, he was still married, so he remained single. At the time, Siobhan couldn't imagine why his wife would leave him. He had boyish good looks, you could even call him striking. And he was everything: basketball coach, English teacher, catechism teacher, youth group leader. She wasn't the only one who admired him.

Mr. Hiller had been a great lover of Italian art, and was the first person she knew who thought about art at all. At least, art that wasn't a velvet oil painting of a stag with its hoof uplifted or trees in their fall colours. The kind of art he liked was foreign, old, obscure. When he taught catechism class, his discussions veered into enthusiastic lectures on sculpture or painting. He especially liked the Baroque period — all that outpouring of emotion. Siobhan sat at the back of the class but listened with toe-curling concentration. She just knew that he must be very smart to know so much about so many things. If she was ever going to be a photographer, she reasoned, she better listen to every word, because who else had such a *passion* for smart things?

He had explained to her the importance of *The Ecstasy of St Teresa*, and pointed out the way that Bernini had captured religious ecstasy. "You have a good eye for these things, I can tell," he'd said. "You'll be an artist yourself one day. Maybe a painter." She had nodded earnestly but in the back of her mind wondered if the replica's expression wasn't just a bit silly. But Siobhan had reminded herself that she just didn't understand art like he did. So she placed it on her night stand and with a furrowed brow, worked hard to appreciate it. After all, who else had singled her out and encouraged her the way he did? Maybe that's why she wrote to him in prison, because, in spite of everything, she felt she had to thank him. Now she looks at the plastic figure and sighs. Why does she keep it anyway?

Once she has the room set up the way she likes it, she locks the cupboard again. A call to Mandy will cheer her up, she figures. Crazy Mandy.

Her friend picks up on the fourth ring, her voice as smooth as a receptionist's. "Hello, Mandy Sweet here . . . "

"I figured that. We just got in. What's up for tomorrow?"

"It sure took you long enough to call." She can hear her friend sitting down heavily, sighing into the receiver. "How should I know what's happening? I just called Lance, but he's never in. No one tells me *anything*."

"You know more than I do. So what's next?"

EVAN EATS A LATE DINNER WITH his mother and Gerald. He figures that to sit at the table with both of his parents for the first time he can remember will not be a big deal, so he doesn't let it become a big deal. He doesn't ask for details from Gerald, who doesn't volunteer any. Which is just fine. They talk about the latest standoff between the loggers and environmentalists up the Slocan Valley. Evan can see the loggers' point — you have to make a living somehow. His mother doesn't see their point at all. "There's always another side to the story," he says. (She's used that line on *him* before.) "Someone just needs to go in there and do something. End all this sitting around and talking," he says and gets up from the table.

Sitting always makes him restless, so he runs water for the dishes. The washer in the faucet is loose and water leaks over the counter. "For pete's sake, Mum, how long has this been like this?"

"Oh, I don't know," she murmurs. Knowing her, it's probably been leaking for months. Every time he comes home, he has to fix an appliance, change burnt-out light bulbs, or throw out something broken. What does his mother do all day? The counter underneath is probably rotten already. With the sink still half filled with soapy water, he finds a wrench and takes the faucet apart. Typical half-assed hippie construction, he thinks as he inspects how the fixture has been installed. He will have to buy sealant.

"I'm driving into town," he says after he finds his mother in the living room.

"What for?"

"I need to get some supplies. The sink is dysfunctional."

She looks at him as if he's crazy. "It works just fine. I've never noticed anything. And what's the rush? Nothing's open at this hour anyway."

That's something that's always irritated him about living near such a small town: everything shuts down so early. In the city, you can get something done with your life, instead of sitting around waiting for the stores to open. He likes to get down and fix what needs to be fixed, without second guessing.

He drains the sink and stalks out the back door. Only briefly does he register the rural setting: a single coyote howl, the breeze still soft though the sky has darkened. More importantly, there has to be a tube of sealant somewhere in the shed. His mother and Gerald are in the living room — doing nothing much probably. Talking, even laughing. He slams against the shed door with his shoulder. Damn thing always sticks.

As he roots through every dusty pile, he comes to the conclusion that his mother is making a big mistake in taking up again with Gerald. At first, he'd thought, whatever, it's their business. But now he can see that Gerald can only be bad news. He has only ever cared about his film documentaries or, fleetingly, about his young protégées. What could Gerald possibly do here on this country road? There are no film-making schools anywhere nearby, and nothing much to make a film about. He'll end up a financial sponge. Evan's mother could lose everything. For that matter, Evan could lose everything. It had all been working out just fine with Gerald a long-distance phone call away.

But his mother never did anything for rational reasons. She'd be horrified at the thought. She'd always let her life unfold organically (or was it biodynamically?) and it never really mattered what Evan thought. She didn't consult with him before trying every crazy diet — vegan, macrobiotic, hypoallergenic — when he'd been starving for real food. When he was barely weeks old, she was doing pot and mushrooms to open her consciousness, as an act of defiance against the dominator society. He spent his formative years at fundraisers for causes he didn't even understand. Whenever she volunteered for the latest community crisis, somehow he ended up "volunteering" too. She continued sewing lousy wrap-around pants well into the eighties because that's where she was, creatively speaking. It didn't matter that no one bought them, that she couldn't afford ski lessons for him or new clothes. She just did whatever made her happy at the time. And apparently, still does.

His mother comes out as he wrestles to close the door. One more thing he will have to fix. "What are you doing out here? I need to tell you what I've planned for Tuesday," she says. She holds a pottery mug in her hands and the steam drifts into her face. "Some of your cousins will be here, you know. Come in and talk with us."

"I've already talked. There's no sealant, but you've got paint in there that's rotting. Is there a depot in town?"

"You just got home, Ev. Relax a little. You're always so . . . wired, like a city person."

"I live in the city. That makes me a city person. And there's nothing wrong with getting something done." Together they walk back to the house, but Evan stops before going inside.

"Listen Mum. About Gerald, I really think you're making a mistake here."

She lifts her eyebrows and sighs. "Naturally," she says.

"No seriously, you have to protect yourself. He left you once already so how do you know he won't do it again? And he's penniless. He'll bleed you dry."

"He has a few projects on the go." She peers at him in the dim porch light. "Don't you think I've thought of these things already?"

"No, I don't think you have. You're not being rational." He's heard about old people who make rash decisions — going to singles' clubs, getting married — because they're lonely. He's never thought of his mother as that old. But clearly, she is not seeing clearly at all. Maybe she feels sorry for old Gerald, maybe he's another bird with a broken wing. She has always been too soft hearted, too inclined to take those broken birds in. "Just think about what I've said and if you want him to leave, I can talk to him."

"Don't," she says. "Don't do anything, Evan."

He works out for an hour with his old set of weights, then stretches in the living room. First he has to move aside the clutter of houseplants, Guatemalan pillows, Indonesian throw rugs and Mayan clay pots. He's happy when Gerald leaves the room. Evan hopes that he's not spending the night. Surely Gerald hasn't moved in already, but he doesn't want to ask, because that would mean speaking to the guy. His ears strain for the sound of a car pulling out of the driveway, but instead he hears water running in the bathroom, then heavy footsteps moving down the hallway towards his mother's room. He shudders. When his mother comes in to say goodnight he concentrates on touching his toes and barely mumbles a reply.

꿈

He falls asleep quickly, but wakes to the rustle of cedar boughs outside his window. They are not so loud as to wake him though. So what has? His back aches from the lumpy mattress; he scissors his legs under the thin, pilled sheets. This is what getting back to the land really means, he thinks. Never being comfortable again. Never being able to afford decent sheets on a decent bed. Hippie shit. He rolls over, then a high squeal makes him sit up in alarm until he realizes it is only the creak of a hinge. His mother's giggle is followed by a lower-toned chuckle. The squeak gets louder and faster. The giggling continues. He feels ill to his stomach. He pulls the pillow over his head and hums loudly. An old Pogues tune.

In the morning, he's more tired than when he'd gone to bed. He stumbles into the kitchen and puts on a pot of water. He searches the cupboards, but finds no coffee. Instead he finds glass jars filled with loose and lumpy herbal teas, decaffeinated organic orange pekoe — what's the point? — a Swiss coffee substitute and an ancient tin of chicory. In the freezer there are plastic containers of cooked beans, mashed squash and stewed rhubarb. Perfect, just perfect.

He casts one last look around. The tins, jars and knife block sit in the arrangement that Kristy had left them so many years ago. The kitchen still feels like her room. At one time, she'd dreamed of being a professional chef, and spent her last year with them experimenting. Apart from one or two disasters, the food was delicious.

He remembers how, not long after she made the basketball team, she'd changed almost overnight into a girl with confidence and ambitions. All her lanky clumsiness disappeared when she was on the court. It sickens him now, when he thinks back to how Mr. Hiller set up extra practices. The thing was, she really could play and for a while she'd bloomed. Then something had happened — and she reverted to that awkward, dark girl again.

After her death, they'd pieced most of the story together, based on what came out during the trial and some guesswork. Hiller had encouraged her, gave her every attention, convinced her that, with his help, she would be a star. He'd started out as simply her supportive coach. Slowly, yet steadily, he'd closed in on her, as he'd done with several girls before. He would wait until they were of age before turning the relationship into a sexual one. Apparently he'd told her that she was special to him, but that they had to keep the true nature of their relationship secret. He must have convinced her thoroughly, because she perfected an independent, silent exterior and betrayed nothing. By her grade ten year, Hiller had won her trust so completely, she'd do anything for him. He'd been carrying on this same routine for years. But he must have got sloppy, or too confident. With Kristy, he couldn't quite wait until her sixteenth birthday —

Evan turns away. He just can't think about it.

The bedroom at the end of the hallway is quiet except for the muffled sound of snoring. Naturally. He walks out the back door and strides over the two steps that have been broken for years. His mother's car keys, as usual, sit on the dashboard where she won't lose them. Security is not much of a concern in these parts, but getting to town is. The car is covered in mud, he notices, and the clutch still fussy. Just because she lives on a dirt road doesn't mean she has to let the car slide into disrepair. Mud damages the paint after a while. Wet leaves have probably been moldering under the hood since fall. One day, she'll open it and wonder where the rust came from.

There are no signs of human life along Bonnington Road as he drives down the dusty track to the highway. Even the dogs barely have the energy to bark at the car, much less chase after him. Doesn't anyone have a reason to get up in the morning? Does no one have a job? This area used to be a back road with only a few houses breaking the thick bush. Now it looks more like a subdivision; a suburbia without an -urbia; sprawl without a city to sprawl around. Peach and teal plastic siding is the décor of choice — a far cry from the black tar paper of the old Doukhobor houses, or the weathered wood of hippie shacks.

Once on the highway, he drives towards the closest gas station. The man behind the till eyes Evan's blue silk pyjama bottoms and fleece sweater with suspicion. Years ago, Evan would have worried about getting beat up for wearing anything "different." The man lifts his baseball cap, resettles it on his head and raises his eyebrows, but Evan refuses to show the slightest reaction. Instead he grabs the largest cup he can find and drains the glass coffee carafe. "You're out," he says, lifting it in the air.

"That's an awful big cup you got there," the man replies.

"Yeah, well, it's early," Evan says as he puts a toonie on the counter.

"Nearly seven already," the man grunts. "Guess you had a rough night, eh?"

Evan shrugs and leaves the change. Typical of gas stations, the coffee is thick and bitter, but at least it's honest. It's not coffee trying to be a dessert.

He balances the cup between his knees and drives back to his mother's property. When he walks into the house, he can tell she's awake. Every window and door is open and she's standing on her head in the living room, balanced on a purple velvet pillow. His weights lie scattered around her. "Good morning," she says as he falls onto the couch. Then her eyes narrow and she slowly lowers her legs until she crouches on her knees. "That's not a styrofoam cup, is it?" Her voice is muffled by the pillow.

"Yeah."

She turns to face him, her shoulders slumped. "Evan! You know how much I hate it when you use disposable packaging. The cupboard is full of mugs. How am I going to get rid of that now?" She gestures to the cup in his hand.

"Throw it in the garbage."

"It's styrofoam!"

"It's one cup!"

They glare at each other.

Gerald storms into the room. "Hannah!" he cries. "You cut the lemon lengthways again. Do you know how hard it is to get the juice out when you cut it lengthways?" Grizzled white hair floats like a cape behind him, then settles to his shoulders as he stops. As usual, he wears a pair of faded jeans rucked up to the low curve of his belly. His chest is bare to reveal a thick mat of grey hair. Evan looks away.

From his few childhood visits, he can recall how Gerald lurches into each day by drinking a glass of lemon juice, cayenne pepper and maple syrup. He swears by it, claiming it jumpstarts every useful digestive process that Evan prefers not to contemplate.

"*I'll* squeeze it then," his mother says, sighing audibly.

"But why did you cut it like this in the first place?"

Evan gives her a look to say, you asked for this, but she is already trotting off to the kitchen. Gerald is an old man, stuck in his crotchety old man ways. Does his mother really want to live with such an insufferable guy?

He listens to them talking in the kitchen — his mother's voice calm, Gerald's belligerent. This is what she calls "negotiating." He has never seen her like this before — placating, indulgent. And frankly, he doesn't see why Gerald can get away with such a tantrum, when *he* never can. He's always thought of his mother as a strong, independent woman. Those qualities used to irritate him, but now he wants that independent mother back. How can she possibly want to deal with this for the rest of her life?

He'll have to do something, because he can't stand listening to them much longer. It's up to him to point out what's going on, because obviously they can't see for themselves. He finds them both huddled over the kitchen counter. His mother measures out a teaspoon of maple syrup saying, "Enough?"

Gerald scratches his belly. "Just a bit more." His voice is calmer, but verges on pouty. Evan can't remember seeing his parents in a domestic scene like this, their heads close together. There is something horribly wrong about it, something that makes him feel as if the floor's just tilted.

"Mum," he says. "He can make his own drink." Who lectured him on the principles of equality? She doesn't reply. "Gerald, what kind of stunt were you trying to pull there? You think you can charge around giving her orders in her own house?"

"We've come to an agreement," his mother says.

"Well, I don't agree with *this* — " He gestures at them. "Just remember this isn't your house, Gerald."

"Take it easy," Gerald replies.

His mother continues to stir the concoction and Gerald reaches for it eagerly.

How can she regress like this?

❧

Like a barn, Evan's consciousness had been raised, lickety-split, in a community effort. When he was four years old, his mother took him to her monthly consciousness-raising meetings with the local women's group. The group, of course, would never forbid children. How could they empower single women if they turned away their small boys? So while the women met in the living room, Evan played with someone's three-year old in the spare room. The babies stayed with the women, breastfeeding their way towards increased awareness.

The meetings, his mother explained, liberated her. They left her shaking and tearful. *These are good tears,* she was careful to explain. But she still needed her space afterwards. The power, she explained, came from bearing witness to the injustice of the patriarchal world, the atrocities committed every day in ordinary homes. *We have to stand up and be counted,* she said. So, in every meeting, each woman would stand and recount a personal story, then the others would respond with the motto, "A woman is not an object."

The seeds of harmful attitudes were planted early, so he needed to understand about these things now. Evan would grow up to be a new kind of man: an aware man.

"What's an object?" he asked her one time.

"It's a thing, like a chair. A chair is an object you sit on."

He was horrified. Did this mean he could never sit on her lap? This frightened him. Who would treat his mother like a chair? Why?

At the time, Evan's passion was race cars. It would have been tanks and bomber planes if he'd known such things existed. He hugged the collection of second-hand toy cars to his chest as they drove to a meeting. Once they arrived, he lined them up in a row by his knees. He drooled with excitement. Consciousness-raising meetings meant three hours of unsupervised play time with his ace cars.

He experienced a euphoric hour. Only he and the car existed. *Brrrrmmm.* But then he felt a tickle in his bladder. He had to pee. He clutched his crotch to make the feeling go away and pushed the car across the plywood floor. "Brrrmmm, brrrrmmm," changing pitch as the car sped up. Soon, the burning in his bladder was unbearable. But he had no idea where the bathroom was. On their many visits to strange houses, his mum always went with him to the bathroom. There had been too many accidents. Then nightmares.

He tiptoed into the living room and sidled up behind her chair.

" . . . this went on for years," a woman said tearfully. Her reddish hair was parted in the middle and hung in long sad waves on either side of her face. "I've always had such terrible PMS. My breasts just ache. He knew that. But he'd come up behind me . . . "

"Mum," Evan whispered. "I have to pee."

" . . . when I was at the stove, cooking dinner, and he'd grab my breasts." The woman demonstrated on herself, a grimace on her face. "And he'd squeeze as hard as he could, and pinch my nipples."

His mother gasped. Her cheeks were wet.

"Mum, *come on.*"

"Shhh." She inclined her head towards him and whispered. "It's down the hall. You're a big boy now."

"And it hurt like hell." The woman crumpled over and her hair swung forward in a red veil. "He always laughed. Thought it was the greatest turn on. Of course, it always meant he wanted sex, but I wasn't in the mood . . . "

~ 73 ~

A collective murmur of "No," rose from the circle. Evan tugged on his mother's hand, his legs squeezed together. He couldn't go alone. The hallway was dark. There could be a stranger down there. She knew how it freaked him out. He did *not* want to pull down his pants in an unknown room, all by himself. She had to be with him. "No, *you come with me.*" He stamped his foot.

The woman leaned back. "But he always got his way. I'm sorry, I can't go on today." Her neighbour reached out to squeeze her hand.

"Mum."

"I said shhh."

"A woman is not an object," they all said in somber tones.

"You're not listening to me!" His voice rose with each word until he shouted. Powerless to avoid what was happening, he felt a warm trickle down his leg. "Now!" His feet stamped as a pool formed. The tearful eyes of everyone turned on him. He cupped the offending instrument through his wet trousers and returned their collective gaze. He was doing something far worse than peeing on a stranger's rug. He knew this. But it was not his fault.

Now, after all that effort to raise him, her fussing over Gerald's lemon water is bringing his awareness down. He wants to tell his father to leave, but he doubts either of them will listen.

Now Evan wonders if his mother will also change her mind about who owns the property. If Gerald is part of the "family" — which up until now has been a family of two — he'll bring all his messy attachments and relations with him. That includes India, the daughter of Gerald's last official girlfriend. Is India part of this newly-made family too?

Evan always assumed the house would be his one day, one thing he could count on. But with Gerald around, that all change? Evan can easily imagine his father convincing his mother to sell the property to raise money for the next documentary. The Plight of the Alpine Squirrel, or some equally worthy cause.

The thought leaves a bad taste in Evan's mouth. He walks out of the kitchen. The sink needs fixing. Then he will drop by Lance's.

WHEN LANCE ANSWERS THE KNOCK ON the door, he doesn't question why Evan is in town, nor why he has dropped by at such an early hour. Lance suspects that, like he and Jason are entangled, so he and Evan are interconnected in some way that neither of them understand. While Lance will forever respect the wisdom of the forces that brought him and Evan together, he also wonders, with a small dose of despair, if entanglement is forever.

Evan stands on the doorstep and shuffles his feet. "I had to buy sealant," he says, and holds up a tube. "Do you know anything about caulking sinks?"

"No," Lance replies. "I haven't got to the sink yet." He'd ripped up the kitchen six months earlier and still uses the hose and washtub in the basement. Life was much more optimistic six months ago, and inertia was not such a strong force in his life.

"How are you, man?" Evan says. " I thought we could hang out for a while."

"Sure, come in."

The frustrating thing about entanglement is that this complete interactivity of two or more beings does not make conversation any easier. This has always puzzled Lance. A strong sense of kinship, of connection, surges against his chest.

In his mind he reaches out to Evan in a way that acknowledges all they've been through together. They should have so much to say to each other. They are linked after all. But for a few minutes, they just stare at each other. Lance's hands remain at his sides.

Then Evan looks away and clears his throat. He paces out the house, inspects the framing and knocks on supporting beams. "Cedar?" he says loudly.

"Fir," Lance replies.

"Of course." Evan nods and fingers the wood. "Hey, guess what, my mum and Gerald are back together."

Two more entangled beings, Lance thinks, but something tells him this is not an appropriate response. He chews his bottom lip. It's not that he lacks the desire to communicate with his old friend, just the skills. It used to be easier, but their friendship has rusted over by now, the social greases worn away by the intervening years. Lance often misses the nuances in interpersonal communication: the rhythm of conversation, conventions of speech, carefully controlled advances and retreats.

Between the inner Lance and the outer world is a thin but very real membrane that keeps the two separated. He feels himself bump up against this invisible bubble and mentally staggers back. Out loud, he says, "Of course."

He thinks to ask Evan how his mother is doing, but this only leads him to memories of Kristy, how she and Evan's mother got along so well. The weather should be a safe topic, but last winter's heavy snowfall leads to thoughts of Kristy and her white boots, which leads to . . . He stops himself and grabs onto the wooden beam in front of him as if it will save him. "The grain of this wood is fascinating, have you noticed?"

Evan gives him a puzzled look and is about to say something but changes his mind. He looks as if he, too, searches for a safe topic. "So, uh, how's the rocket?"

Ah, the rocket. Lance's shoulders ease down as he strides to the back of the house. "I'll show you."

Linda wanted him to throw the rocket out, but he could never bring himself to part with it. He has worked on it since he and Evan were thirteen years old. It's been modified and rebuilt many times, at first with Evan's help. They'd seriously believed that a rocket would transport them out of their miserable teenaged lives. Once they perfected the design on a small scale, they would build a module large enough for a teen. But they never even came up with a model big enough for Laika the dog. These days, it sits under a blue tarp. Lance tugs at the grass that grows tall around it.

"The paint's peeling off," Evan says, Curls of acrylic paint crumble as he brushes the cardboard-tube body. The lettering, Laika, is barely legible. But still, just looking at the rocket has the power to lift Lance's spirits. It never mattered where the rocket would go, or when, if ever. The existence of the rocket itself means that the possibility is always there. Apart from that, the rocket is a source of endless conversation with Evan. At last they can talk freely and easily. They reminisce over previous launching attempts and the hours spent in the shed. Evan worries about its bedraggled appearance, though there is something about decay that secretly appeals to Lance. He'd be sad to clean it up. The peeling paint is entropy in action.

Evan finds a few sheets of sand paper and scours one balsa wood fin. "If we just buff this baby up, we could try a test launch this weekend."

Evan was always keen on the bodywork, never the motor.

"Oh no," Lance says. He fingers the sand paper in his hand. "No. I don't want to launch it."

Evan stops scrubbing and stares at him, incredulous. "What's the point of building it then?"

"Oh, I know it will work. I don't have to prove it." Well, it sort of works, apart from a minor flaw here and there.

"Why not?"

Lance shakes his head. "I know it has the potential, that's enough for me."

"Come on, get serious. We've got to try."

"It's not ready." His hands tremble and he drops the sand paper.

"I can help fix it up."

"No. It'll never be ready." The great blank expanse that is Evan's face shimmers before his eyes. He gulps. "I really don't feel comfortable talking about it."

The rocket's construction never worried him, but there are bylaws against launching rockets in residential areas. At least, there should be. The noise would attract the neighbours, who would phone the police. The police would come snooping around, asking questions. They would want to know who he is. He can't let that happen.

He will only ever launch the rocket into the space of his imagination, because the biggest fear of his life is that one day he will be arrested. If he were, he would be deported to the US. His parents are both draft dodgers who came to Canada during the Vietnam war. Lance, born south of the line, is not technically a Canadian either. And then there's the small plot of marijuana at the back of his parents' property. Oh, it had seemed so simple at first. Of course it's organic and high quality, for personal use only. Now that his parents have, in effect, disappeared from the face of the earth, the plot has become choked with thimbleberry bushes and knapweed, but the original crop is still there, growing wild.

Then too, neither he nor his parents has ever filed their taxes. It's important to understand, Lance argues (to himself, as he replays these arguments over and over in his head) that in every other way, he and his parents are law-abiding citizens. They are merely looking for the chance to live their lives as they see fit in a peaceful environment. It's very simple.

This is the reason he smiles politely at Jason Lashinski, keeps his anger in check, and will never launch the rocket. To end up in the police station is the last thing Lance wants. He'd almost gone into the station with Kristy all those years ago, hadn't he? That would have been the end of him, but was, in a sense, the end of her.

"I have a terrible headache," he says to Evan and presses his fingers to his temples. He closes his eyes. "They come over me sometimes. They can be incapacitating."

"Okay, okay. Take it easy, man."

With his eyes closed, Lance stands immobile in the grass. He listens as his friend clears his throat then, after a pause, lets himself out the side gate.

Evan

BEFORE EVAN IS AWARE OF IT, he's driving down Granite Road towards Nelson. He drives loops through the town, past the stately, the ivy-covered courthouse, the low-slung mall crouching on the lakeshore, and across the orange bridge towards the north shore. At Six-Mile Beach, he swings a U-turn and heads back into town. The sights do not bring on waves of memory or anything corny like that. They do not affect him much at all. They are just buildings. Streets. Stop signs. He drives up hills and down, the routes so familiar he does not even have to think of where to turn. The old high school looms up on his left but he barely glances at it. Shrugs. It's simply a brick building, smaller now than it once seemed.

So much, he tells himself, for hanging out with Lance. That turned out to be a bust. Lance has always been a bit wacky, but that had never mattered because he was fun to be around. Back when they were kids, Lance was the one to take risks, to pull the weirdest stunts, and he never worried for a moment about the consequences or what anyone thought. But now he never does anything except go to his dead-end job and come back to his unfinished house. It's as if he's lost his nerve. What happened?

He wonders where to go next, then finds himself on the familiar route to Siobhan's house.

SIOBHAN

SIOBHAN WAKES TO BANGING DOORS AND breakfast noises. Her parents' car is packed by the time she makes it to the bottom of the stairs. Her mother kisses her cheek on her way to the front door. "Sweet Girl," she says then frowns. "There's no point in you driving all this way on the one weekend we're out of town."

"I'll be here when you get back. You'll get sick of me quickly enough," Siobhan says and follows them out the door. "You'll be happy to have your house back to yourself once I've gone."

Her mother lists specific instructions for watering plants, the weekend rotation of household chores, which prepared meals are waiting in what compartment of the freezer. As Siobhan stands on the sidewalk, every instruction slips out of her mind. She thinks of how the pavement presses into her bare feet, how her pyjamas flutter in the morning breeze.

Her mother sticks her head out of the car window and waves. "Have a wonderful time. Be a good girl." Siobhan waves back. Does her mother think this incantation will ward off the wild drug-addled orgies that her youngest daughter would otherwise be having?

"Likewise," Siobhan says. "On both counts." She turns back to the house.

"I'll say a prayer for Mandy," her mother calls out as the car pulls away.

Once inside, she falls into her father's chair, and pulls the lever to lift the footrest. It's an ugly chair, not as comfortable as she'd remembered. The fake leather is too hideous for this day and age. Do her parents not realize this? She tries closing her eyes, but she can't fall asleep. One ear is open for the sounds of Rat the cat. He should be stalking into the room any minute now, but then she remembers that he's dead. A movement out of the corner of her eye makes her jump, but it's only the curtains in the breeze.

She wanders the empty house, holding her breath in the unusual silence. Without the noise of other people, the house is a foreign landscape, strange in its eerie familiarity. She opens the door to each of the four bedrooms. *What a mess Mum has made,* she thinks. Not that it's untidy. That's the problem. It's organized to the point of lifelessness. That's it, she decides, it has lost its essential funkiness. The record player is tightly packed into a corner of the living room, speakers side by side. It's covered in a quilted throw. Have they never heard of *stereo?*

Usually, as soon as Siobhan enters her parents' home, she is overcome with a mysterious yet overpowering lethargy. No matter how tidy she is in her own apartment, at her mother's house she collapses on the couch with a groan, incapable of lifting a finger. She might contemplate gathering up the dirty cups off the coffee table, but the thought alone will exhaust her. For the duration of her visit she will be struck down with a bad case of Living With Mum.

This time, a sense of purpose surges through her. She unplugs wires and rearranges the speakers to allow for the best sound. They will thank her when they come home. The phone rings but she ignores it. No one with any decency should call at this hour, so she certainly isn't going to answer. Maybe it's Michael who, since they've moved in together, insists on daily checkups whenever they are apart. He's sweet to be concerned of course, but there's something fuddy-duddy about the routine of it. Her parents don't even have an answering machine and she's suddenly delighted with that fact. Oh, the joy of being unreachable.

Michael was the furthest thing from fuddy-duddy when they'd first met five years ago. She had been shopping at the Sally Ann when they both reached for the same jacket. This impressed her right away. By the time they'd left the thrift shop, he'd written his phone number on her hand, with the agreement that they'd share custody of the jacket. It was an obvious ploy on his part, but she'd willingly fallen for it. How gallant, she'd thought, how original. He was in his final year of film school, three years out of Ontario and more BCish than she was: unironed, uncombed and unscheduled. She'd never realized it before, but now that she thinks about it, since that day he hasn't stepped into a thrift store. She can see how he's been reverting to the preppy look of his private school years, even gleaning fashion tips from the style pages of the *Globe & Mail*. Lately, he'd been talking a lot about getting real, about growing up. It was fine to live like a bum while they were students, he told her, but they're older now.

A couple of weeks ago, when she'd bounced back from the vintage clothing store with her latest find, he'd smiled indulgently, but shook his head. "Check it out!" she cried, twirling around in the forty-year-old, tulip-skirted dress. "Only fifteen bucks!"

"The clothes make the man," he replied and when she pointed out that she wasn't a man, he shrugged. "Still. Clients can't take you seriously in an outfit like that."

"But it's perfect for an opening," she replied, though she knew he was right. The brightly-coloured pattern didn't exactly say "professional." Besides, when was the last time she'd gone to an opening, much less one of her own work? She hung the dress in the back of the closet and joined him at the table where he was working on their five-year business plan.

Getting real meant setting goals and making realistic plans for their future. The plan included moving back to Ontario, where Michael's father had offered him a partnership in his real estate development company. After two years as a cameraman and still only doing day calls, it only made sense for him to accept. In Ontario, they'd be able to buy a house some day, something they could never do in Vancouver with its sky-high prices and limited job market. She'd be lost without Michael, she reminded herself. Penniless, at the least.

She stares at her parents' old furniture, and feels dull. Bored. What is she doing as a photographer anyway? Nothing. Well, not exactly nothing: she's paying bills. Getting and spending, that's what she's doing — but she could get tired of the tidy little life she and Michael are creating. As a teenager, she had such huge ambitions of making the big time in photography. People would see her photographs and be changed. Would be amazed. But after a few early disappointments and years of frustrations, those ambitions failed to inspire her, leaving her crushed and hopeless instead, a failure. So, with Michael's help, she got hard headed about life. She left art college behind and got down to being practical. She cultivated commercial clientele, threw out her snobbish arty ideals and got down to the bread-and-butter jobs. After a couple of years, she bought a real couch on credit because she could actually get credit for the first time in her life. What peace of mind. The real couch made her feel considerably better about the shitty East Vancouver house she shared with four other artists.

Then, she and Michael had moved in together. They found a cute, affordable suite — still in East Van, but not shitty at all. She threw out her crumb-infested, fuse-blowing toaster oven because he had a new, stainless steel microwave. The day they bought a cappuccino machine together, she knew she'd crossed some invisible threshold. She was a real person, finally.

But in spite of this, after she waves Michael off to work, she has taken to lingering over her morning latte. She's been getting to the photography studio later and later each day. She finds excuses to run pointless errands along the way. Last week she sat down in the unlit studio, and for an hour or more stared at the shuttered windows, asking herself, *now what?* and *what was my point, again?* She doesn't want to go back to idealism and scrounging, but is this dull feeling the only alternative?

She rubs the sleep out of her eyes. Enough of angsting. Her stomach rumbles. Leafing through the family collection of vinyl, she finds an old Supertramp album, a favourite when she was seven years old. She puts it on the turntable. Breakfast music. As she wanders into the kitchen, she hears someone pound on the front door.

Evan stands at her door and knocks like crazy. Knocks and knocks and knocks, not knowing why he's ended up *here* of all places. He just wants to talk to someone uncomplicated. He wants a conversation with no undercurrents, no traumas, no obligations. Siobhan has always been cool. Hanging out with her is as easy as hanging out with a guy. He's hungry. He'd pulled up and saw movement through an open window, so that decided it.

The door swings open and she stands there and blinks. "What are you doing here?"

He shrugs. "Driving around, tried to hang out with Lance." He doesn't bother to elaborate. She wears an old tank top and baggy pyjama bottoms that hang off her square hips. Her hair falls to her shoulders and, at the back, is slept into a bird's nest. Her shoulders are startlingly bony, wide and sharp. He notices a small cluster of moles on the white skin of her collarbone and can't take his eyes off them. Have they always been there? Why has he never noticed them before? Oh. Yes. Because he's never seen her naked. She is one of those rare women: one he's known for years, who still talks to him and counts him as a friend. The kind of woman who steps to one side and says, "Well come in then. I was thinking vaguely about eating. Interested?"

"Yeah." He walks past, fists in his pockets. He scans the walls, the bookcase, the framed assortment of family photos. Studio photos of the family dog. A grey cat on an orange bedspread. Siobhan on Santa's knee in the mall, though by the time the mall was built, she was already too big and embarrassed for Santa's knee. The carpet is thick brown shag, the hallway walls the colour of dark honey. *Is it possible that Siobhan's attractive?* he wonders. Is she beautiful, or just plain? He's never thought about it before. He glances back at her. She looks different.

Not that she makes an effort to attract, not so far as he can tell. She pushes past him into the kitchen, then raises her arms high to reveal stubbly armpits. She yawns. "Gawd, my parents woke me up at the crack of dawn." She rubs her face and scratches her head, which messes her hair further. Round-shouldered, she slumps to the fridge. He pulls out a chair and sits at the yellow melamine table.

"Would you like eggs?" she asks into the fridge.

"Sure." Then he hears awful noises coming from the living room. Noises best left un-amplified. "Am I hearing what I think I'm hearing?"

"What, me slaving my butt off to make your breakfast?" She slams the fridge door.

"No, late seventies crap music. Is that what this is?" He gestures towards the living room. "There are lots of new recordings out there you know. Music has advanced in leaps and bounds in the last twenty years."

"It's all my parents have, seventies crap and eighties crap. All in vinyl."

Two thickly carpeted stairs separate the sunken living room from the dining room, which he takes in one long stride. He might be acting like an asshole — there she is, making breakfast — but he can't stop it. He comes by it honestly. And besides, the music is truly awful, falsetto voices, cheesy guitar riffs. He had the album once, or did Gerald? Fall-coloured afghans cover the couch and chairs, all in polyester knits that promise static shocks. Once the needle lifts off the record, he feels better. He runs his finger across the spine of each album. They are stacked neatly, but in no apparent order. He wants to hear something that will take him elsewhere, somewhere comfortable. Choosing a record has always been a weighty decision. Part of his mind argues that the choice is meaningless. No, music is not meaningless at all. Each album is a conversation. It's loaded with memories and emotions and reflects the personalities of everyone involved — her parents for keeping the album, his for choosing it, Siobhan's for responding. The right music sets the right mood for the right sequence of events to happen. And those events would be . . . ? They can be whatever he wants them to be, provided he chooses the right album. His neck aches from craning it sideways. He pulls out a classic Meatloaf album and sits on a chair to read the liner notes.

In the next second, he feels a tap on his leg and opens his eyes to see Siobhan standing over him, a plate in each hand. She looks at him quizzically. For a second, he can't make out where he is. He has that panicked, disoriented feeling that comes after a deep daytime sleep. For a while there — a minute? an hour? — he'd been far, far away. The dream is forgotten instantly, but leaves him with a warm feeling. He feels an intense longing, the urge to scratch a deeply-buried itch.

Instead, he stares at her uncomprehendingly. She puts the plates on the coffee table. "You okay? Sorry I woke you."

"No problem." She has made the eggs exactly how his mother does — over easy with the eggs on the toast, not on the side, and rings of tomatoes. Is there something significant in this, he wonders. It strikes him as an omen; he can't move.

She curls her legs under her and sits cross-legged on the floor. "So, did Mandy get hold of you?"

"Huh? No. Maybe."

"Well, we're having lunch at her place. Come on, eat, it's getting cold."

"Wait a minute, Siobhan. I mean . . . Do you always make eggs this way?" He searches her face. "I've got to know, it's important."

She tilts her head. "You know, I used to think Lance was the weird one and you were almost normal."

At this, he sits on the floor opposite her and eats. Perhaps everything that happens to him is meaningless after all. Life is a series of coincidences and there's no higher meaning. He's too serious about everything: his mum, Gerald, Kristy, Siobhan. As soon as he starts to care so much about everything and everyone, he gets into trouble.

She has a funny little smile on her face, but keeps her eyes lowered. It's strange, he thinks, to eat breakfast with a woman in her pyjamas when he hasn't slept with her. Now, he wishes he had. A woman he's known since she was flat as the Prairies, who spewed her way through their grad party, who might even have saved him from drowning one time in the Kootenay River. To sit there with her is strange, but whether in a good or bad way, he can't say. At the age they are now, he thinks with a start, his mum and Gerald had already broken up and had a five-year-old kid. Him.

Whoa.

"So, you have any plans for while you're up here?" she says. "I mean, other than . . ."

He fiddles with the fork in his hand. "Not really. I might help my mum fix some things around the house, but . . ." he shrugs. "Haven't thought about it."

"Yeah. I was thinking of developing and printing some of my old photos while I'm here. There's still darkroom gear in the basement."

"Wicked."

"But now I'm too lazy to do anything. Nelson does that to me."

"Yeah." They eat in silence.

"I'm looking forward to seeing your mum. She must be lonely living way out there by herself."

Fuck. For a second, he'd forgotten about Kristy, or Gerald and his mother. He gets up and carries their empty plates into the kitchen. She follows, then pours a glass of juice and rests a hip against the counter as he washes the dishes. She's saying something about photos, or negatives, or whatever she's saying. He dries his hands, but something bugs him. What exactly is he doing here? He needs to know if the look she is giving him is one of simple confusion, or an invitation? He doesn't want to stand there with a dishtowel in his hands. He wants to go upstairs and lie down on her bed and he wants her to hold him. He is so tired. He wants to put his cheek against that constellation on her collarbone. He knows there's a guy she lives with, a guy who seemed pretty cool the one time they'd met, but this is more important. Evan's purpose is suddenly crystal clear. His life has lead him up to this moment. To Siobhan with her dirty-blonde hair and long toes and sharp collarbones.

"Siobhan?"

"You want some juice?"

"No." He shakes his head, impatient. "I was just thinking. This may sound strange — " He grabs her hand, which is cool in his.

"Evan?" She peers into his face. "Is something bothering you?"

Just then there is a banging on the back door and they jump apart. "Just a sec," she says, but moves away reluctantly. He stares at the ceiling and takes a deep breath.

Lea stands in the doorway looking way too fashionable for Nelson, hair combed, makeup on. Her clothes are what most people would call an outfit: a blue fluffy skirt thing and a short-sleeved shirt that would probably be described as "oatmeal" or maybe "ivory", but to Evan looked just this side of dirty laundry. The tiniest steel-grey earrings dangle from her ears.

"I *called*, Bon. I phoned three times but no one answered." Lea stops when she sees Evan. "Oh, hi. I didn't realize you were over."

He lifts his chin in her direction but, before he can speak, Siobhan breaks in. "It was you! What were you calling so early for? Of course I wasn't going to answer the phone. I'm on holiday here. We're on Kootenay time."

"I thought we'd go for coffee before seeing Mandy. And everyone. But I guess you're all here." She cranes her head to look into the living room.

"I'll make you coffee. We've just had breakfast." Siobhan opens a cupboard.

Evan leans against the table. "I was driving by," he says, "this morning."

Lea wipes crumbs off the table. "Sure."

"Coffee's on. Listen, I should have a shower. I think I reek. Give me a minute, guys, okay?"

As Siobhan pounds up the stairs, Evan returns to the living room and listens to her heavy footsteps move from one room to another. To her bedroom perhaps.

Lea sits on the edge of the couch, but neither of them speak. He does not look at her, not directly. She stares at an embroidered verse mounted on the wall, a saying from the Bible surrounded by pink and purple flowers. "But if ye do not forgive," it says, "neither will your Father which is in — " Upstairs there's a squeaking noise, perhaps of Siobhan sitting on her bed.

"Is Lance here?" Lea says finally.

"No."

She looks away again. Her hands are folded neatly in her lap, her back straight. She's pulled her hair back into a fancy kind of ponytail, a style he's never seen before. "I couldn't sleep," he says. "At my mum's. So I came into town."

She smoothes a wrinkle in her pants. "Sure."

When Siobhan comes down she is wearing a sleeveless flowery number. He's never thought of her as a flowery kind of girl. She and Lea go back into the kitchen to make coffee, but he doesn't want any. Instead, he stretches out on the couch and pretends to sleep. He tries to tune out their conversation, but he must have fallen asleep again, because Siobhan has to wake him up again, tickling his foot. "Come on, Sleeping Beauty," she says. The view down her shirt flashes before his eyes, just before she straightens. It startles him. That constellation again. "We're going over to Mandy's. You drive," she says with a slow smile, then turns away abruptly.

Lance: Anti-Matter

Lance opens his eyes to the rocket, one fin half polished, the sandpaper Evan used lying on the grass beside. Maybe his friend is right; maybe it's time to launch it once again. His parents, Frank and Stella, are safely underground now, so he no longer has to worry about them using the rocket for their own purposes, as they once did. That reminds him, and with his stubby carpenter's pencil, he writes a note to himself on the back of the sandpaper: it's time to take a load of supplies to his parents. The grocery list rarely varies: sacks of brown basmati rice, tofu, onions, miso, bunches of carrots and kale. They grow their own mushrooms, which, like them, live without ever seeing the light of day.

He folds the note and shoves the stiff sheaf into his back pocket. On the way through the house, he picks up his keys from the counter by the sink. What did he need to get? Oh right, basmatic rice, tofu, onions . . .

It had started innocently enough, as these things do, in the mid-eighties. Stella invited their new neighbours, recently escaped from the war zone of LA, over for a cup of chai. The two couples hit it off immediately and started regular movie nights: *All the President's Men, The Boys From Brazil, Fat Man and Little Boy.* The neighbours knew that it wasn't safe even in the wilds of Bonnington. American helicopters flew low overhead all summer, to take photos of potential grow-ops and plot drug raids. What people didn't realize was that the invasion of privacy wouldn't, and didn't, stop there.

The many contrails that criss-crossed the blue skies were not, as they'd innocently supposed, exhaust from passenger planes. They were gases released into the atmosphere by CIA planes. The CIA is in the business of mind control. They fear individualism; don't want the people to think. How better to stop the thinking than to poison the air the people breathe? Soon, the people would become so complacent, the American government would be able to monitor their every movement, read their mail. The government would soon control their very thoughts. And the people would allow it. The neighbours started to wear face masks with heavy-duty carbon filters. Frank and Stella started to dig the underground module.

Meanwhile, Lance was in grade twelve, on the brink of freedom. He tuned out most of the post-movie conversations. He had enough to worry about.

Then one afternoon, he carried the rocket across the backyard, unaware that his parents and neighbours were watching his every move. His goal that day was to see if the launch pad would still support the weight of this latest model. A simple goal, until his parents got involved.

Within days, and before Lance could believe it, a payload of sensitive gas gauges and a tiny camera had been strapped to the rocket. Between the four adults, they'd bought all the necessary supplies and convinced Lance to lend the rocket to the cause. If the CIA were resorting to surveillance, well then they would use counter-surveillance. It was still a free country, the neighbours said, last they checked.

Pressed into service by the protectors of freedom, the rocket was now a worker, an airborne seeing-eye dog. No longer a pet project or a toy, it was a soldier in the war against oppression. He kept his mixed feelings to himself and christened the rocket Laika, after the first Russian dog sent into space.

By the time his parents finished their underground module, Lance had decided to move out. He took the rocket with him. By then, the rocket had failed in its counter-surveillance mission, and he'd lost the desire to solve its design flaw. And Kristy was gone. Everything was different.

For the first few years after that, Frank and Stella retreated underground only when danger signs were present: buttermilk cloud formations, heavy plane traffic. As time wore on, they only felt safe when underground. Now, they hadn't been out in broad daylight in almost a year. Without Lance to deliver their food, they would starve.

Lance smiles awkwardly at the cashier as she rings through the groceries. He's worked with her for years but can never bring himself to strike up a conversation. What if she wasn't interested in talking to him? Instead, he watches her place each item into his faded blue canvas bags, then slips out the door. He hums to himself as he heaves the bags into the passenger seat beside him, then turns the van around to head out of town, towards his parents' place.

As he drives down the highway, he winds down the window and glories in the feel of the warm wind through his hair. The road curves between the Kootenay River on his left and the mountainside on his right. Silver-blue flashes of water wink at him as he zooms by. He gears down as he reaches the turnoff towards his parents' property and steals once last glance at the river.

The grass on their driveway has grown long since his previous visit. He'll have to mow it before he returns to town — one of the many tasks he performs so that no one gets suspicious. In their strange way, his parents still want to maintain the semblance of normality.

He pulls back the blue tarp that has been thrown against the house in a casual-seeming sprawl, then raps against the door in the ground with the coded series of knocks. After a couple of silent minutes, he hears a few dull thumps. Then the door swing sopen and his father's startled face stares up at him through the gloom. The cool, dampness of the underground room is a shock to Lance's system and he shivers. Inside, it smells of onions, pot and the peculiar earthy odour that now clings to both of his parents.

His father's eyes light up when he sees the thick bundle of newspapers and magazines tucked under Lance's arm. Over the next two weeks, Frank will read them cover to cover, then clip and paste key passages into a scrapbook. This is his elaborate way of compiling evidence to support the intricate, labyrinthine line of argument that proves every fear he has for the present or future. Lance has given up denying his father this perverse pleasure, so hands the papers over without comment. Maybe this week, the news will be hopeful.

He unpacks the groceries with his mother. There isn't much to talk about anymore, and silence fills up more and more of their visits. His parents don't do much themselves and anything he does causes them to fret. That leaves the current news as the only topic of conversation, but Lance isn't about to resort to such small talk himself.

Over the past year, his parents have grown suspicious of anything that could allow the outside forces in: telephone, fax, CB radio, or worst of all, computer, but hey still read, and listen to the news on the radio obsessively. Hasn't he heard about identity theft? He doesn't have a credit card, does he? Not an internet account! "I worry about you, Lance," his mother says, "out there every day." She waves to the ground above her head. "I worry so much."

She used to be an avid gardener. In the spring she asked him to bring packets of seeds, but now he sees them lying unopened beside the bed. He peers down at his mother's pale face and says, "Stella, you need to get out more." There's still a trace of colour on her cheekbones, but it's faint. She's taken to smoothing her hair flat against her head to mask the oiliness, but this only emphasizes the new thinness of her face.

She glances over her shoulder at Frank and frowns sadly. He would never let her take such a risk.

Lance can't blame those neighbours of long ago, who have since moved further north. He suspects that they only tapped into something that had lurked in the psyche of his parents for some time, a geyser of disappointment. The age of Aquarius had not come after all and the future looked worse than they'd ever imagined.

With a final sigh and a farewell embrace, Lance climbs back out to face the brittle sunlit future. After he mows the lawn, he drives home. He looks up at the sky and thinks of the mother ship. Once again, he wishes it would come to take him home. More than ever before, he's on his own.

Lance can't shake off the heavy feeling as he pulls into his driveway. The empty day yawns before him. He kicks through the long grass of his backyard to stand in front of the abandoned rocket. In a sense, his parents ruined the rocket for him all those years ago. But the innocent cardboard tube also reminds him too much of Kristy's last night. He looks at it with an accusing eye, as if it were to blame for what happened.

Today, Evan's unwitting enthusiasm forces him to look at the rocket as simply a rocket. A miracle of physics and engineering. He picks up the sandpaper once more. Perhaps, after all, he will fix its problem of early recovery.

In the back shed, he finds the rocket toolbox. Inside lies a crumpled piece of paper. He doesn't need to open the box to know that it contains a diagram, the solution to the rocket's design flaw. He'd scribbled it down in a flash of inspiration late, late on what he later discovered was Kristy's last night, after he'd driven home from that last house party. The last night they'd all been together. The next day, he'd abruptly forgotten the rocket or his solution and so it remained, like a conversation that, once interrupted, can never be resumed. He hadn't even looked at the diagram since writing it down. He studies the box carefully, chewing his lip. He can't bring himself to open it, so he pushes it aside.

If he could only stop thinking of Kristy. All this talk about the rocket has got him wondering what she would think of it. She'd joined them when they'd launched their smaller, beginner models, delighted by the drama of it all. Mostly, what he doesn't want to remember is his last conversation with her, a memory that will always be linked to the rocket. It isn't a logical connection, but there it is. Unbreakable.

He presses his fingers to his throbbing temples. He'll have to finish this later. He heads back inside.

In the middle of his gutted room, he sits on a cushion and surrenders to the persistent, unstoppable memories. He wants thoughts to slip through his mind and leave him, instead of attaching themselves to the sticky burrs of memory. His swamiji, a gnarled but venerable old man from the highlands of India, taught him the technique of surrender. In the two years since his visit, Lance has practiced letting-go every day.

He let go of his houseplants, didn't he? He surrendered his attachment to his old shoes. He let go of all desire for coffee and tea. But of everything, the thoughts are the hardest to let go.

Though he grew up as the single moon between the planets of Stella and Frank, the Jensen universe included more than three celestial bodies. The others were hidden from the day-to-day life of Lance's childhood, because they'd been left behind at the commune. Lance was too young to have any memories of the commune, even though he was born there. The leaving was acrimonious enough that contact was impossible afterwards. Over the years, Lance overheard comments exchanged between his parents and pieced together his own version of the story. Frank insisted that they'd left the commune on ideological grounds: the majority of the members wanted a name and so proposed "The Brother- and Sisterhood of Advanced Communal Living." Frank objected to the word "advanced", because it suggested capitalist notions of progress and hierarchy. At the time the issue was a burning one, and Frank wrote a long and earnest manifesto that defended egalitarian chaos but it was ignored by the other members. This was the official explanation for why they packed up and left the country.

The unofficial explanation, however, is that in the commune, all relationships were open. Unfortunately someone, maybe more than one, slipped out of that opening. At one time the family constellation included another man, another woman, and one other child. They were all abandoned. Who's child was it? Stella's or Frank's? A child left by a mother is a tragedy, a child left by a father, hardly news. A child was left behind, with the other man or woman, and that is the point. Once in Canada, the Jensens' life continued as if nothing had ever happened, as if there had only ever been Stella, Frank, and Lance.

He often wonders what the other child is like. Someone out there shares half his genes. It's even possible that he or she shares all his genes, for the commune believed in co-parenting. Children were not necessarily raised by their biological parents. The commune was one big family. He wonders where the child is and how they are alike. He wants to meet his other half. For years, he believed that Kristy might have been that other child. There was something about her that he had recognized the moment they met, as if he'd caught his reflection in a mirror. It didn't matter that her hair shone like polished chestnut while his hung in lank, pinewood-coloured strands, that her limbs stretched long past shirt cuffs and pant legs, thin and pale, while he had his father's solid build. They could still be related. The thought that she could have been his sister still flickers through his mind now and then. And then, some mornings he wakes knowing that another presence is near, or has just slipped by. On those mornings, he feels strangely whole. Like he did with Kristy all those years ago.

Back in grade nine, he would have quit school if it weren't for one accidental discovery: girls. Oh, he had known girls before, played with them along the back road, but until then he hadn't really *discovered* them. Suddenly girls became a physics he needed to understand.

He wanted to know how they worked, how their parts fit together. How, for example, did they manoeuvre around breasts without bruises or collisions? How did they roll their hips like that, like puppies, and not trip over their feet? How could they flick their hair back and forth and back and forth off their faces without wearing out their arms? Their physics baffled him.

Take Mandy, for instance. (Oh, if he could.) She was a different planet, and he was the astronaut, furiously building a rocket. He wanted to orbit her, be an asteroid and collide with her surface.

Mandy never so much as looked at him. A year earlier, a girl's glance would never have mattered. But one day he'd woken with a thirst for girls like nothing he'd ever known. They were everywhere, yet out of reach: they walked down the hallways, sat in class a hand's width away, and jiggled as they ran around the gym. They had no thirst for Lance, but looked right through him as if he did not exist. He had never before been so invisible, so much like anti-matter. He couldn't figure out how to materialize.

Neither could Evan, who confessed a similar feeling. Lance found two porno magazines in the garage and on weekends, he and Evan studied them carefully. Unfortunately, study did not elucidate anything. Girls were all Lance and Evan wanted to look at. But, as for themselves, Lance and Evan might as well have been figments of the imagination.

Then one day, Kristy talked to him. If girls were stars, it was true that Kristy did not glow with quite the same light as Mandy, but she did have a sheen of her own. She glistened. More importantly, she saw him.

"What're you doing?" She stood over him as he sat on the pavement one afternoon, waiting for the school bus.

At first, he did not recognize her comment for the invitation it was. She merely irritated him. Was it not painfully obvious what he was doing? He did not look up, but replied, "Reading."

"What're you reading?"

"Physics."

"But why? Physics is *awful*."

At this he looked up, startled. "It's beautiful!" She wore a brown skirt that stopped just above her knees. He stared at her kneecaps.

She sat down so that her face came into view. "Tell me why it's beautiful. I don't understand, I'm just a dumb-dumb." She gave him a gap-toothed grin.

He didn't know where to start and felt a blush creep up his neck. He looked around for Evan,, who was nowhere in sight. By the time his friend did arrive, Lance was halfway through stuttering an explanation of surface tension, his face aflame with the ecstasy of it all.

Kristy was not quite Mandy, but she did listen. She laughed when he told a joke — she understood him. Evan was peeved when Lance suggested they invite her to hang out with them, but eventually relented. After that, the three of them went everywhere together.

They were hanging out in Lance's space one night when Evan grew bored with their company and went to the other side of the room to watch a video. She let Lance kiss her once, twice, three times. When he drew back, her expression made her look older than her thirteen years. It was as if she possessed a wisdom he'd never comprehend himself. She seemed to know what to do when he didn't, and guided him gently.

And later, when his hand slipped under her shirt, she flinched but didn't push him away. As his fingers closed over her breast, he knew he'd finally found something that had been lost his entire life up until that moment.

"Do you like me?" she whispered in his ear.

"Yes," he whispered back. In that moment, he really did. "I like you."

She sighed. "Well, I like you because . . . you're so *normal*.".

"Yes," he said, surprised by his tears.

One day later that fall, Lance was late and hurried along the rear wall of the school. It wasn't especially dark or cold that day, but he felt shaded and shivered as he brushed by other kids. He was thinking of what he and Evan would talk about on the bus, when he would next see Kristy, that his shoelace was undone. He was about to stop and tie it when his legs buckled underneath him. Then he was face down on the concrete, wondering how he had got there. His collar was yanked violently and he was dragged upright. The guy with the dirty blond hair held a fist full of his shirt and was twisting it around. Instinctively, Lance grabbed the boy's wrist and tugged at it.

"You come near me again, I'll beat your head in," the boy said and brought his face close. "Don't look at me, you hippie faggot."

Lance continued to struggle, pushed at the boy's chest, but couldn't break free. The boy shook Lance's jaw, then shoved him down again. He fell on his side, his hand crumpled under the weight of his body. The guy's two friends said nothing but kicked at Lance's legs.

He leapt up and gasped for air, his eyes burning and throbbing. He thought his head would explode. "Fuck off," he croaked, then coughed. "Just — " Three pairs of hands slammed his chest against the wall. With a flash of pain, his head jerked to one side and then he was on the ground again, on hands and knees. This time, he didn't get up. The three forced laughter as they stood over him. "Spaz," they said and spat on the ground near his head. "Girlie boy."

Just then, a crowd of girls came around the corner, talking loudly. The boys jumped away from Lance and bounced high on their toes as they retreated, still swearing at him. Again, Lance forced himself to stand and saw that one of the girls was Kristy. The other girls gave him a wide berth and looked in the other direction as they dragged Kristy away. She glanced back and her expression mirrored the terror and embarrassment he felt. He averted his eyes and gathered his fallen books, one by one.

On the bus, Evan whispered fiercely in his ear. "Why did you have to say anything to those guys, Lance? Why can't you just lay low?" His eyes were wide with fear. "Shit Lance. They know you're my friend. You'll get us both killed." Then he slid away and pressed himself against the window.

No, Lance repeated to himself. No to them all. No to everything.

But "no" didn't stop Jason, the bandana boy, from finding Lance again, beating him up again, or chanting "hippie freak" and "faggot" across the hallway whenever their paths crossed. Lance learned to look over his shoulder and keep quiet. He couldn't tell Stella and Frank. "I fell on the soccer field," he would say, to which his mother would reply, "I've never liked organized sports."

Before then, he hadn't had cause to hide anything from his parents. A whole new part of his life had opened up which was outside the boundaries of their awareness. Each school day was a journey that led him so far away from them that he came back a changed person. His parents remained the same. They were too simple to grasp what was happening. Even though school filled him with terror, he couldn't quit and go back to home schooling. Frank and Stella no longer knew who he was.

With Kristy, Evan, and their new friends Mandy and Lea, he went out on weekends. He was the New Lance. On Sunday afternoons, they hung out in Gyro Park and parodied the children playing on swings. He wasn't a kid anymore though he wasn't sure what he was instead. He was half way between what he had been and what he wanted to be, in a kind of un-Lance land. All he knew was that, after only a couple of months, his friends knew him better than his parents ever had. They were his family.

"You have to promise to be my friends forever," he said to them one evening. This was the most important, the most serious, thing he had ever said to anyone. "I will cease to exist if you stop being my friends." And he would. There would just be no Lance without them. He would lie down and die if they stopped hanging out with him.

Lance, Kristy, and Evan sat in the back row of the town's box-like theatre and watched movies. One Friday night in May, they saw *Back to the Future* with Michael J Fox, a Canadian actor, a boy who'd grown up right here in BC. His role was to be a typical American teenager, but he was not what he seemed. He was not so typical. He climbed into a car and drove into the past and then into the future, and when he returned, his parents were none the wiser. A zipper of recognition ran up Lance's spine. He couldn't take his eyes off the screen.

They walked through the dark streets of town afterwards. He reached for Kristy's hand, but she evaded him. She had been sulky and quiet all evening. He had been thinking that he should go out with another girl. She'd seen the others beat him up and when he looked in her eyes, all he could see was that scene replayed over and over. She could find a new bruise instantly, even one covered by his shirt, and she would run her fingers over it, knowingly. He feared she felt sorry for him.

That night, Stella picked them up in town and drove them back to Lance's home. Evan's mother would pick up Kristy and Evan there, so he sat with them while they waited.

"I don't think I can go out with you anymore, Kristy," he blurted out into the silence. "I don't like you."

It took her a while to respond. "But . . . I thought you did. You said you did."

Lance blushed, knowing that Evan was hearing this. "I lied," was all he could reply. Just then, a car horn honked and Kristy ran outside. Evan stood up slowly and grinned at him.

Lance can't think of that time without a burning flush of shame.

Lance's eyes fly open. He feels the cushion under him and takes in the hushed light of his empty house. He needs to get outside. He needs . . . quarter-inch nails. That's it, he must have finishing nails.

Lance jumps onto his skateboard and glides down the hill from his house towards the building supply store. The deep blue of Kootenay Lake and Elephant Mountain opens before him and for a moment, his mind is empty. He stops short when he enters the parking lot. There's Jason, helping another man load lumber into his truck. Lance flips up his skateboard, tucks it under his arm and walks towards him. Just the thought of Kristy has made him resolve that there will be no more dodging in his life, no more missed connections. He stands beside before his former classmate for a few minutes before he's noticed. Jason turns with a slightly puzzled expression and Lance looks him full in the face. "Hello, I'm Lance," he says, at a loss for how to begin.

Jason grins to show his chipped, cigarette-stained teeth and holds out a hand, "Hey there Mr. Lance, what can I do ya for?"

"I went to school with you. You . . . " Lance falters. He doesn't know if he can go on. Jason is shorter than he is, he notices, not by much but enough that their eyes aren't level. Lance still feels overpowered.

Jason takes one step back. "Is that right, hey? Well, you need anything, you give me a shout," he says with a crooked grin.

"You used to . . . three times . . . " Lance can't finish. Jason gives him a worried look, then jerks his chin up as a goodbye and walks away.

How many times has he been in the store to buy tools or materials? But he is completely forgettable. He stands in the middle of the parking lot, stranded. He feels erased. He looks around him: men busily concentrate on their errands, oblivious to his existence.

Eventually he throws down his skateboard and starts back up the hill towards the empty, gutted shell of his house and his desert-like bed. In this town, which clings to the side of a mountain, getting around by skateboard is more of a devotional practice than a practical transportation option. It's like one of those self-scourging tasks an ascetic monk would do as meditation. Instead of ten thousand prostrations or sun salutations, Lance pushes himself and his skateboard up the long slow hill, and thinks all the while of his swamiji, or Kristy, and sometimes of the other child. After a time, he does not feel quite so alone. When he arrives at his house, he sets up a pillow, candle and wicker screen to create a small quiet space. He sits down to clear his thoughts and lower his pulse.

EVAN STANDS IN FRONT OF LEA'S car and jangles the keys in his hands. "Where does Mandy live, again?"

"I'll tell you where to turn," Lea says.

"You sit in front," Siobhan insists and climbs into the back seat before Lea can reply. "So, how are your folks doing, Lea?" She's babbling, she can tell.

Lea lists the details of her arrival the night before, her parents' probing questions and reactions. Though Siobhan nods and answers, she shakes inside.

She thinks of how she stood over Evan, a plate in each hand while he slept in her father's chair. His face takes on a whole new look when he sleeps. Something soft and endearing has the chance to surface. It frightens her. So she'd been overly breezy and efficient with him and, yes, she has to admit, teasing. What kind of dork flirts with an old friend like that? *Damn it.*

"So . . . is Mandy okay?" Evan says.

"What do you mean, okay?" Siobhan crosses her arms over her chest and shivers. "She'll just be Mandy, like she always is."

"But she's . . . " His hands trace the outline of an extended belly through the air and he glances at Siobhan meaningfully in the rear-view mirror. "You know. Full of weird hormones."

"She's not sick, she's having a baby," Siobhan says irritably.

"It's still a little weird," Evan says as he turns onto the street.

The distance to Mandy's house is only a short walk, but the drive feels long. Siobhan steps out before Evan has the chance to turn off the engine, then straightens the hem of her shirt. Is it too revealing? But it's summer for heaven's sake. No one is going suspect anything. *Suspect what?* she asks herself angrily. *Don't be silly.*

She is the first to the front door and knocks as Lea and Evan take the stairs slowly, one at a time. They both look up and down the street, uneasy. The door opens after the third knock.

"Cripes, it's the crack of dawn." Mandy fills the doorway, clothed in a blue T-shirt that stretches tight over the outline of her belly button.

The sight of her pregnant friend, so big and *matronly*, startles Siobhan. She stifles the urge to laugh. Behind her, Evan huffs in alarmed surprise.

"It's almost noon," Siobhan says and follows closely as her friend shuffles down the hallway to the kitchen.

"Like I said." Mandy puts on the kettle, then sits down heavily at the table. Lea pulls out a chair, and looks at the kitchen cupboards with interest. Siobhan listens to the sounds of Evan as he walks through the house, his steps heavy and measured.

"I wait for, like, *ever* for a phone call from you guys, then you show up before I've even had a cup of tea. I just can't win."

"Nice place you got here. Where's this Mick guy?" Evan stands in the doorway.

"Huh? He's, I don't know, probably sleeping at home. He gigs at the Zoo until two on Friday nights . . . morning . . . whatever. Lapsang souchong okay with you guys?"

Siobhan and Lea exchange glances.

Evan presses on. "Oh, so he doesn't live here?"

Siobhan gives Evan a hard look, which he ignores. Can he be more obvious? And why is he so concerned anyway? Mandy just smiles vaguely and lifts the lid of the teapot to peer inside. A gust of air from the open window blows the smoky fragrance towards Siobhan, and it cuts through the scent of unwashed dishes.

"So Mandy," Lea says eagerly. "Are you all organized for the birth?"

Mandy pours the tea into four mugs. "I guess so. Not that you can ever really be ready."

"What's your plan?" Lea presses.

"Well." Mandy pauses to blow on her tea. "I'll have it here, of course." Lea lets out a small gasp. "If it all goes pear-shaped, at least the hospital's only five minutes away. Mick went to the prenatal classes with me, so he'll be my breathing coach."

"Oh good," Lea says though a slight frown still creases her forehead. Evan rolls his eyes.

"I was only going to have Mick and the midwives around," Mandy continues. "I've told my mother I *don't* need her help." She shares a knowing look around the table. They've all met her mother before. "But now that you guys are here, and if the baby arrives before you go back, I was thinking maybe you could . . . stand watch, kinda." Her face is hopeful.

Siobhan catches Lea's eye and raises an eyebrow. She turns to Mandy. "It's not like we'd be much use to you. I mean, I don't know anything . . . "

"I don't want you to be useful," she says. "Just supportive. You know me, I like a party."

"Well . . . " Siobhan says.

"Sure, I'll be there." Lea gives Mandy's hand a brief squeeze.

After a pause, Siobhan pushes her doubts aside and says, "Okay, okay."

Mandy turns to Evan with an impish grin. "You're completely insane," he says. She nods. "Why would . . . I mean, seriously . . . " He swallows then mutters, "I'll think about it." Her smile widens. In triumph, she takes a sip from her mug.

Siobhan looks down at her own cup and hopes that the baby arrives late. For a few long moments, they quietly drink their tea and wonder what they've got themselves into.

"Hey," Lea says into the silence. "Have you heard about Mr. Hiller? I read an article in the paper last night."

"Yeah, imagine dying in prison like that." Mandy says. "I mean, sitting in grade ten English class, I never thought he'd end up *there*."

"Asshole," Evan says, his lips a thin, hard line. "He deserves to rot in a worm-infested cesspool." He sits in the chair beside Siobhan. His knee nearly touches hers.

"But worms don't live in the water," Lea protests.

Siobhan squeezes her legs together. "He was still a good teacher," she says. "And a good coach. We all liked him — before, that is."

It's Evan's turn to giver her a hard look. "Who gives a shit what kind of teacher he was, after what he did?"

"I just meant . . . forget it."

"Take it easy, Evan," Mandy says, and lays a hand over his. "It's not like he hurt *you*." Siobhan looks down at their hands.

"How do you know? How can any of us know for sure? He could have picked any one of us."

"I think he just means it affected us all." Lea draws her shoulders up as she says this, a conciliatory, we're-in-this-together gesture.

"No, that's not what I mean. You have no clue what I mean. None of you do."

Mandy gasps. She withdraws her hand to place it on her belly. "The squirt kicked." Her fingers lift slightly where they rest on the taut dome of her stomach. "Again! It's the most unbelievable feeling."

They all stare at her belly as if it's something to be feared. Something about the conversation — Mr. Hiller and Mandy's pregnancy mentioned together — makes Siobhan uneasy. She stands up and puts her mug in the sink. "So, where is Lance, anyway? Did you call him, Mandy?"

"I left messages. I haven't actually talked to him in ages."

"Maybe I'll swing by his place to see if he's home."

"He lives up on Granite Road now you know."

"I'll go." Evan rises.

"No." With a hand firmly pressed against his shoulder, Siobhan pushes him down, then immediately lets go. They stare at her. "I'll take Mandy's car. Where are the keys?"

I look like I'm running away, she thinks, and runs out the door. In the car, she rolls down the window to get a lungful of fresh air. She realizes she's speeding and slams on the brakes. *Oh God*, she thinks, *I wanted to move my chair closer to his. I wanted to punch him in the face.* As she drives to the outskirts of town she argues with herself. What does he know about what Hiller was really like? *And why do I care what he thinks? I never have. Shit head.*

She has a sudden urge to call Michael.

EVAN

MANDY WATCHES SIOBHAN'S RETREATING BACK. THE door slams. "What's her problem?" she says.

"Siobhan's hard to read," Lea says.

"Yeah, always so secretive." Mandy places a hand on the table and heaves herself up.

"Take it easy on her," Evan says. Now that he's got over the shock of seeing Mandy pregnant, he follows her with his eyes as she moves around the kitchen. Even when she was thirteen, she'd oozed a savvy kind of sexiness that few women ever possess, no matter what their age or how beautiful they are. It's hard to say what he likes about her, but everything about her suggests warmth. Her skin is the colour of dark honey, her crazy curled hair a darker honey tipped with gold.

"You were the one who was just — " Mandy braces her hands on either side of her belly. "Ooof, the squirt kicked again. It's never been this active before."

"Oh sugar, Mandy." Lea pulls out two books from her bag. They are adorned with brightly coloured sticky notes. In times of stress, Lea turns to research and fanatical organization. She flips one book open. "I've heard that an overactive foetus, in the final trimester, could mean that . . . oh, what was it? How close is the hospital?"

Evan rolls his eyes. "Dial down, Lea," he says. "It's all right." Come to think of it, there is even something pretty cute about Lea, with her put-togetherness, that hairstyle that needs to be mussed up.

"Yeah, listen to Evan," says Mandy as she pours another cup of tea. "Evan always knows what to do."

"Give me a break." He flushes, wonders if she's referring to how he never knew what to do about Kristy. Yes, he really should have stayed in Vancouver. Life is simpler there.

"But I've read up on it," Lea continues. From her purse, she produces a pair of glasses and slips them on. "I'm not worried or anything, it's just good to be prepared."

Evan pushes his chair back to stand and says, "Just leave it alone, Lea." He paces the length of the room, then picks up his mug and slides it down the counter with a clatter.

"My, we're grumpy today," Mandy says. "She's just being a concerned friend."

"Yeah, yeah." He leans a shoulder against the doorjamb and folds his arms across his chest. "Sorry." The row of Japanese teapots on top of the fridge catches his eye and he gazes at them without really seeing them. But he can feel Mandy's questioning look trained on him. The silence stretches.

"My mum's making such a big deal about this ceremony shit," he finally says. It's easier to blame his mother. They're all thinking about Kristy, he's sure of it. She might as well be sitting in the room. He avoids his old friends for this very reason. Now, with them all together like this, it's inevitable that the conversation will swing around to her. But they don't even know the half of it. He and his mother never told anyone that Kristy was one of Hiller's victims. They'd only found out themselves when the police had come by to question them after Kristy died. Now, he just can't bear to tell Lea and Mandy.

"Yeah," Lea says. "Parents can be weird."

"She must miss Kristy still," Mandy says sympathetically.

"Yeah. Mum's started sorting through Kristy's clothes, and they're all over my room." He thinks back to Siobhan's comment, sticking up for Hiller. What was that about? He moves to the sink and wipes down the already-clean counter.

Mandy twists in her chair. "Did you ever know for sure if the crash was her fault?" She falters. "Sorry, that sounded awful. I didn't mean it like that . . . "

"I . . . " Lea starts. "I've always wondered about that too. Did they ever find out how her car . . . " She falters, then looks down at her cup, which she pushes back and forth across the table.

"I miss her, you know," Mandy says. "We used to hang out on my mum's couch and talk for hours. She would make the most amazing frozen peanut butter tofu pie and we'd eat half of it just sitting there." She catches his eye and waits for him to say something.

He remembers eating pie with her, the cold shock of it in his mouth before it melted. Sweet, nutty. Damn. He turns to stare out the kitchen window and places his hands firmly on the counter.

"Yeah," Lea continues, "She made tzatziki, too. We all thought it was so exotic back then." She laughs at herself then swallows. "I remember the night she . . . "

" . . . drove off," Mandy finishes for her, barely audible. It's as if neither of them can say the word "died." "Was . . . was it really an accident, Ev?"

He can feel their stares on his back, and when he turns around their expressions are fascinated and horrified at the same time. He looks from one to the other, takes in their round eyes. They can't leave the subject alone. They feed off it, insatiable, and he is no better. He pushes himself off the counter, unable to look at them any longer.

Restless, he paces through the rooms of the house and scans the pictures on the walls without seeing them. He needs to get out of there, not just sit around and drink tea. The women talk in low tones in the other room. He stares out the front window waiting for Siobhan and Lance, but after a few long minutes, returns to the kitchen. "Listen, I'm feeling pretty bagged. I think I'll pass on lunch and drive back to my mum's."

"There's a couch in the play room. Did you see it?" Mandy says with forced cheer. She and Lea stand up, strained smiles pasted on their faces.

"Yeah, I saw it. I'll just go." He can't stick around there any more. He needs to get away from their questioning eyes before he spills the whole story.

"Well," says Mandy as she follows him to the door, "this is totally lame. I wanted us all to hang out together."

"Maybe later."

"What about a barbecue this evening, at Lakeside Park?" She puts a hand on his arm, a bit too insistently.

He mumbles agreement and she hugs him, saying, "I'll tell Lance and Siobhan when they get here. You'd better be there, buddy." He can barely get his arms around her, her belly huge between them.

The gearshift rests comfortably in his palm. It feels solid, sure and he tightens his grip as he gears down. He searches his mind for safe, distracting thoughts. Images of Siobhan's flower-covered breasts, and the feeling of Mandy's belly pressed against his abdomen, even the scent of Lea's perfume, crowd his mind. *A woman is not an object, a woman is not an object*, he chants to himself, over and over.

What is his problem? Four weeks ago his most recent attempt at a relationship had gone bust. Not that it was anything serious, just a possibility really, but nurtured over weeks of careful manoeuvring, crafty tactical advances and high hopes. Michelle. She had all the signs of being perfect and he thought he was finally getting the hang of this young, urban, available-guy living.

He'd appeared at the right events and bought the right drinks, talked for hours with no hint that he expected anything for it. He'd laughed at her jokes, self-consciously perfecting a chuckle that sounded pleasantly surprised by her wit. The jokes had been funny at the time, but became less so in retrospect. They'd gone roller blading around English Bay, for dinner on Grouse Mountain, mountain biking on Mt Seymour. He was sure she was a serious catch: an aerobics instructor. Every inch of her was beautiful, firm. Her long brown hair shone, her lips were naturally full, she had a sense of humour (at least he thought so at the time). She was gutsy. They had common sporting interests.

But when the much-anticipated moment came — at her apartment, after a dinner that he cooked and dishes that he washed, after a bottle of champagne — it came as a fizzle, not a pop. He couldn't explain what hadn't worked, other than it just didn't feel right. As they'd rolled on the couch, it struck him that her laugh was something like Kristy's. He could have just been imagining things, but he'd left as quickly as possible, claimed an early morning deadline, and drove around town for hours. Got some take-out pizza and ate it in his quiet, white apartment. Then he washed it down with a tall frothy beer.

Now he's having weird, irrational thoughts about his old friends. They make him think of Kristy even more than a familiar-sounding laugh ever could. Something's wrong with him. Thoughts of Siobhan's white skin float through his brain, but he pushes them aside.

He turns up Bonnington Road, but drives past the road that leads to his mother's house. He couldn't stand to be around his mother and Gerald just yet. Near the border of the property, just before the dilapidated fence that separates his mother's land from the neighbour's, a footpath snakes up the mountain. It follows the western edge of the property towards the creek which serves as the back border. Halfway up the mountainside, in a small clearing, is the shrine to Kristy that his mother made. Evan pulls over into the grass and parks the car, and after sitting in its stillness for a moment, heads up the path.

LANCE: ENTANGLEMENT (BROKEN)

LANCE SITS. HE SITS SOME MORE. After a time that cannot be measured, pretty much everything dissolves. Everything is interconnected but nothing matters. The particle is a wave and the wave is a particle and Lance bobs up and down. He feels weightless; he feels a deep giggle rising. He feels not just peace, but silence.

Then there's a knock on the door.

When he opens it — the silence of another time and space still hanging off him in tendrils — he sees Siobhan. Anxiety has carved fine lines in her face. Her body hums with it. He feels a strong urge to reach out to her and so he kisses her on the lips.

She jumps back. "Hey," she says and laughs nervously. She blushes and looks down at her feet, then steps into the hallway with a brisk air as if shaking off her embarrassment. "I've come to get you," she says and looks around. "Wow, you sure gutted the place." She walks around the central room. Her footsteps echo on the unfinished floor. They are as loud as gongs in his ears.

Before Linda left him, they had knocked down every wall possible so that the downstairs could be one large communal room. She had wanted the room filled with the happy sound of children — their children. Lance simply avoided the subject every time she brought it up. The thought of being responsible for another being filled him with terror. He'd turned his energies to the renovations. The supporting beams are all they left untouched. The upstairs was going to have an open floor plan as well, but she left him before they got that far. In the months since her departure, little has been done. The walls are still unplastered, the floors still rough, piles of tile collect dust in the corner. The task no longer delights him.

"I'm just finishing *siddhasana*," he replies. He can barely form the words. His mind still clings to silence.

"Sure," Siobhan replies tentatively.

He needs to sit down for a bit so returns to his cushion. She sits next to him and crosses her legs awkwardly. "Can I wait for you to finish? What are you doing?"

Perhaps she will understand. They had been close friends at one time. The silence, the stillness, is so beautiful that he wants to share it. Perhaps she needs it more than he does. "Look at the candle," he says. "I've seen something very beautiful." There are few people he can say this to without fear of them laughing at him. He hopes she is one of those few. He wants a sign that she understands him, that he's not alone. In a way, he muses, it's a relief that Linda left him before he screwed things up, the way he always does. He's hurt enough people already. Linda probably saved him the trouble and herself a lot of grief and heartache. But he's tired of being alone. He takes Siobhan's hand and places it on her knee in the correct position.

"Empty your mind," he says and closes his eyes. They sit there for a few minutes, but he can hear her heavy breathing, nails scratching at skin, the movement of her head. He heaves a great sigh and struggles to hang onto the feeling and pass it on to her.

THE SILENCE IS KILLING HER. MURKY sheets of plastic muffle the brilliant sunlight. Siobhan steals a glance in his direction. It's as if he doesn't quite rest on his cushion. He almost hovers. He's one of those light walkers too, moves as if he weighs nothing at all, despite the fact that he's heavyset. At least, heavy about the hands and feet. They are almost too large for his body. He moves like one of those first biplanes, ponderous and weighty but at the same time, airborne.

She thinks back to the kiss, though she shouldn't be surprised by it. Lance never makes the same distinctions most people do. He'll hold anyone's hand, even Evan's, though Evan's pretty jumpy about that. When she'd first seen Lance kiss his own mother on the lips, she was sure there was something pretty sick going on in the family. But he did it so matter-of-factly and never seemed strange about his mother in other ways, so she came to the conclusion that's just the way his family was. After a while, she got used to him. Though he can still catch her off guard.

Her feet go to sleep and she longs to move. Sitting here like this is ridiculous. It isn't like her to do anything as weird as this. She shifts her legs until she finds a comfortable position.

Something about the room, the wicker screen, something about hearing his breathing without seeing him reminds her of sitting in a confessional. She mumbles, "I have had adulterous thoughts." But she isn't even married. "I am living in sin," she says out loud. She looks at him. Deep in their smudgy sockets, his eyes are closed. "Ha," she answers herself. "It sounds silly to say that, doesn't it?"

Outside a child bicycles down the road and calls out to her friend, "Wait for me!" The sound of beads rattling on the spokes are loud in the room.

She has a mental image of what the two of them must look like, silent in darkness, and in one way the scene is totally ridiculous. Embarrassing. But then, there's something relaxing about sitting there. Her mind drifts to the first time she ever talked to Lance. Meeting him was like opening a door to discover that a new, tospy-turvy world existed on the other side. That was the day she ran away. She'd just turned thirteen. What a horrible age.

On her thirteenth birthday, Siobhan did not get the trampoline she'd asked for but a pinafore dress with a sensible woolen turtleneck to wear underneath. A *pinafore*, not even pedal pushers or leg warmers like the popular kids wore. She had dreamed of bouncing on the trampoline, higher, higher, higher, until she flew out of this horrible, ugly town and her boring, miserable life. Without a trampoline, she would have to walk instead. One morning, instead of taking the familiar road to school, she cut through town to the highway that headed west towards Vancouver. Once she reached the city, she would be a world-famous photographer. In her backpack was an envelope with three hundred dollars saved from her paper-route money, which she would use for the first weeks until she was discovered and became famous.

Head held high, she passed the big ugly box buildings of downtown. What a boring town: the mill closed, the tiny hilltop university too, so all anyone could talk about was jobs, or rather, the lack of them. Way back when her parents were young, things got better every year and everything was groovy. But now it was the mid-eighties. If the hole in the ozone didn't get you, the nuclear bomb would. Siobhan couldn't wait to leave. "I'm thir*teen* already," she'd said to Lea the day before. "I've grown out of this town." It did not matter that the big ugly box shells were being peeled off the downtown buildings, one by one, to reveal the finely-tooled stonework, stain-glass windows and wood detailing from the silver rush days. What was once covered with blank, monochromatic sheets of siding was now a row of grandmotherly buildings, decked out in lacy frills. The buildings looked down on Siobhan with disapproval, telling her she was making a stupid mistake. She wouldn't listen to those old ladies, because she was moving up in this world.

But the road to Vancouver is long. After an hour's walk, she wasn't even at Grohman Narrows Park. Not to be discouraged, she pulled out her camera. She was a real photographer now, so she could find something artistic in anything, even here. Something bleak, but meaningful. She fiddled with the shutter and aperture dials, then focused on the toes of her boots against the asphalt lip of the road. No, that was just boring, not desolate and heartbreaking like a really smart photo should be. Nothing for her future fans to marvel over. She lowered the camera and contemplated the stretch of road she now inhabited, a spot by the highway that she had only ever seen from the back seat of her father's car as they whizzed past.

In fact, her father could have driven by this spot the evening before, while she waited at home for her family to make a big fuss over her first year of being a real teenager. Her mother had tried, had made her favourite meal of hamburgers, but all day Siobhan waited for her father to do or say something — she wasn't sure what — that would acknowledge that she had turned a corner in life. She was almost a woman, surely. She had a trembly sense of anticipation about what this meant. She was a new person, shiny new. She wanted her dad to notice. And thirteen — *thirteen* — that had to count for something. Her father was a man of few words or gestures, and even fewer encouraging ones. Before dinner he shook his newspaper and held it high in front of his face. After dinner he had an important errand to run and with a pat to the head and a quick "happy birthday," left the house. Instead of a key to the magical unknown, Siobhan got an elbow in the side from her brother Matthew, who plopped onto the couch beside her and said, "Thirteen's an unlucky number, you know. The witch's number."

Well, thirteen was also practically adult. With a confident toss of her head she closed her eyes and stuck out a thumb. Held it out there, thought brave, confident thoughts. A cold wind blew over her knees laid bare by the birthday pinafore. She heard gears shift down and tires crunch on gravel. A battered white pickup pulled over just behind her. A tent of plywood filled the back box and it was painted white with block letters in black: POVERTY AND SHAME SHALL BE TO HIM THAT REFUSETH INSTRUCTON. IT IS ABOMATION TO FOOLS TO DIPART FROM THE DEVIL. A COMPANON OF FOOLS SHALL BE DESTROYED. EVIL PURSUETH SINERS: BUT TO THE RIGHTEOUS GOOD SHALL BE REPAYD. PROVERBS 13:18–21.

Oh no, the Jesus-freaks. They lived somewhere out in the Slocan Valley but were a common sight around town. They drove their trucks of warning slowly up and down the main street every day. They were even known to shop in the grocery store, though she'd never seen them up close herself. The young guy in the truck waved at her, smiling, while a woman opened the door, then scooted over to the middle of the bench seat. Jesus-freaks were harmless, right? Siobhan debated this as she walked towards the truck. They were Christians after all, weren't they?

"Hop in, little sister," the woman said, a dreamy expression on her face. "Where is your journey leading you?"

Love thy neighbour. Judge not, lest ye be judged. Right? *Right?* She slid onto the seat. "Um, Vancouver?" She tugged on the seatbelt, but it did not budge, so she just clung to it.

"That's a long way, girl. We're going as far as Bonnington."

"Close enough."

The woman was young, not much older than Siobhan's sister, with pale eyes and two blonde braids. Round, brown-rimmed glasses dominated her thin face. The man's face was harder to see, covered by a black tangly mess of beard. As he pulled out onto the highway, he turned to her. "Are you a friend of Jesus?" he asked.

"Oh sure."

"But has He entered your heart?" The woman enquired, and lay cool fingers on her arm.

"Yeah." At this, the two exchanged a worried look. Siobhan added, "I'm Catholic. We go to church every Sunday."

The woman frowned with concern. "Then you don't *know* Him. We do. Jesus has been reborn and lives with us now in Slocan Park. This is Simon Peter — " she gestured to the man, " — the Rock of the Church, the foundation upon which the true faith shall be built."

"And," Siobhan said cautiously, "who are you?"

The woman blinked. "I'm Cindy." Cindy continued to regale Siobhan with stories of the wondrous miracles performed by Jesus of the Slocan Valley. Her face lit, she squeezed Siobhan's arm. "Oh," she said. "*Oh.*"

As Cindy's rapture overtook her, Simon Peter grew sullen and ran fingers through his long hair. "But we will never truly know Jesus," he mumbled. "We can never be close to him." Cindy didn't seem to hear. Simon Peter's control over the car grew looser and looser. He slowed to a crawl, then jammed his foot on the accelerator. They whipped around hairpin corners. The truck lurched to the left, to the right.

"You can drop me off anywhere," Siobhan said as Cindy enthused and Simon Peter mumbled behind his mustache. "I don't mind." Maybe the Jesus-freaks belonged to a cult. She'd heard about such things. They could take her three hundred dollars, tie her up and do unthinkable things to her. Images swarmed her imagination, a grisly collage of every rumour, news clip and nightmare she'd ever known. "Right here would be fine." Her voice rose.

"Jesus is our Lord and Master," Cindy said. Simon Peter brought a fist down on the steering wheel, but said nothing. Siobhan's heart pounded in her ears.

"Hey, Peter, this is the turnoff!" Cindy's dreamy look vanished and she pointed to the right. He swerved off the highway and geared down with a loud grinding sound. The truck laboured up the steep dirt road, stuttered, then stalled.

Before the dust could settle, Siobhan was out the door, slipping on the gravel, slithering down the slope of the ditch into a patch of rose hips. Cindy stuck her head out the window and said, "Are you okay, little sister?" but Siobhan bravely waved them off.

She ignored the brambles that scratched at her and called out, "God bless!" An incantation, a good luck charm. Reluctantly, Cindy turned away. The truck pulled away in a puff of dust. As her heartbeat slowed, Siobhan inspected the wounds on her legs. Once again, she cursed the birthday pinafore, which left her legs bare. She shuddered — she'd come too close to evil but, luckily, had slipped out of its grasp. Maybe this is what happened when you were teetering on the edge of adulthood.

She climbed out of the ditch and looked around. She was far enough up the mountain and away from the highway that traffic was a muffled moan in the distance. Hemlocks grew thick on either side of the road, but she glimpsed houses through the branches. Overhead, an eagle circled, or was it an osprey? She squinted at it, sighed, then started to walk up the hill. She walked and walked.

Eventually, the road sloped down again. Behind her, she heard the scrape of tires against gravel and then a boy on a bike whizzed past. He screeched to a halt, then straddled his bike with one foot on the ground. She recognized him, that light brown hair hanging in his eyes. She stopped a few feet away. "Hi," she said. It was all very quiet up there on the mountain.

"You're from school, aren't you?" he said and flicked his hair with a twitch of his head.

"Um, yeah. How come *you're* not in school today?"

He shrugged. "Didn't feel like it. Stella says I don't have to go when I don't feel like it." They looked at each other, then away. There was no one else for miles around. "How come you're not in school?"

"I'm going to Vancouver."

He nodded. Her stomach growled, loudly, so she folded her arms over her middle.

"You're going all the way today?"

She nodded.

"Stella's driving to Castlegar this morning. She can give you a ride."

"Who's Stella?"

"My mum."

"Why don't you call her 'Mum' then?"

He looked at her funny. "Because her name's Stella." They eyed each other warily.

"What's your name, anyway?"

"Lance Jensen."

"Oh. I'm Siobhan Campbell." She waved her hand weakly. He pushed off, then pedalled in slow motion. With a glance over his shoulder, he said, "You want to sit on the handle bars?"

"No." She followed him down the road and along a short driveway. Three small buildings sat close together, joined by plywood walkways. The outside walls were unfinished, covered in black tar paper. Cautiously, she followed him into one of the buildings and sniffed the air. It smelled like hippie — incense, garlic, a hint of apple in the background. Lance disappeared around a corner. The room appeared to be a kitchen, but enormous pillows dominated one corner. Half-burnt candles lined the windowsills. The colours of the room were bright and cheerful despite the layer of dust everywhere.

He came back with a pear in each hand and sat down at the table. She sat opposite. He put one pear in front of her, then sliced the other with a knife, and watched her as he slipped a piece into his mouth. "What are you going to do in Vancouver?" he said around the slice.

"Be a photographer."

"Cool, can I see your photos?"

With a shake of her head, she pulled the knapsack close to her stomach. She'd heard of strange pagan groups who lived in the mountains, people who performed rituals at midnight. And she was thirteen. The half-burned candles behind her took on ominous meaning. The boy before her just smiled eagerly.

"What do you take photos of?" He handed her the knife, tip first. Startled, she leaned away, then took it. Slowly, she drew the blade through the fruit in her hand.

"This and that," she said. "Nothing really. My pictures are kind of . . . moody."

"Cool. Do you play Dungeons and Dragons?"

"No."

"I can teach you."

"I should probably go."

"You want a sandwich?"

Despite herself, she nodded. He moved around the kitchen like he was used to doing so. Starving, but making sure she witnessed him take a bite first, she ate the sandwich he had placed before her. Grass-like bits hung over the edges of the bread and her tongue rolled around a kind of cheese she'd never tasted before. She suspected he didn't have parents after all. As he ate, he asked questions about her family, friends, what she did all day if she didn't play Dungeons and Dragons. Sometimes he wouldn't wait for an answer, but shared his own. She told him she would become famous. He nodded, picked crumbs off the table with a wet finger. She licked her lips.

The sandwich finished, she stood up. "I really should go now."

He followed her out the door, continued the conversation as if she weren't leaving. On his bike, he wheeled circles around her. She trudged down the road. He wouldn't stop talking. "D&D is super fun," he said. "You'll really like it." She feared he might never return to his hippie house. She wanted him to leave her alone. "I could show you how to play in ten minutes. No, eight and a half, tops."

As she reached the asphalt of the highway, she waved him off. "See ya later."

He skidded to a halt at the edge of the gravel and balanced on one foot. He watched her cross the highway, then called out, "It's not hard to learn!"

She turned away without responding. One foot after the other after the other, Siobhan walked on. The adventurous life began to be a drag. She was tired. After what seemed like an age, a car whipped past her, blinked its lights, then slowed down. She ignored it until she heard a familiar voice call out her name. She turned around and saw Mr. Hiller walk towards her, his face creased with worry. "What are you doing way out here?" he said. Ah, Mr. Hiller from church and school. She could hardly wait until she'd be in his English class.

"I'm fine," she said though her lip trembled. A wave of guilt washed over her. "I'll get in trouble with the principal, won't I?"

He put a hand on her shoulder, then stroked her hair. "We'll see what we can do."

Relief made her knees weak and meekly she followed him to the car. It didn't take much prompting before she told him everything about her awful first days of being a teenager — skipping the bits about possible cults and pagans — and he nodded sympathetically. "It won't always be so bad," he said reassuringly.

By the time they turned into the school parking lot, Siobhan's tears had dried. It was almost time for lunch break. She barely had a moment to wonder why Mr. Hiller had been on the highway on a school day, when he cut the engine. "Look Siobhan, I could say you were helping me with a youth group activity, but you'll have to go along with the story. This really isn't moral. I don't like being forced to lie for you."

"I'm so sorry," she said. She wanted him, of all people, to respect her. She wanted to thank him. He seemed to understand what it was like to be thirteen, when her parents obviously didn't. Reluctantly, she slid out of the door that he held open and dawdled by the car.

"Did I tell you I cut myself, too?" she asked and pulled up her skirt to show him the scratches on the inside of her thigh. In that instant, her flash of confidence evaporated. She hesitated, confused, and glanced up at him for approval. The insides of her legs burned and she had the sudden urge to pee. Fear and a strange excitement churned in her stomach. Something in her — something she didn't trust — terrified her.

His mouth was open but the lunch bell jangled before he could speak. The parking lot came to life with kids swarming like bees.

Relief flooded her limbs and she released the hem of her pinafore, but couldn't move. Her heart pounded in her ears as her eyes remained fixed on his handsome face. His expression was unfamiliar, his eyes flickered over her as if measuring. She lowered her eyes quickly to break his gaze. Something made her back away. At that moment, she heard one familiar voice above the others, and twirled around. "Hey, Lea," she hollered. "Wait up!" She ran two steps before she remembered her manners and turned back. "Thank you, sir," she said. "I appreciate you helping me out." He simply nodded, his mouth a thin line. She was so lucky he'd driven by, she told herself as she ran after Lea. Really lucky.

Now, the thought of that day jolts her out of her trance. She opens her eyes. She can't believe she wrote letters to the man for all those years. "Lance," she says. "If I tried to comfort a weak man in his time of need, does that make me weak too?" He doesn't reply but perhaps she doesn't want him to. "He wasn't completely bad, that's the point. I mean, that was the point. I mean . . . Oh, I don't know what the point is anymore."

"We're a wrinkle in the ocean of consciousness," he says. "We're a wave. I saw it."

She looks at him finally and can barely make out his profile in the dim light. "What do you mean by that?"

He shrugs and turns to face her. "I don't know. It's like a dream you can't quite remember when you wake up."

She eases her legs out from underneath her. Sharp pains prick her feet. "Don't get trippy on me, I can't handle it right now."

"I can't help it. I say what I mean. It's the truth."

She knows him well enough to know that he's serious. It was a mistake to come here, or maybe the mistake was that she'd followed his lead. Awkwardness creeps in. She rubs the blood back into her legs. "I came to pick you up," she says. "We're having lunch at Mandy's. You got her message?"

He looks at her, confused. "Message? What kind of message?"

They find ten messages on his machine, accumulated over weeks.

Unconcerned, he leaves the room to move the wicker screen and shrine. He rests his forehead against the photo of a smiling man and closes his eyes. Siobhan is left to listen to those who have been trying to contact him — Mandy, a woman she can only guess is his ex from her angry voice, Evan, Lance's mother, a man from work. Lance joins her in time to hear the last message, which is from Mandy: "Lance, pick up the phone. I know you're there. Everyone's in town finally, so get your butt over here. Tomorrow. Lunch. My place. Call me and don't be such a dope."

In the car, he rolls down the window, adjusts his baseball cap, and wriggles in the seat. "I work Tuesdays to Fridays now. The early shift."

"You're still at the co-op, right?"

"In the back room. I'm not a people person." He sticks his head out the window, lifts his cap and yells back at her, "Not that I lack compassion."

It's difficult to imagine him in a regular job, though he has bills to pay like everyone else. *Something*'s paying for that house.

"I'm off coffee now. It prevents the absorption of nutrients, you know." He opens the glove compartment.

"Hmmm."

"We were going to put gables in the attic, open up that space." As he says this, he leafs through the papers he finds in the glove compartment. His voice is deadpan, nonchalant, but he keeps his eyes averted. Then his hands fall into his lap. "I guess I'll do it myself. One day. It's a big house, hey? I suppose I'll get a dog. Or twenty cats." He giggles but ends with a sigh.

"Yeah." She has an urge to put a sympathetic hand on his arm. "It sure is a big house," she says and brakes before they turn onto Mandy's street.

LANCE: THE UNCERTAINTY PRINCIPLE

LANCE AND SIOBHAN WALK IN THROUGH the back door, startling Mandy and Lea who sit at the kitchen table, lost in thought. Mandy quickly recovers and her face is transformed by a wide smile. With some effort, she stands up. "Lance, I thought we'd never see you again!" He kisses her and she says airily, "It's lovely to see you, dahling." As he moves to kiss Lea, she turns her face. He embraces her nevertheless.

He hasn't yet figured out why they are all there, but doesn't want to be awkward about it and ask. For them, it is natural to gather like this, as a group, simply to sit around and talk. Once, this kind of activity might have come naturally to him, but now it seems like something out of science fiction. This is how, he supposes, they observe each other, how his old friends measure each other, as if observation could help them to know one another better.

But so often the very act of observing a thing changes it. Surely this is just as much the case with people as it is with atoms. Here, he thinks, is the uncertainty principle in action. As soon as one variable is measured, the other is changed and cannot be known. So the expectation that something will be true — probability — is more exact than actual observation. The rules of the sub-atomic world, he reminds himself, reach beyond, perhaps even to love and relationships. He tells himself to just be with the uncertainty, instead of resisting it.

Well, okay, he thinks, he can sit around and observe too. With a rush, he realizes he's overwhelmingly glad to see these people. He won't question why they have decided to meet here, now, for seemingly no reason. He hasn't been around a group of friends for so long, he hadn't realized how starved he was for their company. Now his mind is so occupied with this revelation that he can't think of anything to say. He can only reach out for a hand — it happens to be Mandy's — and hang on.

"Didn't you get my messages?" she's saying.

"He never checks his machine," Siobhan replies with disgust. She grabs his head in her hands and shakes it. "That's what machines are for, you nut bar." He giggles, enjoying the feel of her palms against his skin.

"Come look at the play room," Mandy says and drags him along. "I've been dying to show you."

Each room in the house is small and cluttered, making it appear less than it is. He takes in the narrow doorways, the hallway lined with photos and bookshelves, the too-big pieces of furniture. Mandy can barely fit through the hallway and not just because of her pregnant belly. Her personality is too huge for this cramped little house. In all ways, she is ready to burst out. She's too large to be contained. The walls are painted in colours too vibrant for the limited space. Anyone who looks at the red living room walls can see that the colour needs to stretch out. This makes him sad for Mandy's sake. He wants to see her expand, to see how far she can go.

They all crowd into the room. "I didn't want to be prejudiced," she says as she gestures to the yellow paint on the walls, the green baby blanket, the purple rug on the floor.

Pieces of a baby bed in a heap on the ground. She points to them and says, "That's supposed to go by my bed." His eyes are drawn to a large framed mandala, the only decoration in the room. It's bright and multicoloured with a symmetry that's just right in its lack of perfection. He could look at it for days. "What a great mandala," he says. It seems to spin before his eyes.

Mandy turns with a start, as if surprised to see it there. "Yeah. My dad bought it for the baby. It's a Nepalese design." She snorts. "Isn't that ironic?" The others exchange glances but don't respond. They all know that Sean, the baby's father, left for Nepal.

"It's a bit tight to play in," she admits with a shrug. The room is more of a large closet than anything. "But what can you do when you live in a shoe?" While he walks around the room and presses his palms against the walls, he listens to her voice as it rises and falls like a bird call. He presses his ear to the wall; wants to put his arms around the room. It wouldn't be that hard.

"Can't you find a bigger house?" Lea asks.

Mandy twists her mouth into a pout, then catches Lance's eye and breaks into a grin. "I've been working like hell to clean this place up," she says and holds up her hands, wiggling gold-painted fingernails. "Fingers to the bone."

"Should you be painting when you're pregnant?" Lea says, her brows drawn together.

"Mick did the actual painting. But still, it was so much work."

"It looks great," says Siobhan as she walks around to inspect the room.

"Yeah," seconds Lea. "Fabulous."

Mandy crosses her arms over her stomach and sighs in irritation. "No, tell me what you really think. This took me ages."

"Beautiful." Siobhan makes her voice as encouraging as possible.

"I'm very impressed."

"That's a bit better. Don't you like it, Lance?" Mandy pushes out her bottom lip. She's not happy herself, he reasons. There's something she's still searching for.

"You need more space," he says.

She hits him in the arm playfully, but he can tell she's offended. "Thanks a lot. Make me feel even worse about it, why don't you?"

"No," he continues. "I mean that as a compliment."

She rolls her eyes. He wonders how to explain to her, but while he struggles for the words, she waddles the two steps to the far corner of the room and calls over her shoulder, "Can someone help me put this co-sleeper together? I can't even pick it up." She tries to bend down, but her stomach gets in the way. She plants a hand in the small of her back and slowly eases up again. "Ooof." She makes a joke about it, but he can feel a great sadness in the room. Something is not in balance, but there's no way he can know what's out of kilter. He could knock out the north wall to open this room up, if the bathroom weren't in the way. His eyes roam the walls as he considers the options.

Lea presses the co-sleeper's instruction booklet into his hand and he grasps it tightly. "You're a handyman," she says with casual bravado, though he senses shyness underneath. They have not seen each other for so long. "You put it together."

He is pleased to be asked and feels a blush rise up his neck. He is nevertheless doubtful at the same time. "I'll try," he replies. There are many things he has tried to put together, but he can't say whether he's ever truly succeeded. Once, long ago, he thought he could put Kristy back together, but it's probably more accurate to say that he broke her apart. Or at least, he hadn't saved her from falling apart. He squints at the pieces of the baby bed on the floor, then looks at the booklet to see how they fit together.

He has barely started the assembly when Mandy calls him into the kitchen for lunch. She serves pinkish tomato soup and he studies his bowl in bewilderment. Overcooked, too salty and taken from a can (as the empty tins on the counter confirm), the soup might as well be space food. Nevertheless, he follows their lead and crumbles snow-white crackers onto the soup. With gusto, he eats two bowlfuls while the other three talk. Then he concentrates on a stack of crackers and smooths butter on their surface before popping them whole into his mouth. He will be sick for days, surely. After she eats, Siobhan mumbles, "I should go, I need to . . . make some calls," and leaves abruptly. He glances up just in time to see her turn away. At this, a slight frown mars Lea's carefully made-up face. She shoots a worried look in Mandy's direction.

The three of them linger around the kitchen table talking about not much of anything but, then again, saying more than Lance could ever hope to express. He cleans up as Mandy sighs over the burdens of being pregnant and he smiles, just to hear another voice.

EVAN

EVAN WHISTLES TO BREAK THE SILENCE that crowds in on him, to ward off the quiet, accusing trees. Thimbleberry leaves slap against his thighs as he negotiates along the half overgrown trail. He ducks to avoid Douglas Fir branches. Long before he can see it, he hears the creek, feels gusts of cool wet air as he winds through the trees. He hasn't ventured this far back for years.

In the months before Kristy's death, Evan's mother, Hannah, subscribed to the doctrine of radical honesty. All throughout the winter and spring of his graduation year, radical honesty moved like a rototiller through their everyday lives, scouring the foundations, unearthing that which had not seen the light of day for many years . . . all for good reason, as far as Hannah was concerned.

"Sometimes the only route to change is through revolution," she said. "The blade of grass must bend all the way to the other side before returning to the middle." This said after the confession that she'd never, in fact, approved of his choice of girlfriends, "They're insipid and never challenge you," his music, "It's loud," or his bleached hair, "The colour makes you look sickly." She'd hoped for better for him, hoped to raise a revolutionary spirit. "You don't have to fit in, do you?" she'd say as her eyes welled with sadness.

That spring Kristy moved into an apartment in Nelson, so that she didn't have to drive to town so often. Not long after, Hannah's sister Sally, Kristy's mother, broke up with her latest boyfriend and came to stay with them to recover. She stayed with Evan and Hannah out in Bonnington, not with her daughter in town. No one questioned it, Sally was in no shape to be a mother, not after so many years. The whole subject of Kristy was carefully avoided, despite Hannah's honesty doctrine. Honesty still had its boundaries, apparently. Meanwhile, Evan suspected that Kristy was having a relationship in secret, and that was why she moved to town, though he never asked.

Evan came home every afternoon to see his mother and Sally sort through old photo albums and wonder aloud how they had got to where they were. "I'll never do to you what my father did to me," his mother said. "I'll never hold you back like that." Look at what a traditional, repressive upbringing had done to Sally, kicked out of the family home at seventeen while pregnant with Jack. How many years had passed before she could talk to her parents again? And Hannah, forced too early into the arms of young Gerald. What a disaster. There were tearful phone conversations and coffee dates between Sally and Kristy during which Sally purged herself of all that weighed heavily on her heart. Or so Evan assumed. After three months of this, Sally returned to Fernie just after graduation, raw and vulnerable, but relieved of her burden. Her confessions, regrets, and indictments lay heaped in a pile, left behind.

From what he could tell, by the time Sally left Bonnington, she and Kristy were getting along for a change. This was a relief to them all, especially to Hannah who, over the past five years, had conditioned herself to fret over her neice. Not long after Sally left, though, Kristy called her in the middle of the night, distraught. Something must have happened during that conversation, because Kristy never talked to her mother again. Sally started to phone Hannah daily, then Hannah would call Kristy, but hardly ever got through. Kristy talked in monosyllables, when she talked at all.

Later, Sally claimed they'd argued over something trivial — her hairstyle, how much time she put into basketball — about nothing. Evan wonders what really happened. Why did Kristy call Sally in the middle of the night like that, when for years, she'd confided in Hannah rather than in her own mother?

The papers reported the accusations against Hiller around then. At the time, Evan and his mother didn't make the connection between Kristy and Hiller. He'd been more concerned about the his mother's burden than what might be going on in his cousin's head. In his blinkered state, he could only see himself. Somehow, through the torrential downpour, the blistering heat, the howling tornado of radical honesty, he managed to graduate. Even Kristy did. Then Evan got a real-live legitimate job in construction. He saved for a car — a new car, with a tape deck and leather seats — and his first mutual fund. His life would soon take off and he wanted to be ready for it.

One day, the police arrived at their door to ask them what they knew about Albert Hiller. They were speechless. Barely a month later, Kristy was dead. Evan and his mother sat at the kitchen table for hours at a stretch and stared at their hands, around the room, bewildered, everything now meaningless. He could feel himself slipping away, and he was terrified.

To save himself, he focused on the logistics. "Mum," he said, "We've got to be practical about this." Yes, yes, she agreed, with a ragged sigh.

Sally decided Kristy should be cremated, though she left the chore of actually arranging for the cremation with Hannah. Sally delegated long-distance, and called at all hours. They were too raw to think, chafed by the reality of what had happened, and stumbled along in a numb haze. Days and nights melded into an endless string of painful minutes. Evan drank tall glasses of vodka and lemon and couldn't be bothered to hide the bottle from his mother. It was the only way he could sleep, and she didn't notice anyway.

Together, Evan and his mother cleared out Kristy's apartment. He moved the furniture and heavy boxes but left the rest to her. He couldn't afford to miss any more work, he told himself. He'd need the money once he moved out.

Once the apartment was cleared, he and his mother could not agree on what to do with Kristy's possessions. Evan could hardly look at them. Her things just sat there and screamed out their Kristy-lessness. The battered couch and salvaged bed frame assumed a menacing air. The clothing was the worst, disembodied yet still exuding his cousin's smell.

"She'd want to give these away," he said. Without Kristy to give them shape and meaning, her clothes seemed even shabbier than before. Evan surveyed what remained of her life: all junk. "She'd want to start afresh."

"No," his mother said as she rubbed her thumb across a vintage, moth-eaten velvet skirt. "She loved this. She'd want her things around her." She picked up an earring and smiled at it wistfully. So the clothes ended up in boxes in the spare room of their house, where they waited for Evan to move out so they could clutter his room.

Sally insisted that Kristy's ashes be interred in the Fernie cemetery — "close to home" was how she put it. Hannah hung up the phone and paced the house in an uncharacterisitic rage.

"She was home here," she said to Evan as she collapsed into a kitchen chair. She stared tearfully at her hands splayed across the wooden tabletop. *"Here."*

"What do you expect? Sally's a fuckwit," was his reply. In the end, Evan and his mother drove the six hours to Fernie with the small urn containing Kristy's ashes in the back seat, their silent passenger. One of Sally's friends had organized a service in a local funeral parlor. Evan stared at his sneakers throughout the perfunctory service. It felt all wrong.

Late that night, as they neared the turnoff to Bonnington, his mother finally spoke. They'd make a shrine to Kristy at the back of the property, on the edge of a small clearing where a couple of lilacs grew. Kristy had loved to tramp through the bush, after all. "But," Evan argued, "she wanted to move to the city."

"No," his mother insisted. "Kristy was an independent soul. She felt a strong connection to the land."

Hannah had a small plaque made by a friend who was a stone carver. She invited Gerald, to Evan's surprise, and Kristy's father, Uncle Stan, who had been purposely left out of the Fernie service, and his children, Jack and Sara. She asked Evan to invite Kristy's friends. He got as far as Lance and told himself he'd phone the others, but couldn't bring himself to do it. So it was a small group that hiked up the hill one September afternoon to the spot Hannah had chosen. She asked Evan to speak, but he refused, terrified he might embarrass himself by crying. While the others held hands, Evan stood apart and stared stony-faced at the plaque he'd placed in the earth. No one was really able to say much. They spent a lot of time in silence, not meeting each other's eyes. As they walked back down the hill, Evan wondered what was the point of that little ceremony.

Now, Evan scans the bush for the break in the trees and the lilacs. His mother had insisted Kristy loved lilacs, but he couldn't remember his cousin saying anything about them one way or the other. And by the time of her funeral, he'd already forgotten how she smelled or the curve of her cheekbones, much less her preference of trees. He had the uncomfortable feeling they had all reinvented her, each of them shaping her into whatever it was they wanted her to be. He rubs his eyes, as if to clear away his thoughts. When he looks up again, he sees the clearing.

The ground around the granite plaque has been cleared, recently from the looks of it. A carpet of fir needles has been sprinkled around but, otherwise, there is very little to indicate what's there. Except the lilac trees, whose flowers, at this time of year, have turned into dry brown seedpods. He pauses a while, looks down at the grey granite, around at the ground-cover and up to the trees. With a swipe of his hand, he clears needles from the headstone. A long forgotten rain shower had turned a season's worth of forest dust and debris into polka dots which lay scattered across the granite surface.

He crouches there until his legs go numb, then slowly stands. He'd wanted to come here on his own first, before whatever it was that his mother had planned took place. His pain was his alone, and he resented his mother for inviting others. He can't go back to her house now, it would just make him morbid. He needs to go get drunk with someone, and he thinks of Siobhan. He rubs his hands over his shorts to clean them, then heads back down the mountain.

ONCE HOME FROM MANDY'S, SIOBHAN WANDERS in circles. She had to get away from her friends, had to find some space so that she could think. Tired, she cannot sleep; restless, she has nowhere to go. She can't face the possibility of running into someone she knows and she's in no mood for small talk. At the front window, she stares out across the sunny street to Elephant Mountain which crouches before her. She can't go out there, everyone in town either knows her or thinks they do. She could never be blissfully anonymous in Nelson.

The phone rings and she answers it impatiently.

"Why haven't you called?" It's Michael.

Though she'd thought of calling him earlier, now she's disappointed to hear his voice. "Sorry, I've been busy. Mandy invited us for lunch. Lea came over early."

"Well, I've been waiting for you and I have things to do today."

"Well, okay then, what's going on?"

"Good news. I've booked our flights for a trip to Toronto."

"What? I thought we decided we can't afford that. We were going to think about it for a while. Can you cancel?"

"Look, if we're going to move there, it only makes sense to take a look around first."

She is suddenly and unaccountably irritated. "Oh, so the decision has already been made then. I thought I had a choice in the matter."

"We talked this over, remember? It's a great opportunity for us."

He's right, of course. A partnership with his father would set them well on the way to a comfortable life. You don't just throw an offer like that away. She feels panicky, out of control, though not certain whether it's the move that bothers her. "A great opportunity for you maybe, but what about me?" she says, her voice rising. "All my contacts are here on the west coast." She wonders who she will know in Toronto other than Michael.

"Don't be unreasonable, doll." She hates it when he calls her that. "It might take a while, but I'll be making enough to get us by. We'll be together, remember."

He sounds so reasonable on the other end of the line. Here she is, barely able to hold the phone, her hand shakes so much. At one time, she would have jumped at the opportunity to go somewhere as exciting and far away as Toronto.

"We're just checking things out, okay?" he says.

"I guess so."

"Anyway, the tickets are non-refundable."

"Oh," she says. "I guess we're going then."

"I'll show you around," he says. "My folks will love seeing you again."

"Yeah, sure."

"Maybe one of these days I'll even get to meet your parents," he says, then with a forced chuckle adds, " Ooo, the mysterious parents."

"I should probably go," she replies. "We're having a potluck tonight. I have to get ready."

"Huh?"

"I'll call you later." She hangs up then glares at the phone a long while.

She climbs the stairs to her old room. She needs the satisfaction of putting things in order, so she goes to the locked cupboard. Maybe Lea is right. She'll sort through this mess finally, clear out her stuff.

The room has a closet and cupboard. Long ago, when the pain of sharing a room with her sister was at its most acute, she had annexed her half of the bedroom and declared the cupboard hers, the closet, her sister's. At least the cupboard has a lock. It's still locked and only she has the key, the rusty skeleton key that she is never without.

With some fiddling and twisting, she opens it. It smells dusty in there. Dusty and . . . something awful. A moulded or desiccated rose of forgotten significance falls at her feet. She finds a sticky bottle of perfume that she once thought beautiful, then a favourite pair of runners from her track and field days. The closet is jammed full: papers, books and old clothes in a messy pile. She pulls everything out onto the floor then finds some cardboard boxes. With a sigh, she sits down to sort through everything, piece by piece.

The letters are the hardest. It's impossible to throw them away. She unfolds notes passed in high school. The agonies and embarrassments still make her cringe. "Bon-bon, I can't stop thinking about Evan. Why did he dump me like that? Doesn't he like me anymore? It's been a week already and I'm still a wreck. Please talk to him. You're his bud. Ask him if I have a reason to live. Love ya always, Mandy." Her reaction to that note had been a mysterious flash of anger and she'd never replied. She opens another from Lea: "Bon, should I ask Lance to grad? Just as a friend, I mean. Girls aren't supposed to ask, are they? Your buzzing friend always, Bee." Their relation-ships are still too complicated, too tiresome. Nonetheless, she re-folds each letter and throws them in the "to keep" box. One day maybe she will laugh at them.

A photograph slides off another pile and she catches it. Slightly blurry, it's of all of them dressed up at a party. She can't remember what they were doing that night. Their faces fill the picture: Lance, Mandy, Lea, Evan, and herself. Her own face is wobbly with glee, her mouth wide open, but Evan stares darkly at the camera. A tiny bandaid crosses his chin. Frowning, she strains to remember what had been so significant that day. Nothing. Maybe they were all drunk. She looks at his face again. They've known each other so long. It's a rare thing, she realizes, not to have to explain yourself to someone. He already knows who she is. She feels more herself around him than with so many others. That's got to mean something. She puts the photo to one side and picks up a stack of letters bound together with elastic. The last two are from Mr. Hiller. Her fingers shake slightly as she unfolds them and she chides herself, *don't be so dramatic.* She reads through them both.

They had always been short and chatty. "I am enjoying the baseball series on TV," he wrote. "It is the sport I most loved as a child. It was invented by Canadians, did you know that?" He always tried to teach her something, even from his prison cell. He never so much as suggested that he was in prison, or that, for example, he watched TV with other inmates. No hint that he'd done anything wrong. He talked mostly about the past: when he was young, when she was young, anything but recent events.

She'd always believed what she'd been taught in catechism, that you should love your enemies. Had she got it wrong? She doesn't like to think about him, but as she looks at the letter in her hand, she can't keep the whole sad mess out of her mind.

When Mr. Hiller had first been charged with ten counts of sexual assault, the whole town recoiled. Then, quickly, people divided into two camps: those who said they'd always been suspicious from the moment they'd laid eyes on him, and those who did not believe the charges could possibly be true. Seriously now, people were getting charged right, left and centre these days, but that didn't always mean they were guilty. A man couldn't look at a child anymore without being labelled a molester. Society was becoming too suspicious, paranoid. No one believed in plain old goodheartedness. He'd done so much for the community after all. They knew him well, he wouldn't do something like that.

At first, Siobhan belonged to the second camp. It just couldn't be true. As the trial wore on, the second camp quickly lost members and those who remained fell silent. A very small group continued to be supportive. They were organized informally by his sister, a quiet, devoted, and increasingly sad woman. They gave him shelter in that time between the sentencing and the beginning of the trial, when he was still a free man according to the law, though not according to public opinion. He could not walk the streets safely. Even those who had never met him would recognize his face from the newspapers. It was a small town after all, and when had a terrible thing like this ever happened before? This wasn't exactly Chicago. This was beautiful, historic, sleepy Nelson where half the people were unemployed and not even the pot growers disturbed the peace. They just hung out.

Siobhan had felt personally offended by the accusations. Up until then, the world had been a welcoming place because there were selfless, generous people like him in it. Mr. Hiller — not the man himself, but the idea of him — had unconsciously become her reference point, a peg planted solidly in the ground when everything else was so variable and unknown. Then that peg had been ripped out and she was left to hang in the breeze.

One night, after an argument with friends about it, she'd written a letter to him to say that he'd always been good to her and she would always remember that and if ever there was a need for character witnesses, she would say something kind about him. She felt better after writing it all down. She cried and felt indignant, then angry, then defensive, then calmer. The act of writing was cathartic. She folded the letter and slipped it between the covers of her locked diary, which she hid at the bottom of her locked closet. It's not as if she would actually send it. She didn't have his address. He was in hiding after all.

The whole thing felt deeply unfair. Why had those vague, nameless, faceless beings brought this about? Who were they and why did they stir up trouble like this? They were being purposely nasty. Some people were just messed up from day one and had to blame someone for it. Some people always had an axe to grind, a chip on their shoulder. Rumours flew around about who the victims might be. Of course, legally their names couldn't be published, but people speculated. She didn't want to know who they might actually be because it was none of her business.

But she'd always known that you had to do the right thing in life, and that doing the right thing often meant you had to take the hard road. Sometimes it wasn't obvious at first what you were meant to do. This belief, coupled with a natural sympathy for the underdog and the desire to please and be pleasant, got her involved. Accidentally.

It happened not long after the initial accusations were made, during teatime after Sunday mass. Her mother had left early, complaining of a headache. Siobhan stood there with half a cup of tea in her hand and wondered how she could make a similarly hasty exit without seeming impolite. Then Mr. Hiller's sister had approached her, the nice young teenager that she was, a girl who made the effort to come to church when so many kids these days were too busy driving around in loud cars, swearing and drinking until all hours. Miss Hiller's sad, sad eyes pinned Siobhan as if she were a mounted butterfly. Inevitably, the conversation worked its way toward the thing that made Miss Hiller's heart so heavy: the unfair accusations. The world would never be right for her again. She could not sleep at night, thinking about all the ill will directed at the brother who had practically raised her since their parents died. He'd had a hard life as it was, with his wife deserting him those many years ago. Living alone when he should have had a family, still faithful to his marriage vows.

Siobhan murmured sympathy and support and, by the time the teacup was empty, agreed to keep his spirits up by writing to him. Miss Hiller would forward mail to him, wherever he was at the time. Siobhan left the church hall with an address written on a piece of paper and felt like she was either bravely doing something right for a change, or something . . . well . . .

He replied almost immediately. It was so good to hear from her. He, too, described a sense that the world had been turned upside down, that it would never be right again. He was confused, and couldn't understand how people would doubt him. He prayed daily for meaning, for deliverance. So she replied with the written equivalent of murmured sympathy and support.

Then he was convicted and sent to jail.

After a couple of years, the whole Hiller business bored her. She moved to the city. She went to art college to unearth her creativity and discard her dull past. She had ambitions, was busy. She redefined herself in every way. After longer and longer pauses, she would send off a reply to his letters but it was a painful duty, like giving blood. She never mentioned to anyone that she wrote to him. Her friends would never understand. The shame did not reflect on them in the same way that it reflected on her. They weren't Catholic. And it wasn't anyone's business. Part of her instinctively knew to keep the correspondence secret.

After a while, though, Siobhan began to wonder. Had he really been as good as she remembered? Maybe there had been something not quite right about him after all.

Really though, she didn't think about him too much. Mostly, she got busy with her life.

Besides, it's not like she was ever actually involved in the situation. She'd never wanted to put a face to Mr. Hiller's victims, or a shape to his guilt.

It's over now, so just forget about it.

She throws the letter onto the floor and stumbles down the stairs to the kitchen. After she puts on the kettle, she opens the back door and stands on the step. She needs fresh air but in the end, it does not comfort her. The kettle whistles but is ignored. Finally, she unplugs it and wanders into the living room. She puts on a record, turns up the volume, then drifts back to her room.

She continues to sort, efficient now, almost angry, and throws as much as she can into a green garbage bag.

She doesn't hear Evan until he's in the doorway. "I said, hey!" he hollers over the music.

"Oh holy shit." She drops the bag and whirls around. With a half-closed fist, she whacks his shoulder. "Don't you ever scare me like that again, you asshole."

He takes a step backwards. "I knocked but the music is so loud. Your back door is wide open, you know."

Overcome with a strange relief, she crushes him in a hug. "It's so awful, Evan. It's been such a shitty afternoon."

"What's going on?"

She steps back quickly, glances around, pushes a strand of hair off her face. What *is* going on? "I'm cleaning up. Moving the last of my stuff out finally." The record ends. They stare at each other in silence.

"Can I stay here tonight?" he says.

LANCE: SCHRÖDINGER'S CAT

AFTER THE LUNCH DISHES ARE DONE, Lance searches Mandy's cupboards for cookies until he finds half a box of stale ginger snaps. He hasn't eaten a store-bought cookie in years and though they taste like sweet cardboard, he grabs a handful anyway. Now that he has finally stepped out of his house and into hers, he doesn't want to leave. He thinks maybe he'll stay there forever. *Is this some kind of falling in love?* he wonders. Eventually, Lea gets up to leave, so he and Mandy follow her to the door. As a unit, they shuffle down the front stairs, gathering on each step before they lurch forward, like a stumbling, three-headed animal. Lea chews on her lip and squints into the sunlight. She takes in a breath as if to say something, breathes out, looks down the street, opens her mouth, then closes it abruptly.

"What?" says Mandy.

"Nothing," Lea replies, then with a swish of her ponytail, turns her head to peer intently up the street. She takes a deep breath and in a rush blurts out, "Do you guys think that Kristy might have been . . . " She trails off.

"One of Hiller's victims?" Mandy finishes.

Lea nods. Lance does his best to block their voices out and stares hard at the sunlight that streams through the trees.

"Yeah, I'm sure of it," Mandy replies. "Shit, you'd have to have your head buried in the sand not to figure that one out."

She pauses, takes a breath, then exhales slowly. "You know, I helped her find that apartment here in town. Helped her move in even." She runs a hand over the high arch of her stomach and sighs. "I was jealous of her, living on her own like that. Thought she was setting up some sort of love nest or something."

"Why, did she say she was . . . going out . . . with someone?" Lea asks, uncertain. The childish term, "going out," hangs in the air, perverted now, and slimy.

"Sort of. She hinted he was older than us — but not that he was *old*."

Lance squints into the sun and hopes that if he keeps silent, they won't ask him questions. He wonders at Lea's sudden curiosity. In high school, Kristy had been too much of a fringe character. Socially speaking Lea had been too close to falling off the edge herself. For the sake of survival, Lea only hung out with those above her, like Mandy.

Lea smoothes the hair back off her forehead, then fishes through her purse until she pulls out a tube of lip gloss. "Don't you feel guilty for not asking Kristy more about it?" she asks, and looks at them.

Mandy shakes her head. "Well, maybe at first. And I'll always feel sad. Not guilt anymore, though. I was just a kid. I had no idea." Lance marvels at her words. How can she make it sound so easy?

Lea's face clouds over with confusion. "I never really knew her myself," she mumbles and takes the last step onto the sidewalk. "Now that I think about it."

Mandy follows her. "No." They ponder this in silence, before she continues, "She wasn't Hiller's only girl either. Jeez, hey?"

Lea sighs, like you would over a distant tragedy, something terrible but remote. "Sometimes, when something good happens — like my university grad — I'll think of her, and feel sad she'll never have the chance to have these experiences. But . . . " She lifts her shoulders in a shrug.

Mandy turns to Lance. She is beautiful. "You're awfully quiet, Lance." He looks at the ground while she presses a finger against his shoulder. "Kristy said something to you, didn't she?"

He blinks painfully. "Yes," he says.

Lea whips around and gives him a hard look. "What?"

And Mandy says, "Why didn't you tell us?"

Lance shrugs. In all the time they'd been together, he hadn't told Linda, either. Never even mentioned Kristy to her. But he'd found out about Mr. Hiller when Kristy went to the police station to give her statement. Not that he'd known that's where they were going. He had tried to offer her a ride, then sensed she was upset, so ended up following her. As if he could help. What had he been thinking? Back then, when he was a teenager, he really believed he could change the world. He thought if he just put some effort into it — laid down on the logging road in protest, wore hemp clothing, opened his heart and consciousness (it was all the same thing to him) — the big problems would be solved. He thought he had the power to save the earth *and* the people on it.

He no longer believes this. He is twenty-eight now and his only ambition is to cause the least amount of damage possible during his time on this planet. He is an affliction on the earth and on the people around him, as experience has proved. He must be isolated. And anyway, all is already lost . . . humanity and the earth. His reduce-reuse-recycle lifestyle won't ever make a difference, and even with an increased consciousness, he is still lonely and fucked up. Maybe all is lost because he betrayed Kristy that night. He's given up trying to figure it out, it's too painful. "I was thinking," he says as he steps out of the porch's shadow and into the sunshine, "of building a shelf in the baby's play room. Doesn't that sound good?" He flings out his arms.

"Lance," Lea says in a disapproving tone. "What do you know?"

"Does it matter?" he says finally, his back to them. "It's not my story to tell. I'm going to get my tools, Mandy, and some wood. I'll be back soon."

"Okay," she says with a sigh.

Okay, okay, he repeats to himself as he warms in the sun. *No matter what happened, I'm going to be okay.*

He heads towards his house; he needs to pick up his van and tools. It's a long walk, across town and up the long hill of Granite Road and Lance can't help but think back to the night Kristy went to the police station. For years, he has pushed all thought of that episode out of his mind. At least, he tried to.

What he remembers most clearly are the boots she wore, white leather with a fringe of tassles down the back. Stupid. The late spring evening was chilly and wet. He had stopped in the gas station for a drink just before heading home. When he stepped out of the gas station's store, he saw her leaning against the side wall, in the shadows.

He hadn't noticed her around school much lately, had even wondered if she'd dropped out and no one had told him. Now that he thinks about it, why didn't he bother to ask Evan if something was up? He'd been too self-absorbed, or maybe still ashamed about dumping her those years earlier. She hadn't deserved it.

That night, though, the glow of her cigarette and the white gleam of her boots caught his attention. He walked over without questioning why. He felt so clumsy standing before her, so awkward, the way you do when you've ignored a friend for too long.

He barely recognized her. She'd changed when he wasn't looking. She stood with her shoulders rounded forward and her eyes down. Her arms were crossed over her chest and the wrists that poked out from her jacket were delicate and bluish-white. The cigarette teetered between two long fingers.

He couldn't stop looking at her. Her dyed-black hair, her tired, old-looking eyes surprised him. At a loss for words, he'd offered her a ride.

Of course, she refused. He couldn't blame her but, at the time, he felt offended and would have walked away if she hadn't pushed off the wall and stormed off before he had the chance. Guilt surfaced and before he knew it, he was following her towards downtown.

"I'm glad I ran into you," he'd said to her retreating back.

"Fuck you!" she'd said as she whirled around to face him at last. It stopped him short. "You don't give a shit about me and you never did. You're just like my cousin. 'Kristy's such a spaz,'" she'd said in a perfect imitation of Evan's sneering tone. "'Let's ignore Kristy.'"

He still feels nauseous at how she'd seen through him. He had said those things, but never thought she'd overheard. He tripped after her and tried to apologise. He was a good guy, she had to see that. As he stumbled along, he stared at the heels of her white boots flashing ahead of him.

Then . . . then when all he was thinking about was how to redeem himself in her eyes, she'd started to talk. Haltingly. They fell into step and walked side by side.

"I'm such a loser," she'd said.

"Someone finally loves me," she'd said. "And then it all goes to shit."

"We just want to live our lives together," she'd said.

She grabbed onto the sleeve of his jacket and hung on. She turned her face away, but kept a lethal grip on his jacket. They passed the aquatic centre in silence; its concrete hulk sheltered them from the wind.

Her footsteps slowed until Lance felt he had to drag her along. Her hand on his sleeve squeezed convulsively. Lance could sense she was filled with darkness. Fleetingly, he was curious, but only in the way he would look back at a car wreck, or suddenly gain interest in someone whose parent had died or who had contracted a fatal illness. The fascination with raw misery. But mostly, he was scared to find out what lay deep inside her, didn't know if he could handle exposure to it.

At that point, he saw that they were headed for the police station.

A car horn honks and Lance jumps. He had been standing deep in thought on the edge of the highway. His heart races, though he can't tell whether it's from the picture of Kristy so clear in his mind, or the car that swerves around him.

When he had looked up at the police station, he'd stopped. He couldn't believe she'd go in *there*. He can still feel the tug on his arm as she tried to drag him along. He simply couldn't go in there. He'd heard of police dogs who could smell pot smoke that was weeks old, who could sniff you out even if all you'd done was stand by a smoker. His palms had gone sweaty and his heart pounded. He'd started to back away, all thoughts of Kristy gone. Her hand on his sleeve reminded him that she was there.

"Come in with me, please," she'd said. "I can't do it alone."

And then she'd said, "Lance, they want me to give a . . . statement. They're going to charge Al . . . Mr. Hiller.

They don't understand that we're in love. He told me he loves me. We're going to live together."

The blood roared in his ears and he could hardly hear her. He couldn't believe what she said and he still can't believe it now, ten years later. At the time, it was too impossible to contemplate. It was dangerous; it was the kind of thing that made everything else senseless. So what had he done? He'd turned and left her there.

Lance stands in his driveway and chews on his lip. His van sits quietly on the gravel, rusting away. *He'd just left her.*

With deliberate, measured movements, he loads his tools into the back of the van. He forces himself to think of other things — he'll need screws, saw, level. There's a spot by the door, above the change table in the play room where a shelf could fit. He climbs in and while he drives towards the building supply store, he repeats different versions of Schrödinger's equation to himself. Delta x times delta p . . . Psi times x, t. He'd always liked Schrödinger, a physicist who loved Vedanta philosophy.

As he pays for the few bits of lumber (Jason nowhere in sight), he whistles a tune, then slips the bills back into his wallet with careful precision. What can he do about Kristy today, anyhow? Today, he can build a shelf for Mandy. Hopefully, it will be strong enough that it won't fall on her baby and kill him or her. This is all he can do.

He parks down the street in the broken shade of a maple. When he nears Mandy's house, he sees her, still standing on the sidewalk. Her back to him, she peers intently at the ground. When he stops beside her, she puts a finger to her lips. "Shh," she says. "You'll scare him away." She points to a grey cat who sits a safe distance away under a burdock leaf. Hindered by her protruding stomach, she bends slightly, a hand outstretched. The cat pokes his head forward, then thinks better of it and settles back under the leaf. "*Pss, pss, pss,*" she says encouragingly. The cat meows, takes a half step forward, then falters. "Uh-oh," she says. "He's got a bad leg, do you see that?" With a hand against her back, she straightens.

At first glance, the cat is a handsome, sleek creature, but when Lance looks closer, he sees the wounded leg and hip bones that protrude.

"I'm a silly goose." She whispers so as not to disturb the cat, "I'm in no shape to be dealing with a sick animal. Not now." She looks to him for agreement. "He probably has an owner somewhere, huh? Someone who looks after him." Tentatively, the cat inches forward as if he can sense her hesitation. He sniffs the ground. "That's the problem with strays. You think, 'oh, how cute,' then find yourself saddled with a cat for fifteen years. And I can't be doing that. You know what I mean?"

Lance nods. "Yeah, I know." Linda had always wanted a cat, but Lance had stood firm. Pets expect to be cared for. And maybe in the back of his mind, he'd known that a cat would just make breaking up that much messier. Why make it worse?

EVAN

SIOBHAN BLINKS. DID EVAN REALLY JUST ask to stay over?

Evan's mouth goes dry as he stares at Siobhan.

"Why?" Siobhan says, looks at Evan in the doorway like he's crazy.

"Forget it," he says and turns to head down the stairs. She always wants to know why, can never just accept a thing without an explanation first. He'll find somewhere else to stay.

She puts a hand on his arm. "Wait a sec. Look, I was just asking. What's up with you anyway?" She scans his face. "Okay, okay, I don't need to know. I'm being nosy."

"Did I tell you Gerald's moving back in?" he says.

"With who, your mum?"

He nods.

She blinks in surprise and her mouth slides from a grin to a frown. "No, you never said anything about that. Weird."

He nods again, turns away and walks down a couple of stairs. He stops at the landing to watch her follow him. The clean curve of her eyebrows emphasizes her wide-set eyes. It's like he's never seen her before. "Yeah, it's weird all right," he says.

"Well then, we can make up a bed in my brother's old room." This isn't the response he expected. "The extra sheets are downstairs."

"What, now? There's no rush." He frowns. They stand inches apart on the landing. He notices how her white teeth push against her lip — just enough to make her mouth prominent, yet not enough to look bucked. She pushes past him and her breast grazes his arm.

"I guess we should buy some food for this barbecue tonight," she says over her shoulder.

He'd forgotten all about it. "Sure," he replies, unenthused, and follows Siobhan into the kitchen.

"Shouldn't you call your folks first?" she says.

"Don't call them 'my folks'," Evan says.

"Well your mum then. She'll be expecting you tonight."

Maybe Siobhan's parents still treat her like a child, but his mother has never been one to stay awake all night, waiting for him to come home. "My mum's not exactly worried."

"Yeah, right. You're just making her worry to get back at her."

"What?" That's the most absurd thing. She's starting to sound like one of his mother's co-counselor friends.

"Don't you want to talk about it?" she asks. "The whole Gerald thing?"

"No."

"Why not?"

He shrugs. "I'd rather not think about it."

"Doesn't it bother you?"

"Yeah. That's why I don't want to think about it."

She frowns at him, then heads out the back door. They walk down the sidewalk, bumping shoulders. Evan kicks at the debris that collects along the edges of the road. The streets are covered in a layer of dust and gravel, the moraine deposited after a winter of sanding trucks. He always feels like one day he will fall on his ass walking down these hills.

After a while she says, "Michael's parents were separated for a while, you know," and looks up at him with an almost business-like helpfulness.

"Who?"

"Michael," she says. "You know . . . Michael," then turns away.

"And?" he says. "What does that have to do with anything?"

She shrugs. "He dealt with it really well. Michael's very practical that way. He might have some, I don't know, insight." She ends with a nervous laugh and shrugs again. "Never mind."

Grumpily, he opens the door to the health food co-op and she smiles apologetically as she walks in. He glances around the store to push aside his irritation.

He would never shop here by himself. It reminds him too much of being dragged here as a kid. To Kristy a trip to the grocery store was an adventure, but he was always embarrassed by his vegan mother and her scruffy Guatemalan fashion. He runs a hand over his short hair and takes in the scene. The co-op is a window onto the alternative future. In this little world, progress doesn't mean convenient, wired or online, but rather fair trade, animal friendly and organic. Siobhan heads towards the produce while he wanders the aisles and inspects the shelves. This whole alternative scene, he muses, is just as sleek and seductive as a palm pilot. Both versions of progress promote their own brand of sexiness. This place is what every granola-muncher guiltily, secretly craves in their heart of hearts: abundance, excess, the permission to still have it all. He snorts, glances around for Siobhan, then his eye catches sight of a corn chip display. The brand he can never find in the big box stores. They're crisp but have some heft to them. He grabs two bags. When he finds Siobhan, he tosses them into the basket on her arm and says, "This place is such a crock of shit."

One eyebrow lifts as she replies. "Oh yeah? You want anything to go with your crock of shit chips?"

"Ha, ha."

She flashes a grin and the dimple in her cheek deepens. As they wander the aisles and haggle over what to buy, Evan feels like they are edging uncomfortably close to a kind of domesticity. Sometimes he thinks that buying groceries demands a deeper level of intimacy than having sex. More commitment. At least with sex you can close your eyes and shut up. Then he finds himself strangely pleased to discover they both reach for the same salsa. And bread, and cheese. They agree to buy wine on the way back. Oh shit, he thinks.

Back at her parents' house, they both gravitate to the living room and collapse, she onto the couch and he in the chair next to it. He stretches his legs. Her arm dangles into the space between the couch and chair and he is acutely conscious of the way she moves her hand through the air as she talks. They rehash high school memories now — the safe ones — and she laughs easily.

She says, "Remember when you and I and Lance went jumping off those cliffs into the river?" But then a frown flickers across her face.

"We froze our butts off," he says. It's funny now, thinking back on it, but it sure wasn't at the time.

Matching velveteen slipcovers adorn the armrests of his chair and almost immediately, one falls onto the floor. "What's the point of these things anyway?" he says as he bends down to pick it up, nearly colliding with Siobhan's skull as she too bends down. Instinctively, she puts a hand to her eye, then bursts into a nervous kind of laughter. He reaches out to pull her hand away. Their hands dangle in the space between the two chairs. He twirls the ring on her thumb around, as if this is his purpose. He hangs onto her hand, fiddles with the ring, strokes her palm, then says, "We should go swimming there again while we're up here, don't you think?" He stares down at their entwined fingers.

She makes a funny little sound in the back of her throat, then abruptly leaps off the couch. "Shit," she says. "I forgot to do something. I was going to bring something to the park for Mandy, but I've got to . . . Listen," she says and furrows her brow as if concentrating very hard, "I think I'll have to join you guys down at the beach later. This won't take me long, but I really . . . " She tugs her shirt down. "I really should do this thing for Mandy."

Glaring, he leans forward to rest his elbows on his knees. "Fine, then," he says. "I guess I'll get going."

"Here, let me put the food in a cooler," she says and gestures towards the bags on the kitchen table. "I can bring the rest later."

"Don't bother."

SIOBHAN

SIOBHAN PRACTICALLY RUNS DOWN THE STAIRS after she closes the door behind Evan, her heart pounding. Then runs back upstairs to tuck the empty grocery bags into her mother's frilly bag-organizer, like she is hiding evidence. Evidence of what? she asks herself angrily, but does it anyway. Then runs back downstairs and slams the door to the makeshift darkroom. Throws the bolt, then turns to stare at the hulking heron of an enlarger that dominates the table. She remembers how her father helped her set up the darkroom when she was a teenager. The height post is bolted to the table top; the boxy enlarger lens with the negative carrier sits at the top of the post as if hanging its head. She knows that it will soon become a fossil, a relic of her former life. A wave of sentimental attachment washes over her as she strokes the black metal hood.

The familiar motions of setting up the enlarger and mixing the developing chemicals quiets her mind. Soon she hums under her breath. Down here in the back room of her parents' basement, the noises from the street and upstairs are barely-heard rumbles. She can't listen for Evan's footsteps, wouldn't hear them even if he did come back for some inexplicable reason. Because he's not coming back. And she doesn't want him to.

What is this thing she has to do for Mandy after all? The idea had only come to her the instant she'd said it out loud. She is here in the basement because it would be dangerous to go down to the beach with Evan. She would betray herself if she did — she'd find everything he said sidesplittingly funny or would stand too close to him. So she'd come up with the first excuse that came to her mind. A flimsy one at that.

The dynamic of their group had been fixed years ago and couldn't possibly be changed now. They could think about mixing love and sex and friendship when they were young enough that it didn't matter. But now any new move would be serious, would upset the balance beyond repair. And besides, she is involved. She repeats this aloud: "I am already involved. I don't do crazy things. I'm not that kind of person." She yanks open a box. Inside lies the debris of her seventeen-year old self: photos, negatives, and the journals where she kept notes of aperture and shutter speed, light conditions and occasionally, random thoughts. She shouldn't have brought up that time when she, Evan, and Lance had gone cliff jumping. The memory makes her flush.

It was a Friday afternoon, near the end of an unseasonably warm June. Their final days of high school were almost on them, but even so, she couldn't quite imagine life beyond it.

Lance had his parents' car that day. It didn't take much to convince him and Evan to skip. She knew of some pools along the Kootenay River above the dam and described them to the guys over lunch. Kristy overheard them and, uncharacteristically, begged to join in. She'd always wanted to go cliff-jumping, she said. Her eyes gleamed in anticipation of the risk. But when she wasn't looking, they slipped out the back door of the gym. As they pulled out of the parking lot, they glanced over their shoulders to make sure she wasn't following. Siobhan and Evan hunched down in their seats and giggled guiltily.

"She'll be wandering around for hours looking for us," Evan said. "She just won't give up, once she latches onto an idea."

"Poor confused Kristy." Siobhan chuckled and they joined in.

Lance choked back his laughter. "We should have brought her along," he mumbled, half-guilty.

"Nah," Evan said, then stuck his head out the car window. "We're abso-fucking-lutely free!" he hollered to the houses flying by. It felt good to escape, to do exactly what they wanted and nothing they were supposed to do.

The pools were deep enough and the cliffs high enough to be a perfect spot for cliff jumping. They turned off the highway onto a dirt road. Dust clouds blew up around the car but through them she made out a figure by the side of the road and as they came closer, she saw he pushed a rusty bicycle. Precariously balanced on the bicycle was an enormous burlap sack. His pink turban was what she recognized. He was one of the many characters who hung around town, scraggly-haired and wooly-bearded. She'd heard that he didn't have a home, but he always seemed to be happily sipping a cup of coffee in Wait's News or Danny's All-Star Deli. She couldn't figure out his name, because he changed it every few years. Leroy, Samson, Elvin.

He turned to them as they passed and enthusiastically waved and cackled with laughter as if they had just shared a joke. They all waved back. "Hey," she said. "He knows us."

Lance waved but said, "Nah. He's that happy to see anyone."

"Yeah," Evan said. "He buys fruit from my mum all the time and still doesn't recognize her." Then he added, "That'll be Kristy in a few years."

They silently watched the man, who now seemed to mumble to himself. Total loony-bin, Siobhan thought and wondered if what Evan said was true.

She twisted around in the seat to watch him out the back window. She couldn't decide if he looked deranged or as if he didn't have a care in the world. "What's he carrying?" she said.

"Probably what he'll eat all winter," Lance said, unconcerned. He accelerated as soon as they were far enough away that they wouldn't drown him in dust.

"Huh." She settled into her seat. Why were they not fascinated?

To get to the cliffs, they had to hike a short way through bush. The path cut a faint ragged line through the underbrush but it was just visible enough that they could follow it. Pulling up in the rear, she stared at the back of Evan's heel as he picked over the uneven terrain. She took in a deep breath and strained to smell the hot pitch scent of pine. It had occurred to her recently that if she ever went out with a guy, he would have to be like Evan. Not Evan himself, of course not. Though sometimes he was harsh, she kind of appreciated this roughness — it meant he saw her as an equal, as real, not something that required special handling. At least, she hoped so. But Evan was always after some other girl, any girl. She wasn't interested in him, either. They were just friends, after all.

Along the river, they scrambled over and down moss-covered rocks in their bare feet. The diving cliffs were two big flat rocks, one to the right of the other and a few feet higher. "Holy," she said looking down at the pool of black water. "It's got to be a twenty foot drop at least."

Evan hesitated just behind her and looked over her shoulder. "No way!" he exclaimed. "That's eighteen feet, maybe nineteen."

She rolled her eyes. "Okay, okay."

"Who's going first?" Lance said as he tugged off his T-shirt. The waistband of his underwear peeked above his shorts. They were blue-grey, the material frayed. Yuck, she thought and turned away.

"You go," she said.

Evan dropped his T-shirt on the moss behind them and gazed down at his chest. He rested his hands on his hips and tested various poses until, apparently satisfied, he turned his attention to the trees behind them. The choker necklace that Siobhan had made cut across the tanned skin of his neck. She had made one for each of them: beads crafted by a local potter strung along a thick leather thong. Evan's choker was made of pearly white and green beads. She was surprised, and flattered that he actually wore it.

He glanced up and caught her staring at him. Squinting against the light, he lifted a hand to shield his eyes. "Yeah, this is way better than Consumer Ed," he said and drew out the words.

She flushed at the approval, then nodded.

"So, now what?" Lance said. It was just warm enough to suntan, so they lay down on the dry crunchy moss, pointed at clouds and made up stories about what they were. It was almost as though they were on summer holidays already. Siobhan hung onto that carefree, unhurried feeling for a few minutes.

After a bit, Evan sat up and ran his fingers through his hair to brush out the twigs and dry needles. "Shit," he said, a hand to his ear. He twisted around and scanned the ground around him. "I lost my earring." On hands and knees, he ran his fingers over the thick moss.

Siobhan and Lance joined him. "What does it look like?"

"Gold," he said. "It's, like, real gold too."

They pawed the ground but found nothing. Finally, he sat back on his haunches. "It was a present from Kristy," he said, then shrugged. "Worth a lot, I bet. Bummer."

They stood and swiped the dirt off their clothes. Siobhan glanced back at the water and debated whether to leave her T-shirt and shorts on or change into the gym strip she'd brought along.

"Think it's cold?" Lance took a step closer so his toes gripped the edge of the rock. He flapped his arms like a swimmer before competition.

"It's going to be freezing," Evan said and they laughed nervously.

Lance looked from him to Siobhan, a crazed, daring gleam in his eye. The corners of his lips lifted into a grin. With one big step he lunged over the cliff and called out, "Geronimo!" as he hurtled downwards. *One, two, three.* They peered over the edge and watched his arms trail overhead before they disappeared. A mass of white bubbles exploded in the black water. She held her breath.

"Shit," Evan said quietly.

"Come on, it's fun," she said, but her eyes were trained on the water below. Come up, come up, come up, she repeated silently like a mantra. She couldn't back down. This whole expedition had been her idea. She would just have to jump, at least once. Come up. Come up.

With a whoosh, Lance's head popped out of the water. He slung his wet hair around and said something but she couldn't catch the words. "How cold is it?" she called down, relieved and excited again. He didn't reply but paddled with quick strokes to the rocks that lined the shore. Behind her, Evan looked doubtful. He shook his head.

"Just go and then it'll be done," she said. "You'll like it."

"No, you go first."

"You'll never jump then."

"I'll go right after you. Seriously. You can count on me." He nodded several times as he said this.

But he wouldn't, she could tell by the look in his eye. Guys were supposed to be fearless. They were supposed to act before thinking. She counted on them acting before thinking. Through narrowed eyes, she studied him until she heard Lance scramble up the rocks behind them. His grin was wide and goose bumps stood out all over his skin. "It was great," he said. He wiped the water off his chin. "Totally radical."

If she was going to skip out, it had to be worth the risk. She could not go home without having tried. "Evan's not going to jump," she said, hoping to shame him into it.

"You gotta go," Lance said and flopped down on the rock. "You're, like, flying for a couple of seconds."

"Yeah, okay. I'm just getting myself psyched." Evan hugged himself and looked down to the water once more. "It's a farther drop for me you know. I'm taller." He straightened and threw his shoulders back.

She rolled her eyes. "For God's sake." But she'd taken a step back too. Her heart pounded a bit too rapidly for comfort.

"Go together," Lance said. "Count to three and then go. That way neither one can chicken out."

"Hey, I'm not chickening out," she said as she looked sideways at Evan. Maybe Lance was right. If she went with him, maybe Evan would jump. Maybe she alone had the power to convince him, to give him courage. She held out a hand, shyly at first, then brusquely like she didn't care one way or another. "Come on," she said.

He shook his head. "I'm going to jump," he said and gave her an angry glare. "But when I'm ready."

She wiggled her fingers at him. Why won't you come with me, she thought. With me. With a flick of his wrist, he dismissed her outstretched hand. She withdrew it quickly but kept her face impassive. Fine then. He'd made himself clear. Damn him. She turned back to the cliff edge. Without a moment to think about it, she took two strides and launched herself off the rock, arms out at her sides. Damn him, damn him. She fell through the whistling air, then a sharp smack ripped at her arms and cold pulled her down and water rushed painfully up her nose. She surfaced , coughed out water and blinked blindly. The water was cold against her hot cheeks. Automatically she pulled through the water, her legs so numb she couldn't tell if they moved. Oh man, that was stupid. Her arms began to throb.

Through bleary eyes she could see that she was headed away from the shore but before she could turn around, a low-pitched whoosh and sudden swell told her that someone had broken through the water just behind her. She spun around and snorted water out of her nose. A new circle of bubbles mingled with the dissipating bubbles around her, but she couldn't see anybody. She squinted up to the cliffs and saw Lance wave happily down at them. He cupped his hands to his mouth and shouted, but a gust of wind took the words away.

As she sculled with her hands, she spun around and around but all she saw was her own body, then the clear water around her faded into black. She was too scared to kick her legs in case she hit Evan. Where was he? Instantly she regretted the hatred she'd felt towards him moments earlier. She hadn't meant it.

She wanted him to live, to be okay. It had been stupid of him to jump like that, he could have landed right on top of her. Where was he? Come up, come up. Oh God. He'd been down there too long. Her teeth chattered. Her T-shirt and shorts felt suddenly heavy.

A flash of white shone through the water to her left and then disappeared. She floated towards it, then saw another flash. With a deep breath, she plunged back into the freezing water, her eyes wide open. She clutched at the white and flailed until her hand hit something that could have been an arm and she grabbed onto it. With a weak scissor kick she pulled up, but he was heavy and didn't budge an inch. Her grip on his arm tightened. Vainly, she kicked again but thought, I'm no good at this. I'm not strong enough for emergencies. She could feel the blood drain out of her legs. Her lungs burned. He was so heavy, his body a lead weight.

Finally her head broke the surface. With an extra heave, she brought him up. The effort made her sink under once more and she gulped water. She came up spluttering, sharp pains stabbed through her chest. But she saw him blink, his expression confused and vaguely pissed off. She flung her arms around him, awkwardly, her wet body pressed against his warmth. Her legs banged up against his as she struggled to stay afloat. "Oh God," she said breathlessly.

"Hey, I'm okay," he said in a strangled voice. Then after a moment, he grasped her arms and pushed her away. "Let go," he said. "You're pushing me down."

Instantly, she was embarrassed. What was she doing? As she treaded water, she stared at him. "What were you doing down there? What were you doing?" she hollered.

He rubbed the red marks her fingertips had made on his arm, then coughed. "That hurt like hell."

"You were drowning, idiot!" Shamefully, tears burned behind her eyes. "What were you doing?"

"I don't know," he said angrily as if it were her fault. "Fuck that hurts. You didn't have to rip my arm off."

She kicked away from him and swam towards the shore. Her arms moved in slow motion and it took concentrated effort to pull them through the water. As she grabbed at the rocks and pulled herself up, her hands felt blunt and disembodied. The sharp edges of a stone hurt in a distant kind of way. She shook as she stumbled up the cliff towards Lance and thought about what a stupid idea this had been. All of it. He was a jerk. She hated him.

He climbed up behind her and called her name but she didn't reply. "Let's go," she said to Lance. "I'm cold." She stood a moment in the sun, which weakly warmed her while she squeezed water out of her T-shirt. Some idiot had left the towels in the car.

They didn't say much as they trudged back through the bush. Her head filled with angry, half-formed thoughts. She would never . . . and certainly never . . . the last time she'd . . . and he would see. Wearily, she climbed into the back seat. She didn't want to talk.

"Hey listen," Evan said as they bumped down the dirt road. "I'm not saying I was drowning or anything, but . . . thanks, I guess."

"Piss off," she said and stared out the side window.

Her heart pounds and she drops the lid to the box of photos. Oh shit, she can't think like this. In desperation, she focuses on the enlarger, the red plastic trays, the square bottles of developing fluid. With a deep breath to steady herself, she turns to the contents of the box once more. There has to be at least one photo in the stacks of old negatives that will be worth the effort to print. That's it, she'll look for a group shot from their high school years, something Mandy can hang in the baby's play room so that the baby will know what her mother had looked like. Once decided, the idea takes on the utmost importance and requires all of her concentration.

There are three more boxes, each with hundreds of negatives shoved into dusty plastic sleeves. In her teenage years, she had been keen, but so disorganized. Irritated with her former self, she flips through the scrawled labels and messy mish-mash of negatives. Whole rolls taken of doorknobs, kitchen cupboards, shadows, waves, patterns in the sand at Lakeside Park. So many clumsy imitations of famous works by great photographers — Edward Weston, Alfred Stieglitz or Mary Ellen Mark. She used to think her photos were so smart, so deep. But now as she looks for photos of friends, she notices how few there are. Why didn't she record things that really mattered to her?

She used to tell herself that she was an artist and took photos only for art reasons, not personal ones. That would be indulgent. Art was out there in some smart place, somewhere between the top of the head and the sky. It wasn't anywhere near the heart, nowhere that might hurt to touch.

She sighs and forces herself to keep looking. There has to be something salvageable here, something that doesn't cause bile to rise in her throat.

The elastic slips from a package, and she shuffles through colour snapshots of a party. The group photo she'd found upstairs must be from the same occasion. She still can't remember specifics. All those house parties blur into one vague memory. She can tell Lea took some of the pictures. She must have wrestled Siobhan for the camera. Most of them are blurry, headless shots. Then she sees one where she frowns angrily at the photographer (was it Lea? Evan?). She's about to toss it aside when a blurred face off to one side catches her eye. She stands under the bare bulb and squints at it. It's Kristy, she realizes, and feels a cold sweat break out over her shoulders. Now she remembers. That was Kristy's last party. Not that they could have guessed it that night. It was the last time Siobhan, or probably anybody, had seen Kristy. Now she knows that that particular party signaled the end of something. Unconsciously, it became a pivot that her life still revolves around. Life before that night was immeasurably different than after, though exactly what had changed is too slippery to grasp.

At the time it was just another house party. It was the beginning of the summer after graduation, not even a month after the cliff-jumping fiasco, and they were all giddy with release. The doors to the world had just been flung open and the breeze of possibility filled their lungs. They walked in threes and fours down the middle of the streets through town so that cars had to slow down for them.

The party was at Mandy's dad's new place, along the lake's North Shore. He was out of town so Mandy had the house to herself. Siobhan arrived late, came straight from Saturday evening Mass. After church she'd overheard two women talk about the recent accusations against Mr. Hiller. Rumour was that the police had already taken statements and the trial would soon start. The articles in the paper talked about how many victims there might be, more than the ten official charges. She'd rushed past the women, eager to get to the party, tired of all this talk about the court case.

As soon as she'd arrived, she'd poured herself a glass from someone's bottle of vodka and sipped it broodingly as she looked around the room. Though she didn't photograph her friends, she constantly composed pictures of them in her mind's eye, framed everything she saw within the borders of a viewfinder. While drunk kids reeled past and relationships formed or broke up, while people were ignored and feelings hurt, Siobhan lived in a glass bubble. She observed. In order to see this world like a photographer, she had to train her eye, to keep focused. She couldn't get distracted by being involved.

She stared at Kristy from across the room and framed raw and edgy photos of her dark-eyed face. Kristy sat by herself on a couch and struck matches against her fingernails to watch them burn down before she blew them out at the last second. Evan really should include her more, Siobhan had thought, and wondered, does Kristy smoke now? Then someone's laugh distracted her and she looked away. She doesn't remember if Kristy was around after that; she seemed to slip away.

When she'd heard about the accident, Siobhan's first thought had been, I didn't even say hello at the party. I should have gone over to her. Her last memory is that imaginary portrait. Kristy's face carefully observed but never touched.

Siobhan squints at the photo in her hand one last time, then flips through the remainder. For some reason, she wants a photo of all of them, including Kristy. Finally she spies one: a slightly blurry shot of the five of them mugging for the camera. To one side and half out of the frame hovers a sixth face. The features are unmistakably Kristy's. Yup, this is the one. She scrambles around for the negative and holds it up to the light. No scratches.

Upstairs the phone rings, barely audible, stops, then moments later, rings again. She is rooted to the sot, convinced it's Michael. Idly, she registers that her own heartbeat pounding in her ears is louder than the shrill telephone upstairs.

AFTER HE TIGHTENS THE LAST SCREW into the wall of the play room, Lance steps back to eye his handiwork. "Mandy!" he calls.

She comes into the room, stands behind his shoulder and says nothing but "Hmmm." Then she pads out of the room, leaving Lance to wonder if, once again, he has misunderstood something. But she returns with a stack of cloth diapers tucked under an arm and a jar of diaper cream. She places these on the shelf, cocks her head to one side and nods. "Perfect," she says as she links her arm through his. "I can finally get some junk off the floor. It's even low enough that Mick won't bonk his head."

Lance realizes he has no idea how tall Mick is. Or anything about him, for that matter. He furrows his brow. Another variable to factor in.

Mandy continues brightly, "Yup, just perfect. What else could the squirt need?"

"Really?"

"Really. Now, come on, we should go." She squeezes through the hallway and yelps when she bumps her elbow against the wall.

"Where are we going?" He follows her vanishing form and brushes the last of the sawdust out of his hair. Suddenly, she appears in the bathroom doorway and they almost collide. "Oops."

She sighs mightily. "You're unbelievable, Lance. You have a brain like a sieve."

"There are . . . in fact . . . um, porous holes in the cerebellum. In some cases enough that there is a loss of connection, causing synapses — "

She rolls her eyes and hands him a towel. "You didn't bring a towel, did you?"

He gives her a blank look.

"Figures."

Lance helps Mandy into his van despite her protests. As she settles into her seat, Mandy takes a deep breath and says, "Oh, It's good to get out. The house was stuffy, hey?" She fans her face. "Or was it just me?"

They drive downhill to the park on the lake shore, but as they get closer Lance feels a familiar apprehension tighten his muscles. He has never felt comfortable there. It's one of those tamed city spaces, wedged between the railroad tracks and the shore of the thin west arm of Kootenay Lake. The orange bridge marks the eastern border. City parks are too open, the scattered trees too controlled, the picnic benches too strategically placed. The trees are not of a forest he would recognize. For him, a beach is a place you get to by scrambling down a bank. A beach is private. Lakeside Park is public and formal, with an elephant slide in the sand and a dock for boats, railings that demarcate one space from another, cement block change rooms. Bathing suits are required. He has always known that he is not part of "the public" who has the right to use this public park. He is a trespasser and half expects to be escorted off the premises by a man in a black uniform. The place has always been thick with the Jasons of his life.

Mandy is delighted. "Doesn't this remind you of being a kid?" She opens the car door eagerly.

"Yes," is his glum reply. He carries the cooler to the table she has chosen and glances around tentatively. While there are a few families with small children, the beach is populated mostly with teenagers. Their long sleek bodies lounge on towels or stroll in clusters up and down the sand. Girls with flat stomachs wear bikinis and fluff out their long feathered hair. They all come with a boy's hand attached. Prematurely toughened skid kids saunter by in black T-shirts with white, three-quarter length sleeves, the Metallica designs peeling off the front. Earphone cords dangle from their ears and they bob their heads to a beat that is audible above the other beach noise. They are all impossibly young. He can't remember ever looking that young himself.

The scene before him — the skids, feathered hair, heavy metal music — is so familiar. Eerily so. Evidently Lance has entered a time warp. His foot must have fallen too close to the edge of a black hole and he has slipped through the space-time tear. He has landed on the other end of the wormhole. It is not the summer of 1999 after all, but the summer of 1989. He glances around. Then again the little kids wear broad sunhats, he notices, and their mums struggle to slap sunscreen on their thin fair arms. So it can't be the 80s. All the same, the fug of timelessness hangs thick in the air —

"Is Siobhan here yet?" As Lance stares fixedly at the crowd on the beach, Lea joins them and jostles his elbow. He catches a whiff of her floral perfume. "And what about Evan?" She looks around suspiciously.

The late afternoon heat swells around them. "Cripes, I'm hot," Mandy says. "Aren't you guys hot?"

"Huh?" he says.

"I've heard that a pregnant woman's temperature rises . . . oh fiddle . . . " Lea reaches for a book in her bag. "It could mean the foetus is overexerted and in danger of . . . wait a minute!"

With a flick of her hand, Mandy throws her shirt onto the table to reveal a striped bikini top and the sharp curve of her belly, pushed out by the dense presence inside. *A new celestial being*, Lance thinks, *to distort the space-time continuum.* What a powerful gravitational force. "Come on, Bee!" Mandy calls over her shoulder as she eases herself down the few concrete stairs to the beach. "You too, Lance!"

Flustered, Lea trips after her and waves the book. "Careful!" Mandy continues on. Lea watches her for a few moments, returns to the table and tucks the book carefully into her bag. "Oh sugar," she mutters, then bends down to unstrap her sandals, her fingers tipped with neatly manicured nails. "I just don't have a good feeling about this." She follows Mandy anyway. On the bottom step, she teeters in indecision, then gingerly places her painted toes onto the hot sand. "Ouch. Ooo, ooo." She advances down the beach, Lance a few lazy paces behind. Linda, he remembers, would only ever wear a nylon one-piece bathing suit. Never a bikini. She claimed they were a patriarchal construct, designed by men, for men. Lance decides he likes them.

At the edge of the water line, Mandy wriggles out of her elasticized shorts. Her navel is stretched taut across her belly, which is like a balloon about to burst. "You have no idea," she says as she works a finger under the edge of the bikini bottom and tugs, "how tight all my clothes are these days. I'm *always* uncomfortable." With her hands on her hips, she surveys the beach as if she owns it, then wades in. "Come on!"

"Lance, I don't think she should be doing this," Lea says. She glowers at him like it's his fault, his responsibility.

"How are you going to stop her?" Now that he's out of the shade of the trees, the sun pounds against his back. Sweat drips down his sides. Mandy stands knee-deep in water and surveys the cars driving across the orange bridge on their right.

With a glance, he scans the beach. He is surrounded by the din of conversation and boom boxes. The teenagers pay him no attention other than to give him a wide berth. He has developed that energy force — that social antigravity — that repels teenagers. He must be an adult after all. Not even worth a blip of recognition, he has fallen off their radar. Unlike his encounter with Jason, this leaves him feeling weightless. Free. He breathes in deeply.

Mandy waves at the cars on the bridge and laughs when one honks its horn. "I'm having a baby!" she hollers at the top of her lungs.

Lance's shorts hit the sand and, before he realizes it, he's down to his underwear. His shirt quickly follows. "Lance!" Lea says, but he strides into the lake, takes a shallow dive, and cleanly enters the water with barely a ripple.

The water is shockingly cold and delicious. When he surfaces, he hears Mandy's voice. "That's more like it." With a few strokes, they are already past most of the other swimmers, who paddle around in waist-deep water.

"Look," he says as he flips over onto his back. "We're on our own."

"Let's swim out to the middle." She pushes her arms out in a breaststroke to glide past him, her legs gangly as a frog's. Water beads off the thick coils of her hair. "If I sink, will you tow me into shore?"

Squinting, he can barely make out the faces of those on land. At the water's edge, Evan has joined Lea and the two of them peer at Lance and Mandy from under the shade of their hands. Evan's body is a dark block against the brilliant sand, his square shoulders set firmly. Lance rolls back onto his stomach and paddles beside her. He listens to the shudder of the bridge and the water lap over his fingers. The first six inches are warm, but then abruptly it turns chilly. His back is hot, but his belly and feet cold. As he glides forward the water parts to welcome him. From a distance the lake water looks black and dense, but its transparency is revealed when broken down into the little ripples that run over his fingers. Not black at all.

EVAN

EVAN WAITS ON THE SHORE AND sifts sand through his fingers. Too grumpy to go in the water himself, he watches Mandy haul herself out of the shallows and teeter as she struggles to stand. Lea rushes into the water to steady her and ignores the hem of her dress which settles into the water as if relieved. By the time Lance crawls out, the beach is almost deserted, the teenagers heading home for dinner. From behind his sunglasses, Evan watches two young girls shake sand out of their towels and fold them into shoulder bags. They are the kind of girls who drove him crazy in high school, confident in their sexiness to the point of carelessness. One girl slithers into shorts that have barely more substance than her bikini bottoms, then adjusts the triangles of the top, jostling her breasts into position. That kind of precision amazes him. He half hopes the girls will glance his way, but they head off in the other direction.

Mandy used to be one of those girls. As he watched her swim, he could almost imagine she still was, until she rolled over and her enormous belly surfaced. This could be the last time he sees her like this, silly and teenagerish, unencumbered. From now on, a dependent creature will hang on her. The thought makes him sad for himself, then angry, like he's lost something precious in the sand.

Lance collapses belly-down onto the beach beside Evan, water streaming off his long hair and underwear.

"You used to swim in the buff, man," Evan says. "You're getting conservative in your old age."

"There's a by-law against doing that on a public beach like this." Lance concentrates on his hands, presses his fingertips together. Droplets bead on the coarse hair on his knuckles. "Don't want to do anything illegal."

The sun is still warm. Evan has to glance at his watch to remind himself of the time. Though it is close to seven, it feels like afternoon. He thinks of the burgers he and Siobhan bought — they could only get organic beef in that joint — and his stomach rumbles. They'd picked up a bottle of pinot noir as well, the best they could find, something that wouldn't be a complete disaster if served at air temperature. He wants to know what she thinks of it, but she still hasn't appeared. Damn. He'd looked forward to opening the bottle with her.

Lance interrupts his thoughts and says, "I built a shelf for Mandy today. You should see it. What do you think about knocking out that wall between the living room and the hallway? It would really open the place up."

"What's the point, man? It's a rental house. Besides, you can't renovate when she's got a kid around."

Lance settles his chin on a fist. "Hmmm."

"What's the big concern with Mandy's house?"

"She needs more room."

"She won't be that fat forever."

"No, I mean her personality."

"You got a thing for her, or what?" He says this with a laugh, but eyes his friend warily.

Lance wipes the water off his face with a frustrated swipe. His eyes are dark and sleepy, like he'd stayed up all night. "It's bigger than that. I mean, of course I love her," he says and gives Evan a look that is half irritated, half pitying. "But not in a high school way. I'm not talking about sex."

"Okay, okay. Don't get sore." *Mr. High and Mighty*, he thinks and turns to brush dust off his toes.

Lance pushes himself up. Sand cascades off his belly. After a quick glance around, he strips off his wet underwear and steps into his shorts. They stick to his damp thighs. He strides off towards the picnic table and leaves Evan on the beach.

He *would* say something wishy-washy vague like that, Evan thinks. Lance can never be straightforward, never black and white about things. He's the kind of guy who will middle-path his way through life, see everything as grey: love yet not love, friends yet not friends. It's all good, but nothing's really great. That kind of thinking drives Evan crazy. He's hungry. Now that's straightforward. He likes the tangible things in life, things he can grab onto.

The burgers char on the small hibachi that Lea has brought down and when he flicks them onto a plate, Evan singes a finger. *"Great,"* he says, and sticks it in his mouth. Now the burgers will taste of charcoal. They cost an arm and a leg to begin with, now a finger as well.

With a sideways look, Lance eyes the meat with a slight frown, then mumbles, "If you study the digestive organs of the human body . . . um . . . they are those of a frugivorous animal. Plant-eating. Isn't that fascinating?"

"Fru-what?" Lea says.

"Yeah, just fascinating." Evan says and scrapes off the burnt bits. "But for your information, doctor, I'm a vata type," *Ha*, he thinks, *take that*. He can finally benefit from his mother's wacky obsession with Ayurvedic medicine. "So I can eat meat." He takes a big bite out of his burger and says, "Yummm."

"You could be right," Lance says without conviction. "But the shape of our teeth indicates — "

Evan interrupts. "Why should I listen to you, Lance?" He's heard enough pseudo-science from alternative types to last him a lifetime. "Your head's filled with weird astrology shit — "

"Astronomy."

" — crazy theories of alternative realities. "

" — parallel universes."

"Yeah, see what I mean?"

"Can't we talk about anything else?" Mandy says as she passes Evan the bowl of potato salad.

"Whatever." Evan bangs the bowl down on the table before him.

"So, where's Siobhan?" Lea asks him.

He mumbles, "Don't look at me," and takes another bite of burger.

"Well, it's really great to see you all," Mandy says, and Lea murmurs a sentimental response. "I mean, when was the last time we were all together like this?"

Evan closes his eyes. *Oh shit, not this road again.* He concentrates on filling his plate while Lea and Mandy debate the question. Out of the corner of his eye he sees the bottle of wine and, once again, he wishes Siobhan were there.

"No, I don't think so," Lea is saying. "It was the time we all drove to Vancouver for the U2 concert. When was that? Must have been the summer after grad!" She turns to Mandy with a surprised smile as she says this, but then stops. The summer after grad. They all know what happened that summer. "Funny," she says and sits down on the bench. "I forgot all about that. That was just before, um, Kristy's accident."

"It was no accident," Evan says darkly. A flock of Canada geese fly over their heads towards the lake. Their honks fill the sudden silence.

Lea turns to Lance. "What *did* she tell you, Lance?"

Evan's ears hum; the noise of passing cars and distant picnickers becomes muted. *Lance knows?* The words echo in his head. He trains his eyes on his friend, who sits with eyes down and back rounded. His damp hair falls in thick ropes to his shoulders.

"Not much," Lance replies slowly and presses his fingers to his lips.

Evan opens his mouth to say something, but can't get the words out. *How can Lance know when I've never told him?*

"You can't be so secretive," Mandy insists.

It takes a long while for Lance to answer. "She told me she loved him. She didn't believe the charges, didn't want to testify."

Evan groans to hear the words said aloud and tenses for the inevitable shocked responses.

"And then?" Lea prods.

"She never said anything. But I wonder, maybe she changed her mind — "

Lea says, "Hmm," and Mandy gives a slight nod.

Evan looks at them in amazement. "You guys all know. But how?"

"It was just a guess," Lea says, at the same time that Mandy murmurs, "Of course we knew," and puts a hand on his forearm.

He chews his lip. He can feel his cheeks burn and his breath is short and shallow. "I . . . I can't believe she . . . fell for it," he says finally. He studies his fork, twirls it around and around.

"She was lonely," Mandy says. "She needed someone,"

Evan shakes her hand away. "She should have been smarter than that."

"Think what it must have been like for her," Mandy continues, undeterred. "He probably messed with her mind. He was a professional charmer, remember?"

She's so calm about it. Now anger rises from his gut, and his hands start to shake. For ten years, he's guarded Kristy's dark secret, and here they knew all along. Why didn't anyone say anything? The fork spins between his fingers.

Two guys walk by and toss a ball between them. One protests loudly when the other misses. "Yeah," Lea says. "Siobhan really admired him, too."

"Did he — ?" Mandy starts, then bites her lip.

"No," Lea replies after a pause. "I'm sure nothing happened." She shivers, though the air is still warm. "I can't stop thinking about it though, since this afternoon. We were all duped. *I* even liked him. Don't you ever wonder, what if . . . " She holds a cracker between two fingers and takes a nibble. "I heard there was a group who supported him. Throughout the trial and everything."

"*Supporters?*" Evan is already on his feet. "People actually felt *sympathetic* for him? Who were they?"

Lea flinches. "I don't know who. His family, some people in the church I think."

"That man was a sick pervert and anyone who says otherwise is as much to blame. They should all be shot. I'll do it myself."

"You don't have to be so nasty about it, Evan," Lea says and blinks rapidly.

"Oh, come on!" He throws his paper plate down. "Am I supposed to be *nice* about it?"

"No one's blameless. I mean, we're kinda all to blame, aren't we?" she says as she looks at him pointedly, then down at the food on her plate.

"Whoa. *Lea,*" Mandy hisses, as Evan takes one step back from the picnic table.

"It wasn't *my* fault," he says. Mandy glares at Lea, whose eyes are downcast. Lance squints at something off in the distance. It's easy for them to point the finger. They were never involved like he was. "Why does everyone keep saying it was my fault? I was her cousin, not her keeper."

After a few beats of silence, Mandy angrily starts packing the food away. "No one ever said it was your fault, Evan. You did."

He points at Lea. "She just looked *directly at me* and said — "

Lea stands quickly and her hips bang against the table. "Well, isn't it true?" she says indignantly. "She lived with you for all those years, for goodness sake. Didn't you notice anything going on?"

"You — " he starts. What a stupid thing for her to say. "You're unbelievable." He turns away.

As he strides off he hears Mandy's resigned voice. "Good one, Lea."

Fuck it, he thinks as he strides across the grass. He repeats this to himself as he continues to walk, past the cinder-block change rooms and up the slope between the lake and the tennis courts. Hands shoved in the pockets of his shorts, he walks along the ridge that overlooks the water, towards the soccer fields bordering the park. What do they know anyway, and who are they to say anything? He wipes the back of his hand across his eyes. His temples throb, the pressure in his skull so intense it feels like his whole head will pop off the top of his neck. Suddenly, he wants to call his mother, but then he remembers he left his cell at Siobhan's. He wants to tell her that everyone guessed the one thing he'd tried so hard to hide. He wants to ask why he didn't see what was happening to his cousin. Or maybe he just didn't make the connections. With the light beginning to fade, he loops around the soccer fields, up to the railroad tracks. Eventually, he's calm enough to head back. He'll grab the bottle of wine and take off.

As he approaches the park, he can make out the figure of Siobhan walking past the canteen. Her hand is raised to wave at the crowd around the picnic table, her step light and brisk. The sight of her cheers him unaccountably. He picks up his pace, hollers her name as he breaks into a jog. She's wearing a sundress now, with a dusty-blue sweater slung over her shoulders. When she hears him yell, she slows down and turns in his direction. Suddenly, she is beautiful. Slowing as he nears her, he has an overwhelming urge to kiss those full lips of hers. Siobhan is smarter than other women, he realizes, and always has been. Level-headed. Today, he finds that smartness irresistibly attractive.

She holds a framed photograph in her hand. He stops before her and reaches out for it. "What's this?" he says and gives her a broad smile.

"It's for Mandy," she replies, then clears her throat. "I just printed it. Like I said, I needed to — "

He looks down at the image in his hand and says, "Oh great, a . . . " But then he sees that familiar face and his heart thumps against his chest. "Shit, Siobhan, why give her a photo of . . . of . . . "

She swallows and crosses her arms over her chest. "It was the only one I could find." She shifts her weight and recrosses her arms. "I know, it's out of focus. I think I was trying to take a picture of myself, and holding the camera out . . . " She stretches her arm out to demonstrate.

He hands the frame back to her with a shrug. "Sure. Looks great." Obviously she has no idea what went on. With a deep breath, he raises his eyes to take in the trees and the lake. *Just fuck it*, he tells himself again, *move on*. He doesn't even want to waste his energy being mad at them. He's looking forward to that bottle of pinot noir.

So he looks back at her with another deep smile. "You look good," he says, then reaches out to disentangle a strand of hair caught in her eyelashes. At his touch, she freezes. He continues, brushes his singed finger against her lip as if some hair were in the way. She says nothing, but gives him a wide blank stare. "I've been waiting to open the wine," he says. "Come on, I'll pour you a glass."

LANCE: APOGEE

THE WIND SHIFTS SUDDENLY AND A cold gust blows off the lake to where Lance sits. Siobhan offers her gift to Mandy and apologizes for the lack of wrapping paper. Meanwhile, Evan peels the top off the bottle of wine and with forced heartiness says, "Tell me someone remembered a corkscrew before I scream."

By Mandy's muted cry of surprise, Lance can tell something's wrong. When Lea passes the picture to him, his hands start to shake. He grasps the frame more tightly, but still it wobbles uncontrollably until he puts it down. The sound of its clink against the picnic table is all that can be heard.

"Oh God, I've been thoughtless, haven't I?" Siobhan says, then glances at Evan apologetically. "It's because she's in the photo, isn't it?" Lance wants to say something, but his mouth is dry.

Making as much noise as possible, Evan plunks a row of plastic cups on the table in front of Lance and pours wine from the now-open bottle. "I guess you're not having any, hey Mandy?" he says loudly and without waiting for an answer, gulps down a mouthful. "Come on, drink up." Obediently, Lea takes the cup closest to her.

"Is there something wrong, you guys?" Siobhan looks around at the circle of blank faces. "I mean, apart from me. What happened?"

Finally, Mandy picks the photo off the table and gives her a hug. "Forget it. It was a nice thought. Thank you." She quickly slips it into her picnic basket. Lance thinks of Kristy's face, safely covered now.

While the others mumble a toast, images of her crowd his mind. Lea and Evan prattle on about the wine and the weather in nervous, edgy voices, but he tunes them out. They become white noise behind the drama in his mind: that look on Kristy's face, when he'd left her at the police station. He runs his fingers across the lacquered tabletop, as if the smoothness could console him. He plays the memory over in his mind, though this time he rewrites the ending, rights the wrongs. Kristy: his perfect other, his lost opportunity.

He hears Lea say brightly, "Oh! That sure is dry!" Her face puckers as she peers down into her glass.

"It's supposed to be," Evan says.

Lance listens to the *ker-thunk, ker-thunk, ker-thunk* of cars passing over the bridge and concentrates on the sound. Once the sun disappears behind the mountain, the air cools.

Siobhan's voice breaks into his thoughts. "Quick, let's get a portrait before the light fades," and then he hears the whir and click of a camera shutter. "Look over here, Lance," he hears dimly as if from a distance. "Here."

When Evan tries to grab the camera, Siobhan laughs girlishly, then swats his hand away. He's amazed that they have forgotten what had happened just moments earlier.

Lance focusses on feeling his breath rise and fall in his body. The others clatter about as they clear the plates. Then, with a nudge to his shoulder, Mandy says, "Could you drive me home?" and he stands, grateful.

In the car, she lets her head fall back on the headrest. "Ooof," she says and closes her eyes. "That was awful. I'm tired all of a sudden." And she *looks* tired, drawn. Her hands are folded across the apex of her stomach and once again Lance feels its heavy gravitational pull. New life exerts the same gravity, the same pull, as death. He resists the urge to place a hand on her belly.

As he negotiates their way back to Mandy's house, he listens to her breathe. She rolls her head to the side and lazily opens one eye. "I got a postcard from Sean the other day. He sent it to my mum's place. He doesn't even know where I live now. Or about the baby." She gives him a wry smile. "He wouldn't really give a shit anyway."

After a long pause, Lance says, "Did I ever tell you that I have a half sister? Or maybe a brother?"

She blinks at first, confused by the change of topic, then says, "No, I never knew. Where?"

He breathes in, considers, releases his breath. As they turn onto her street, he gives her a small smile. "I don't know. Never mind. It's not important. I've just been thinking about it lately. But — I don't know, maybe the whole thing was just a fantasy of mine."

She squints at him through narrowed eyes, not following. He doesn't elaborate, just parks, opens the door on her side and helps her out of the car. "I'd really like to meet Mick," he says.

"Sure. He has a gig tonight, but said he'd come by after. Can you wait?"

"Might as well. No reason to go back to my place," he jokes.

"Well, make yourself at home then."

As they walk in, he scans the walls once again. He wonders if he could feel at home here, or anywhere for that matter. Despite the obvious lack of space — every surface covered with a pile of this or that — it does suggest home. Maybe it's the dense aura of Mandy-ness that draws him in, an air of acceptance. Surrounded by it, his dark cloud evaporates and he becomes uncharacteristically chatty and expansive. He hasn't felt like this for years, like he could talk all night. She gathers up the magazines piled on the couch, dumps them on the floor, then stretches out on the couch. He paces the room and throws out suggestions for space-saving renovations.

She smiles tiredly. "I'm just a renter. But wouldn't it be nice?"

"Yeah," he replies, but his mind has already skipped ahead to other things.

"Sorry, Lance, but I don't know if I can stay awake." Her eyes flutter shut, but she mumbles, "Go on, keep talking."

Instead, he turns off the light that shines over her head. One hand against the wall, he fumbles the few feet to the other chair and settles into it. Soon he hears deep breathing and he knows she's asleep. He stares into the darkness.

His thoughts drift back to the photo. Why, of all the images from their life together as friends, did Siobhan choose that one? And then her manic photographing around the picnic table, which reminded him of Lea on that night ten years ago, when she had crowded in on him with the camera lens saying, "Come on, Lance, smile." Slurring her words a little. "Be happy," she instructed him. He'd needed to leave the party and had slipped out the back door as soon as her back was turned. Maybe it was because he'd just read about a tribe in the Congo who believe photographs capture the soul. Or maybe he just wanted a breath of fresh air.

This desperate urge to record every passing moment — sometimes he wonders what all the fuss is about. He would like the past to fade into the past. Stay there.

Many times, he'd tried to imagine what made Kristy decide that she couldn't go on. What flipped the switch. He'd tried to imagine what it felt like to be in Kristy's skin, until he could almost feel himself sailing off that bank.

When she'd told him she loved Albert Hiller, his reactions were so confused, he'd walked away. He couldn't believe she thought such a relationship could work, was shocked that he hadn't seen it coming, then disgusted with Hiller, for reasons he couldn't name at the time But in the days that followed, he'd pushed these thoughts aside — because part of him wanted to believe Kristy's story. Why couldn't she be in love? Did he simply doubt her loveability? Not everyone finds someone their own age . . . And so on. To admit the other possibility would demand action.

Then he'd walked into the other possibility.

He'd been clearing the high school gym to make space for a meeting of model rocket enthusiasts. His arms had been full of volleyballs and his mind full of curses about jocks as he pushed open the equipment room door. At first, he hadn't seen anything in the gloom. A grunt surprised him and he'd stared without comprehension at the sliver of white that glimmered in the darkness. Then the white shape came into focus. It was his English teacher's bare ass. He can still picture it, can still feel the shock of recognition. He'd heard a higher, softer gasp, then saw the third person in the room, a tenth grader he vaguely recognized, one of the many Jennifers. She lay prone under her coach. Lance caught just a flash of her perfect, naked breast as he backed out the door.

Just like on the night Kristy took him to the police station, Lance's mind went blank. All he could do was double over and press his hands against his knees. He was ashamed, and still is, that all he could think about was the curve of the girl's breast.

His thoughts were interrupted when the door pushed against his back and knocked him to the ground. Mr. Hiller stood over him, hair disheveled but his eyes steely. He held Lance's gaze as if he dared him to look away. The man's usually handsome face had turned foreign, strangely hard. "Better me than some clumsy young idiot like you," he'd said, then sauntered away, hands in his pockets.

Why Lance never acted on this discovery, never reported him, he'll never understand. Two days after that incident, the official charges were laid against Hiller so, he'd told himself, it didn't matter anyway.

He'd always wondered whether Kristy knew about the other girls. Tonight, at the picnic table, he'd realized that she must have found out. Could he have spared that Jennifer from her equipment-room initiation? If he hadn't abandoned Kristy, would things have turned out differently? Would she still be alive today? These questions make it hard to breathe, to go on. So he closes that door in his mind, locks it shut and looks out into the darkness of Mandy's living room.

Just after two in the morning, the front door opens. With a start, Mandy wakes and swings her feet to the floor, then shuffles forward. A tall man enters and crosses the room in two strides. Awkwardly, he bends down to meet her lips and only then notices Lance. "Holy shit," he says and takes a step back. "Didn't see you there." He's younger than Lance expected, with an unlined face and a soft beard that struggles to cover his jaw. He sets a guitar case onto the floor and glances at Lance with a quizzical expression. Lance pulls his mind into the present, grateful for the distraction. He nods at him.

"This is Mick," Mandy says with a yawn and introduces Lance as the friend who never returns phone calls. "How was the gig?" she asks Mick, then says to Lance, "He's only allowed in the bar because he's in the band. They wouldn't let him in otherwise because he's underage" She sucks in her cheeks and rolls her eyes.

Mick rubs his nose as if embarrassed. He shifts his weight but doesn't move, unsure where to put himself. Mandy takes his hand, drags him across the room, and says "Massage my calves, would you? They're killing me," and proceeds to steer him towards one end of the couch. She arranges herself along the rest of the length, her legs plopped on his lap as if he were a pillow. He doesn't complain, seems relieved to have such a specific purpose in the situation. "Mick is good at this, aren't you?" Mandy says. "All those finger exercises for holding the thingamabop." She holds up an imaginary guitar in the air.

"The neck," he mumbles.

Lance clears his throat. "You play the bass." He states this rather than asking. Mick nods his head several times, but keeps his eyes lowered, shy.

"Mandy loves to dance," Lance says. "Great sense of rhythm." Her eyes are closed but she smiles tiredly.

"I've never seen her dance," Mick replies, and instinctively the two men glance at her stomach.

"You'll see," Lance says. "Soon." He can see it himself, Mandy with her arms high, drifting through the air, as her hips sway from side to side. That loose floaty hippie dance. Mick up on stage, eyes down, nodding his head. But then Mick will glance up and they'll catch each other's eye. That's all, just a quick glance, but it will communicate volumes.

Just the thought of this imaginary scene lifts Lance's mood. "I had a guitar once," he says. "Long time ago." In fact, he'd written a song — a really bad song — for Mandy on that guitar a long time ago. When she was the distant planet he couldn't hope to reach, and he had been heartsick in love with her, wanting to be the asteroid that collided with her surface, dreaming about it on hot sticky nights.

He doesn't want Mandy like that anymore. Yes, he loves her, not just as a friend, but not like a lover either. He shakes the thought out of his head. The best thing he can do for someone he loves is to leave them alone. He's no good at being involved. Look how he's messed things up before.

He watches the pair of them as they sit on the couch, says very little and leaves before they ask him to go.

Siobhan

WHEN THEY GET BACK TO HER parents' house, Evan casually leads Siobhan over to the couch. Oh, Evan is *smooth*. But just as smoothly, Siobhan rises, retreats to the kitchen, says, "I'm still a bit hungry, aren't you?" Then offers him raisins and peanuts.

He stares at the bowl in her hand, and lifts an eyebrow. "No thanks." Sitting with knees wide open, he stretches an arm along the back of the couch. She paces, the bowl held in front of her body like a shield.

She pops a peanut into her mouth. "So," she says. "What were you guys talking about before I arrived?"

"Nothing much."

"Oh? Lea looked like her nose was out of joint."

He shrugs. "Who knows." He picks up a framed photograph from the end table beside him. It's an old hockey team photo from her brother's Pee Wee rep days. "I play hockey now, you know," he says as he peers at it. "I'm not bad, either. Me and some friends, we just play pick-up games now and then, but still, I had to learn the game." He says this smugly. When they were kids, if you weren't a hockey player, you were their enemy. Evan and Lance used to groan about how much hockey repulsed them. Siobhan, with a brother on the rep team and friends who were regularly intimidated by the team, occupied that uncomfortable land in between.

"Yeah, I go with my mountain climbing buddies. They're into skating too. Have I ever mentioned Ross?"

"No." They live in different worlds now. She has no idea, anymore, who he hangs out with in that day-to-day way. The way they used to when they — the whole group of them — were each other's day to day. She could hate his friends. He could hate hers. He continues, convinced she will be as impressed with this Ross person as he is. "He's from Ontario," he says. "Came out for university. We were supposed to go climbing this week, but my car broke down. Oh right, I already told you that." He rubs his chin and glances around the room as if he'd like to find something to distract them both.

"So . . . um," she says. She's tired and should really just go to sleep. Instead she stands in the middle of the room and faces him. Fiddles with the bowl in her hand, then finally places it on top of the stereo. "You found out that hockey pucks aren't such idiots after all, are they?" she says. It's an old rivalry and no longer even relevant, but she's grasping at straws. The once-huge differences between opposing factions are not so great after all, now that they are older. But like an often-repeated joke, she can't resist raising the issue. He just snorts.

"Well, there's more to the game than just scoring," he says finally. "Lots of technique. I've learned that."

"That's bullshit," she says and points a finger at him. "In the end, guys just want to score." Blushing, she hurries to add, "I mean, women's hockey is a totally different game." Not that she's ever really thought about it. He eyes her, a mocking grin on his face. "What?" she demands. "What?"

"I'm thinking you're probably right, that's all."

She frowns down at him, sitting there like a cat that just caught a bird. "You know what I meant, you loser. I'm talking about *hockey*. The skating might be slower but women are better at technique." She'd heard that somewhere, hadn't she? "They're smarter with the defense."

"Sure, sure. Whatever you say."

"I'm serious."

"Okay," he says and eases off the couch to stand before her, arms akimbo. "Show me this defense technique."

"Don't be a dufus. I don't know how to play."

He drops down to hold an imaginary stick, then shuffles around the room, as if pushing a hockey puck across the carpet. "Okay, so I'm coming at you from the side, like so." He lunges but she jumps out of the way. This is the kind of thing the teenage Evan would do.

"I'm not playing your game, buddy." She edges around the room to dodge his fake hockey maneuvers. He doesn't listen, too busy showing off how he is a real hockey player now. No longer a hippie snob about these things.

"You're not even trying. I thought you liked women's hockey." He's laughing at her.

"Cut it out," she says and titters nervously in spite of herself, backed into the corner by her dad's chair. With his shoulder down, he moves left, then right, and catches her off guard. She wobbles off balance, grabs his shoulder, recovers, twists away and throws him off balance. As they both teeter, he grabs her from behind, his arm under her chin, but they stumble against her father's recliner. "Shit." She lets them fall backwards over the arm of the chair, as if helpless. She has him pinned with her weight.

"He shoots, he scores," he says.

"You're starting to irritate me, Ev," she says, wavering. She digs her elbow into his stomach. At the same time, she becomes conscious of his body under hers, his laboured breath, and struggles to sit. He won't let her. Just laughs. Flicks the lever to lift the footrest so they both lurch backwards into the crook of the seat. A vivid image comes to mind of her father looking at her over his half-glasses as he leans back in this chair. "Okay you win, now let me go." He loosens his grip and she slides to one side to balance her weight against the footrest. As she eyes him, she catches her breath. His legs fall over the side of the chair. Lazily, he stretches and tucks an arm under his head to support it. He returns her gaze with a grin. She glances away, then remembers the photos she found this afternoon. "I found these old photos," she begins lamely. "Did you want to see them?" Even to her ears, it sounds like a ruse. *Would you like to view my etchings upstairs little girl, heh heh.* Though in her case, it's not a come-on, but a deke.

"I'm not really interested in photographs right now," he says.

"Well, I'm not interested in hockey players."

"Yes you are."

He leans forward and she is distracted, her attention drawn to his arm as it arcs through the air. In her mind, she sees it as a still image, a velvety silver gelatin print. The clean curve of arm against a blurry background. The olive tone of his forearm contrasts against the paler skin of her hand, brought up initially in self-defense, but then wrapped around his wrist. She sees a series of black and white images, rich with texture and shape. His square-tipped fingers on the back of her neck. The ragged edge of his eyebrows. Dimly, she hears a voice in her head that says she's falling into something bad, doing the wrong thing. But she can barely hear it, because the curve of his ear and jawbone loom large in her line of vision. She automatically reads the light and knows what aperture she would use. She shivers, wonders if she is being coldly clinical. Then again, maybe she is more aware, engaged. And certainly, it doesn't feel wrong to run a finger down his ear, in fact, it feels like she's doing something right for a change. His lips are surprisingly soft, when all these years she's thought of him as a rough kind of guy.

With her eyes wide open, she watches him intently. Evan is one of her oldest friends, she reminds herself, but she's never looked at him this way. No — that's not true. In her mind's eye, she sees the two of them move together on the uncomfortable, overstuffed chair. It's as if she floats in the air a great distance away and looks down at them. Not at the scene of the crime. Not her.

After a while she says, "Stop looking at me like that."

"Like what?"

"Weird-like. Like that." She lays a hand over his eyes. "Just close your eyes, why don't you?" she says. Then later, "This is so *weird*."

Half-awake, she senses something is not quite right. Her bleary, tired mind gropes around for the cause. Then she feels the mattress sway, which reminds her that she's not in her single-wide bunk bed where she should be, but in the foreign territory of her brother's double bed. The lurch of the mattress is Evan as he slips out from under the sheet. She keeps still, her breath even, as if she's still asleep, but listens to his stealthy movements as he tiptoes out of the room, down the creaky stairs. Is he hungry, or leaving? The hinges of the back screen door whine and then the door bangs shut, but even when she strains her ears, she can't hear a car motor start.

She can just imagine him staring down the darkened street, brooding. She sees herself too, with her back to the space he left, pretending to be asleep. Brooding.

Her mind flickers over the events of the past hours. What has she done? She thinks back to those letters from Mr. Hiller that she'd unearthed that afternoon. She has the urge to creep back into her room and read them again, in the hopes that she'll find some answer, something that will wipe away this misery that sweeps over her whenever she thinks about him. Maybe she was wrong to keep it a secret all these years. She feels like a liar, a fraud. Who could she tell though? The image of Evan's face flashes into her mind, of him smiling down at her, looking directly into her eyes.

She blinks in the darkness and listens to her heart pound. She's wanted this for years, not that she had ever admitted it before, not even to herself. She's drawn to the thing that will hurt her the most. Panic and elation make her breathless, but above all, guilt crushes her like a brick against her chest. With a moan, she rolls over and folds the pillow under her head.

What will she tell Michael? She can almost hear the familiar way he huffs in his sleep, like a dog settling down. He's probably doing that right now, in their bed in Vancouver. He's so solid, dependable. Every night, she lies there beside him and wonders what her parents would think of him. Now, she wonders how her parents would judge her if they knew what she'd just done. She kicks the blanket off her legs and wonders if sleep will ever come.

Her eyes open again to bright sunlight that streams through the curtains. With a quick glance over her shoulder, she sees Evan's bulk under the blankets, fast asleep. She slips out of bed and tiptoes downstairs, unable to face him just yet.

In the kitchen doorway, she stops for a dazed moment, then wipes the sleep from her eyes before she fills the kettle. Just as it reaches the boil, the phone rings. Panicked, she unplugs the kettle and quickly snatches up the phone. "Hello?" she says, her voice low.

"Babe."

It's Michael. Without a thought, she hangs up. Her heart pounds. It rings again. She looks at the receiver on its perch, terrified. She couldn't possibly pick it up.

She picks it up.

EVAN

HIS CHEEK PRESSED INTO THE MATTRESS, Evan breathes deeply and surfaces slowly. One hand trails along the floor beside the bed while the other reaches out to swipe across the sheet. The fact that she's not there has barely registered when he hears her voice. "Your mother's on the phone."

The sense of well-being that had lingered through sleep leaves him in a whoosh. "What?" he says groggily and lifts himself up to see where the voice came from. She stands by the bed in the same pyjamas she wore the morning before. He doesn't remember her putting them on last night.

Clumps of hair stick out around her face and she frowns. She repeats, "Your mother's on the phone," and when he looks around for the phone, adds tersely, "It's downstairs," before she leaves the room.

He slides on his shorts, then stumbles down to the hallway table by the kitchen where the receiver lies on its side. He's still not quite awake, and disoriented. Something doesn't add up. He picks up the phone and grunts a hello. "Hi Ev," his mother says breathlessly, then rushes on, "When you come back this way — you will at some point, won't you? Could you pick up some soy milk? At the co-op?"

"Uh, sure." In the kitchen, Siobhan slams cupboard doors closed. Her back is to him.

"Low fat, you know the kind I like."

"Yeah."

"Make it two cartons. And maybe some juice. I don't know what people will want to drink." She sighs. "There's so much to do before the ceremony. I'll have to cut up the cottonwood that blew over last week. It's right across the path to the back of the property. I could really use your help."

"Sure, Mum. Don't worry." Siobhan brushes past him without a glance, then bangs up the stairs.

"Gerald has errands to run up in Slocan City today and since you have my car, well . . . "

"I know, I know." He rubs his eyes. "Hey, how'd you know to call me here?"

After a short pause, she replies, "Oh *Evan*," then says goodbye. She's either really clueless or way too smart. He shivers.

Upstairs, he finds Siobhan in the other bedroom. She closes a dresser drawer and gathers up what's scattered across the floor.

"What're you so pissed off about?" he says.

With brisk, precise movements, she piles papers on the small desk and pats them into neat stacks. "Look, my parents are coming back tomorrow and I don't think they'd be too impressed to find you staying here."

"What?" He crosses his arms over his chest. How old is she, that she cares what her parents think? "You're kicking me out now?"

She finally looks at him, her eyes rimmed in red. "I'm sorry. I'm not kicking you out." She takes a deep breath. "This has got to *mean* something, Ev, or else it's . . . Well, it's . . . " She drags a hand through her hair, then lowers herself down on the edge of the bottom bunk bed. She stares fixedly at a spot somewhere behind him. "I can't be flip about this, I'm not like that. There's Michael to consider. Even if we — " She flushes and looks down at her feet. "I'd still feel guilty." She covers her face with her hands. "I feel guilty for anything and everything anyway," she says from between her fingers. "It gets so I don't even know what I'm feeling guilty about. It's just like with the letters — " She stops, hesitates, then looks up over the tips of her fingers with surprise, as if he's only just appeared. "Ev, can I ask you something?"

He steps backwards, one hand out for something to hang onto, but it finds only air. "Like what?" he says.

She jumps up and strides to the desk. She rifles through the piles of paper and says, "I know you never liked Mr. Hiller — though you weren't in his class, were you?" She pauses mid-shuffle to study him.

He returns her questioning look, wary. He doesn't like where this is going. She seems to decide something and turns back to the piles on the desk to pull out a sheet of paper. "I've never told anyone about this before, but now I'm thinking that you, of all people — " she holds the paper out to him, and he catches sight of the lurid picture in the bottom corner, of a man with his hands clutched around his bleeding heart. The paper flutters in the air between them, barely moored by the fingers that grip it. His hand automatically stretches out to meet it, but at that moment she pulls it back. "Wait a minute, maybe this isn't such a good idea," she says and steps backwards.

They both breathe unsteadily; she looks at the paper in her hand with alarm. Prickles creep up his spine and over his scalp, like a thousand tiny needles. "Let me see it," he says. Now he needs to know whatever it is.

"No."

"Siobhan — "

"No."

He crosses the space between them, but when he reaches out, she twists away. "No, Ev, forget about it," but he wrestles the sheet of paper from her grip and turns his back to her before he starts to read.

By the way — he can barely decipher the handwriting — *send me your phone number. Mine here at the institution . . .* He flips the sheet over and searches out the signature. *Albert Hiller,* it says and he has to read it twice before the name registers. For a moment, Evan is disoriented, thinking the man is still alive and somehow he's missed that fact. Then he sees the date — 1991. *You can call me any time. I would like to hear your voice again.* He drops the paper to the floor. He clearly hears Lea's voice say, *I heard there was a group who supported him.*

For a few long moments, he can't move, just stares at the pattern in the carpet and listens to her heavy breathing behind him.

"What? What is it?" Her voice is low, but startles him.

He squeezes his eyes shut and shoves the heel of his hands against his eyelids until stars explode. Then he throws his arms down and says, "Hiller fucked Kristy," over his shoulder. "You know that, don't you?"

She gasps, fights for air, then splutters, "No."

"Yes, he did. I don't know how long it went on, but it happened."

"No, I mean, I had no idea that she was — " She falters. "Oh my God — "

"You *knew* Siobhan, everyone knew." He walks to the door and leans against the frame, his back to her. This is so typical of her, he thinks angrily. "How could you support him?" he demands. "How *could* you?"

"I — "

"Did he stay here? When he was in hiding?"

"No!" she cries. "I just wrote to him . . . I . . . " Her breath hitches. "I felt sorry for him."

"Couldn't you just hate him like we all do?" He slams a fist against the doorframe.

"I swear to God — "

"Don't say that." He hears her breathe in sharply. "I think I'm going to throw up," he murmurs and pushes himself off the doorjamb. In the other room, he searches for his scattered clothes, stuffs them into his pack, then stumbles down the stairs. He needs to get out. Out, into the blinding sunshine.

LANCE: PREMATURE RELEASE

LANCE WAKES WITH A START FROM a vivid dream: Mandy cooks pancakes or waffles or something syrupy and definitely too yin for his yang. His eyes fly open when he hears her voice call up the stairs to him, but it's just a pair of cats fighting outside. He lies there, terrified. What is he *thinking?*

He jumps out of bed, throws on a pair of shorts and skateboards downtown, where he has a glass of orange and wheatgrass juice in his favourite café. As he looks down into his empty glass, he knows this isn't where he wants to be either. He boards homewards again, makes his way up the steep Granite Road. Sweat trickles down his back as the sun grows steadily hotter.

After he props his skateboard against the wall of the entranceway, he takes three deep breaths, then strides across his gutted front room to the hole-that-would-be-window. The pieces of cut wood lie in a pile on the floor. Against the opposite wall, the window leans back, the ceiling panels reflected in its glass. He and Linda started to work on this just before she left, months and months ago now. For all this time, he's lived in the dim half-light that filters through the plastic. Today he looks at it as if for the first time. What's he waiting for?

The hammer and nails lie in a neglected corner, where he'd last dropped them. With an almost forgotten sense of purpose, he picks them up and gets to work. Exhilaration surges through his limbs as he rips the plastic down and takes a deep breath of the fresh air that rushes in.

It takes surprisingly little effort to install the window. The trickiest part is when he carries it across the room. He goes very slowly, as if he were performing a walking meditation. He slides one foot steadily across the floor before he shuffles the other one along to join it. All the while, his hands grip the window firmly. Once it's screwed snugly into place, he steps back to look out at the mountain and lake below. An unbidden sense of satisfaction floods him. Maybe there *is* something he's useful for after all. He's so inspired, he strides to the shed to cut planks for the sill. Taped to the pile of mouldings is a piece of paper with the right measurements scrawled in Linda's hand. The paper has curled in the months since. It takes him the rest of the morning to build the sill, but the hours slip by. The nails ease in as if the wood had been waiting for them.

Once he's done, he heads upstairs. His gaze wanders up the walls to the tangle of exposed electrical wires nestled in the ceiling. He and Linda had never got around to ripping out the upstairs bathroom, but now he's grateful for that. Lance runs his hand over the porcelain sink. There's nothing really wrong with the room, after all. As he paces out the length of attic, he catches himself. He's been assessing if the upstairs is big enough for two adults . . . and a baby. But no, the space is entirely inappropriate. He angrily stops himself from thinking any further. Buddhists would call this kind of thinking delusion, which only leads to suffering. Or perhaps it's attachment which leads to delusion, or . . . Oh man. He kicks a stack of hardwood flooring in frustration. It was a stupid thought. Who does he think he is, anyway?

He wanders back downstairs, leans against the fir post and glumly surveys the room before him. For a while there, he'd forgotten what a selfish bastard he is, that he's the kind of guy who cares only about himself, and forgets even his friends.

Suddenly, he's exhausted. He drags himself to the bedroom, tugs the sheets loose, then lies down on the bare mattress. Though the sun filters through the plastic still on the bedroom windows, in his mind, it's nighttime. With his knees drawn up, he cradles the bundle of stale bedclothes, just to feel something in his arms.

The night of that last party at Mandy's, he'd gone outside for a break. After years of a kind of manic addiction to friends, parties, and all forms of socializing, he'd grown tired of it. Over the last few weeks of school, he'd been more interested in the six-foot rocket he was building in his parents' garage. He resented anything that pulled him away. For the first time, he built the motor entirely from scratch. It had to be complete before the end of summer. He couldn't explain why it was so urgent. Evan's interest in the project had waned, so Lance worked solo on this mission. It really felt like a mission, one of utmost importance. On the most recent launch, the rocket had released its parachute too early in the flight path. While it still climbed towards apogee, the parachute flapped uselessly by its side, and so the rocket wobbled, then plummeted to the ground. Shit. He couldn't figure out what had gone wrong.

As he leaned against Mandy's house, he heard the music and laughter from inside, but his mind was filled with thoughts of thrust and recovery.

He was fumbling to get his lighter to work when a flame appeared before his eyes. He'd probably noticed her before she struck the match, but in his memory, the flame just appeared as if out of nowhere.

"This what you're looking for?" Kristy said.

He looked up with a faint grin and held the joint over the flame, then passed it to her. He was surprised to see her, she'd been so withdrawn lately. She shifted the brown paper bag she carried to the crook of her opposite arm before she took the joint. The paper bag clinked.

"You going in or going out?" she said as she jerked her head in the direction of the back door.

"Haven't decided yet."

"Still wondering if it's worth the effort, hey?"

He laughed wryly and she grinned. On impulse, he grabbed her hand. Should he tell her about what he witnessed in the equipment room just weeks earlier? Hiller's white moon rising? Would she want to hear that kind of thing? He wondered whether she'd made a statement to the police after all. He'd meant to call her and say . . .

"Go on in," he said. "I'll catch up with you later."

"That would be . . . good," she said, then disappeared inside. Yeah, he really should call her some time.

After a while, he was ready to join the party again. As he stepped through the back door, he bumped into Lea, who grabbed his arm and dragged him inside. "Group photo!" she said, too loudly. "Group hug, group photo."

He just rolled with it for the rest of the evening, his senses fuzzy-edged and blunted. Forgot to look for Kristy, sidetracked by this person, then that person.

He drove home in a kind of trance, while his thoughts circled around and around the problem of the rocket. Then an idea came to him, like a vision. He almost didn't notice the police cars until their twirling lights flashed across his face.

With barely a glance, he registered that someone had gone over the bank and into the lake. Some drunk driver, no doubt.

When he got home, he rushed straight into the garage, found a pencil and notepad and sketched out a diagram and equation. His hand moved feverishly across the paper. It was the kind of inspiration that might turn out to be deranged scribbling in the morning light, but that night, he went to sleep exalted.

When he woke up the next day, the world was an entirely different place.

They found Kristy's body in the lake, still strapped into the half-submerged car. The newspaper report mentioned high levels of THC in her blood, though there was no mention of the alcohol. They could never explain why she'd crossed the lane and gone over the far bank. The man in the car behind her reported that she swerved suddenly, for no apparent reason. Lance remembers how quick her reflexes had been when she played basketball, how sure she was. She'd been known as a cautious driver, too, even when stoned.

SIOBHAN

WITH A PENITENT FERVOUR, SIOBHAN DIVES into cleaning. The debris of the last two days lies scattered around the house. What will her mother think? She lugs the heavy vacuum cleaner upstairs, and vacuums every inch of wall-to-wall shag carpet. Then strips the sheets off her brother's bed and throws them into the laundry without even a glance. While the washing machine chugs away, she dusts, carefully lifts each framed photo and doily to swipe underneath, and places it exactly where it had been before. She scours the kitchen counters with the noxious chemical cleaner her mother stores under the sink, and holds her hand over her mouth and nose against the fumes.

When this is done, she showers. She washes her hair, her fingers carving rough, vigorous circles over her scalp. Then shaves her legs and underarms, and trims her nails. Slightly dizzy from the frenzied effort, she stumbles into her old room, perches on the edge of the bottom bunk, and rests her head in her hands. Wet hair cascades past her face to her knees.

The truth is, she could never bring herself to give Mr. Hiller her phone number. In that last letter, she'd avoided any reference to his request, had breezily slipped in that she would be out of town. A lot. She lost his phone number somewhere in her messy student pad. Oops.

It was a strange time anyway, her last year of college. She'd left another disastrous relationship. Not long after, she'd woken in the middle of the night, heart pounding, with a mind-searing vision of her future self — she would become a nun, the last living Catholic nun in North America. Not that she had any desire to be a nun, but she couldn't shake the notion that it was her unavoidable fate. If you hear the call, you can't ignore it, even if the call doesn't appeal to you. After that, she couldn't date anyone for a long time — men were assholes, after all. She walked around with the thought, *I am a nun. This is my destiny.*

But she couldn't bring herself to give Mr. Hiller her phone number either. She got confused over what was wrong and what was right, and which side she was on. She felt as if, unwillingly, she had become his comrade, on the same side of some demented battle. The thought made her ill. Over the last years, he had retreated into his own earthly purgatory and prayed for hours at a stretch on the cold cement floor. In his letters, he detailed the spiritual routine of his days, practices which stopped just short of wearing a hair shirt or flailing himself with a cat-'o-nine-tails.

No matter how often she told herself not to be silly about it, the thought of phoning him made her feel cornered. When she was a kid, she'd looked up to him, but as the years ticked by, any thought of Mr. Hiller at all made her squeamish. She would think back to when she was thirteen and had tried to run away from home, to that moment in the school parking lot, and wonder what prompted her to lift her skirt like that.

She learned about suppressed memory syndrome and for a brief while, was convinced she suffered from it herself. Maybe Mr. Hiller had molested her and she just couldn't remember. She wracked her brain, saw a therapist, but failed to uncover any lost memories. Nonetheless the idea made her doubt her own experience, her own memory of everything. Either she couldn't see clearly, or she couldn't see at all. Obviously something had happened back in high school right in her midst and she had missed it.

But *Kristy*. Kristy was too smart for him surely, too street-wise. And Siobhan knew Kristy. Kristy was not some unsubstantiated rumour. They had been friends at least, if not best friends. Her death — just her being dead, plain and simple — had been hard enough to deal with. But she was one of Hiller's victims? That was too much to bear.

Siobhan almost wishes something had happened to her, instead. But no, she'd escaped unscathed — had come close, very close, but had sailed right past danger unharmed. Unaware even. If it had been her instead of Kristy, surely she'd have been one of those strong ones, a survivor. It's a sick fantasy, really, a way to escape the fact that maybe she'd suspected something all along, but turned away from it. She just wants to stop feeling so guilty.

Reluctantly, she walks down the stairs. She needs some fresh air, some distraction, some way to get out of her own head. When she walks into the kitchen, her eyes fall to the floor and she is horrified. It's filthy. She grabs a stiff-haired brush, falls to her knees, and scrubs the linoleum.

She leans her whole body into each stroke, but as she moves across the floor, fleeting images pop into her head. Visions of Mr. Hiller who would put a hand on her shoulder for no reason, then let it linger a few moments longer than necessary. At the time it hadn't meant anything because lots of old men were odd that way. But what about the way his gaze lingered on certain girls, when he thought no one was looking? Or the way he'd become so critical in those last years, letting slip, to her parents, unusually harsh judgments on other students, even when Siobhan was in the room. It was as if he believed some people deserved to be punished.

More than anything, these comments had surprised her. But they seemed out of character so she just dismissed them. They were too inconvenient and threatened to dismantle the image she had of him. So she'd ignored them.

She grips the brush so hard that her fingers ache. Her whole body rocks with the motion as she scours the linoleum, as if she could wipe away all those years of denial, all her transgressions. But the floor is old and worn and no amount of scrubbing will ever make it shine. And Siobhan feels no better, even when her arms start to burn with the effort.

EVAN

AUTOMATICALLY, EVAN DRIVES TOWARDS BONNINGTON, BUT then half way there decides he can't face his father, so he swings a fast U-turn and heads back towards town. He feels cold, but sweat trickles down his sides. If only he could get Siobhan out of his mind. He can still see her standing there with her hand outstretched. He feels nauseous and swallows hard. How could she do it? Who is she, anyway?

He pulls into Lance's driveway and cuts the engine. He gets out and slams the door behind him.

There's no response to his first knock, so he presses his damp forehead against the cool glass of the new front window and peers into the dark interior. Nothing. Maybe Lance is running errands, he thinks, so settles down on the step. Idly, he tugs at a handful of the tall grass beside the stairs. A faint creak startles him and he glances behind, but there's nothing there. He turns his attention back to the grass in his hand and systematically rips it into smaller and smaller shreds as he tries not to think about Siobhan, then throws the bits onto the ground. He wonders if now he's lost a friend, too. She is not the kind of person who will slip in and out of his life without a ripple, the way he likes it. He runs fingers through his hair in frustration, then presses them to his face and breathes in the smell of grass.

"Come on, Lance, where are you?" he mumbles and uncurls from his perch on the bottom step. The front window stares into the wreckage of the house, tools and tiles and planks of wood strewn everywhere inside. Structurally, it's a fine building. Now if his friend could just get around to making it livable. If the place were Evan's, he'd be all over the renovations, he'd do it up properly, slap on a coat of paint —

Rectangular holes line the side of the house, with sheets of plastic taped over them. Through one small rip in the plastic, he spies a lump on a bed and, once his eyes adjust to the gloom, he makes out the dust-black soles of Lance's feet. "Hey," Evan hisses as he raps on the side of the house. "Hey, buddy." The lump doesn't move. With both fists, he pounds out a wake-up call against the wall, but gets no response. Shit, the guy's unconscious. "Lance!" he calls out as panic rises in his chest. "Buddy!" He strides through the overgrown weeds to the back door and rattles the handle, only to discover that it falls open with barely any resistance. He finds the bedroom, which is really just a space marked out by studs, and tentatively shakes his friend's shoulder. Lance barely lifts his head.

To hide his relief, he gruffly asks, "Are you sick, or what?"

"No, I'm not sick." Lance's voice is flat, deadened.

Evan lets out the breath he's held. "Well, get up, man. Let's go, let's . . . fix up that rocket," he says. "Yeah, yeah. Come on, get your ass in gear."

At first, Evan thinks Lance hasn't heard him, but eventually his friend rolls up to sit, pauses a moment with his head low, then hauls himself to his feet. "Okay," he says, but doesn't move. "Okay," he says again and slides one foot forward. He stares at it for a full minute. Evan places a hand against his shoulder and gently guides him along.

Together, they walk out to the patch of lawn where, under its tarp, the neglected rocket points forlornly towards the sky.

Evan whisks the tarp off, then tosses it aside. "So, what'd you say was wrong with it?"

"The parachute is, ah . . . " Lance begins, then stops to scratch his head. "It needs to be bigger. To compensate for the additional girth, due to . . . um . . . well, it's too big."

"Well, let's make it smaller."

"Wait a bit," Lance shuffles back toward the shed, flings open the door, and returns with his old toolbox. The clasp has rusted, but after a brief struggle, he forces it open. Inside tools lie jumbled together. On top, a crumpled piece of paper pokes out from under a pair of needle nose pliers. Evan picks up the pliers, then the paper. He unfolds it and squints at the penciled squiggles. "What's all this chicken scratch?"

"The central structural flaw that, ah, precipitated premature recover . . . " Lance stutters. "Uh, the engine lacked power . . . "

"So, it just needs more juice." Evan tosses the paper aside. "And a parachute and a new body." As he pokes at the cardboard shell, a rotten spot gives way under his finger. "Gross." He wipes his hand against his shorts. "Well, that seems simple enough, let's go get supplies."

After a long pause, Lance shakes his head. "I can't," he mumbles.

"Not this again."

"I can't face it." Lance presses his hands against his head and closes his eyes.

Evan grits his teeth. "Come on, man. It's just a *toy*." His head starts to pound.

"It's more than that, Ev."

Evan rubs his temples but it doesn't ease the tension. He taps his fingers against his thigh, his mind crowded with what he'd love to say to Siobhan, his mother, Gerald. Now here's Lance, freaked out over nothing.

"No it's *not!*" Evan explodes. "It's a lousy *toy.*" He's dimly aware he's not angry about the rocket at all, but he can't stop. "You even built it yourself, you just don't have the guts to finish it."

"No, no, no."

"You could do it, you know, if you'd get over whatever lame-ass hang-up it is that keeps you in bed all day, wasting your life." They stand there silently. Lance studies his feet while his lips work around the words he can't say. He won't look up.

"Ah," Evan says with a sigh and throws the pliers down. "I give up."

As he drives down the highway towards Bonnington for the second time that day, he glances at the rocky bluffs on his left. What he wouldn't give to go for a climb today, to think only of where the next toe-hold will be.

He crosses Taghum bridge and checks the osprey nest. No one home. Too bad he can't say the same about his mother' property. From the road, he spots Gerald's car and as he pulls in, he sees his father by the front stairs. Gerald bends over a makeshift sawhorse and cuts boards. The white pennant of his ponytail hangs down, partially obscuring his face. After he parks, Evan tosses the keys on the dashboard and takes a deep breath. He doesn't know how much more he can take. *What's he up to*, he wonders. From the road, he spots Gerald's car and sees his father by the front stairs.

Gerald tips up his safety goggles and turns off the saw. "Hey, there." For a second, his father looks tentative, almost nervous. Evan falters, bites back the smart-ass retort. Then

Gerald brushes sawdust off his arm and says, "So, you're back. About time. We need the place ready for Tuesday." He gestures at the gaping hole where the broken stair used to be. It doesn't matter what Gerald says, there's always a hint of blame in his tone. Finding fault.

Inwardly, Evan squirms. When he was eighteen, he'd built those stairs and been so proud. They'd held together just fine for the first few years. Gerald continues, "Your mother needs someone around who knows what he's doing. Give me an extra hand with this." Gerald passes him a plank of wood, which Evan reluctantly takes. The last time he and his father tried to fix anything together, Evan was thirteen and visiting him in Calgary. The gas line in Gerald's truck had a leak. In the time it took Evan to bring a rag out from the garage, Gerald had set fire to the engine. He'd needed a smoke, he said in self-defense, then proceeded to storm around in such a rage at the whole stupid situation that Evan caught the next bus and cursed his father the whole fourteen-hour journey home.

Now, Gerald shuffles pieces of timber around and barks out instructions. His face flushes with the effort and air wheezes out of his lungs. Evan feels a mixture of sympathy and admiration for his mother. It must take a lot of effort to be attracted to that.

Gerald has to do everything backwards, doesn't know a hammer from a hole in the ground. "Look," Evan finally says. "It'll work better if we nail these pieces together first."

"I know what to do," Gerald says and flicks his skinny ponytail over a shoulder. "I've been doing this kind of thing since before you were born."

"Where? In grad school?" His parents had met at university where they both were in the newly-formed women's studies program. Gerald had shocked everyone by staying at home with Evan in the first year while Hannah taught.

"There's a lot you don't know about me."

"You got that right." How *would* he know anything about Gerald, when the guy had never been around? And why would he bother to find out now? With one quick blow, Evan pounds a nail into the board.

"Not there!" Gerald bellows. "Aw, would you just listen before messing things up?" He grabs for the hammer but Evan won't loosen his grip on it.

First Siobhan, now Gerald. Everyone's out to piss up his leg today. He's had enough. "You don't know shit, Gerald. I built these stairs in the first place."

"And look who has to fix them."

The pressure behind his temples builds. This is what happens when he's around Gerald. He ends up saying and doing something stupid. Then he gets mad at himself and does more stupid things. When he has his wits about him, he simply keeps his mouth shut so that nothing stupid can come out. Around Gerald, he rarely has his wits about him. All the anger he's felt all morning combines with all he's ever felt towards his father and becomes an inarticulate roar in his brain. He reaches the same conclusion he always does: "Fuck off." He releases the hammer, grabs his stuff and steps over the gaping hole where the stair used to be.

"Don't disturb your mother," Gerald hollers after him and sounds too much like a father, too much like the man of the house.

Evan slams the door behind him. He strides through the house towards his old bedroom. As he passes the doorway of his mother's room, he notices her sitting by the window. He hesitates, is about to say something, then realizes her eyes are closed and her hands lie palm up on her knees. She's meditating. He tiptoes past.

Her quiet voice interrupts him. "You can come in."

For a couple of seconds, he stands in the doorway. The curtains are drawn and a candle has been lit. His eyes still dazzled by the sunshine outside, it takes a couple of moments before he notices the two framed pictures on the windowsill beside her.

"Where've you been?" She says and pats the bed beside her.

"I thought you always knew." As he nears, he can make out that one photo is of him and Kristy when they were twelve or so. They're in the backyard, and his arm is draped over her shoulders. He grins cockily and leans into her side. She stands upright, supporting him. In the second photo, Kristy looks a couple of years older, and has her arms around Gerald and India, the daughter of Gerald's last girlfriend. In both, Kristy's smile is instantly recognizable — that gap between the teeth in the front. The second photo puzzles him. He can't remember Gerald ever spending time with Kristy.

"When did that happen?" he says and gestures to it.

"The summer she stayed with her mother in Fernie. Remember?" That was the summer before their last year of high school.

"What was Gerald doing there? What did he have to do with Kristy?"

"Oh, they were always close. You knew that. He and India drove down from Calgary to visit with her."

"Close? What are you talking about? He never wasted a single thought on her. On any of us for that matter."

"Who do you think paid for her cremation?"

He stares at her, speechless. He'd never thought about it. He's about to disagree when she continues. "I had no money back then, Ev. You'd just graduated and wanted to go to university. It was all I could do to scrape together a little to help you out. And Sally . . . " She shrugs. Her sister Sally, Kristy's mother, never had money.

"That can't be true."

She lifts her hands up. "That's just what happened, Ev. What can I say?"

"But . . . " he stutters, then bites his lip, unable to conjure up proof that she's wrong.

LANCE: THE PROOF OF THE THEORY

LANCE LOOKS AROUND AND FORCES HIMSELF to focus on the rocket. Linda always used to tell him he was too indecisive. It's easier to endlessly ponder the options than to commit to one thing or the other. For all her dreaminess, Linda was a doer. Some time when he wasn't looking (or maybe when he'd been staring at the wall), she'd completed a certificate in communications, hadn't she? Then she'd thrown out everything that she didn't need (like him), got the job she wanted, moved on. Here Lance is still staring at the wall, at the rocket, off into space. When he thinks about it like that, Lance would have left Lance too.

You're wasting your life, Evan had said. This came as a surprise. Lance had always thought he was simply relaxed, that he took his time because, well, there was no rush. There was always tomorrow, and besides, he never quite felt up to it today. Or any other day. But maybe ten years *was* a long time.

But, no. How can he get on with his life when Kristy is dead? What right does he have to happiness, when he's responsible for her death? More than anyone, he knew how miserable Kristy was. Back then, he'd been so wrapped up in his own life, he hadn't stopped Kristy's from crashing to the ground.

Ever since the morning when he heard about her car crash, he's felt like he caused her death. Her life and his own became fused together in his mind, as if they stood on either end of the same teeter-totter. It had to be him or her, their combined fate balanced, and he'd pushed her down so that he could rise.

Even if this were true, well, here he is. He can't get away from the fact that he's still alive. Unless he commits suicide himself, or skateboards into an oncoming bus, he'll be here for a while longer. For the last ten years, he's quietly turned in circles, sunk down, like a screw into a block of wood.

He looks at his feet and sees a pair of pliers. He bends down to pick them up and spies the discarded piece of paper. Gently, he places the pliers in the toolbox and snaps the rusty clasps shut. It's true, he does need to fix the rocket, so that it can fly one more time.

With a deep breath, he unfolds the paper and ignores the tremble in his fingers. The smudged pencil lines tell him about the thrust duration of the motor, coasting flight, weight at burnout, and the ideal dimensions for the parachute. He checks the math and his mind creaks as he runs through the long-forgotten equation to check whether he'd got it right. Shit, he had.

He mulls over the steps needed to get the rocket functional again. A square metre of Mylar should make a big enough parachute for recovery. Only when Evan was there did he realize it needed more than a new parachute. It needed a booster engine. A super-sized, jet-propelling, kick-ass engine.

He chews his lip for a few minutes, debating. Then he forces himself to move his heavy limbs, coax his reluctant legs into action, until he's in the garage. It's easier when he doesn't think so hard about every step. With his brain purposely numbed, he climbs into the van, thrusts the key into the ignition and fires up the engine. *It's not like I'm actually doing anything yet*, he says to himself, *I'll just browse around the hardware store.* Nothing committed, nothing to fear.

By the time he finds a parking spot, he has enough energy to lift his head. He strides into the store, then heads for the aisle of screws and hinges and nails.

"Can I help you?" A polite voice calls from over his shoulder.

He turns and looks his former schoolmate in the eye. "Yes, Jason Lashinski, you certainly can."

EVAN

THAT EVENING, EVAN GOES FOR A long run, straight up the mountain. His thighs burn with the effort on the way up and his knees complain all the way down, but he relishes the feeling. By the time he gets back to the house, he feels almost light. He eases down onto the living room floor and works the kinks out of his muscles.

After a while, his mother falls into the couch behind him and turns on the TV. With a frown, she points the remote control at the TV set. She always holds it with both hands, in front of her chest, as if it were a sword that must be handled carefully. She folds her legs into the lotus position and places her hands on her knees. The screen lights up. Evan sits on the floor and leans against the couch.

"This show never makes sense, but I laugh anyway. It sure is a weird world out there," she says then sighs.

Evan squints at the screen, absorbed by the distraction until his mother destroys the moment.

"So," she asks, "how's Siobhan?"

"How should I know?" he grumbles.

"She's coming to the ceremony, right?" she asks. "I hope so. I want all your friends to come."

For a few moments they both watch the screen in silence.

"You know," he says as he cranes his neck to face her, "she wrote to Hiller while he was in prison." Laughter flutters in the background. "Can you believe it?" Bitterness swirls in his stomach and he grimaces.

His mother just presses her lips together into a thin, resigned line. "Well," she says with a deep sigh, "We all do things we later regret."

He glares at his mother. "How can you excuse her like that?" She lifts her hands in the air. "You can't forgive something like that," he says, "It's . . . it's . . . " Furious now, he leaps to his feet. As he strides out of the room, he nearly collides with Gerald.

His father, a steaming mug of chai in each hand, falters and steps backwards. "Whoa there kid," he says as Evan's shoulder brushes his own. "Relax."

Evan bites back a remark and leaves them to shake their heads at him.

That night, he lies on the narrow single bed of his boyhood room, and listens for that squeaky hinge, for the wind in the trees, for anything that will distract him, but it's unbelievably quiet. Though he strains his ears, he can't even hear the hum of the ancient fridge. Sleep is a long time coming and throughout the night, he tosses from side to side on the bed, unable to find a comfortable spot.

He can feel the closet filled with Kristy's clothes as if it were moving across the room towards him. He turns his back to it, tells himself he's getting as flaky and wierded out as Lance. No matter what he does or what he tells himself, its presence rises darkly behind his back. As he tosses, a mess of contradictory thoughts crowd through his mind. He tries to find a simple line through them all, but by the time the first light peeks through his window, he's ready to give up.

With a sigh, he throws off the covers, drags on a pair of shorts and walks out into the early morning. The geriatric dog from the property next door limps across the grass towards him and wags his tail hopefully. Evan pats his head and they walk down the dirt road. The dog hobbles behind on arthritic paws, half eager and panting with joy, half exhausted. Locks of matted fur hang from his sides and quiver as he ambles along. "What a galoot you are," Evan says to the dog and pats him on the head. "We need a long walk, buddy. That's what we need."

When he and the dog return, his mother is behind the house, with the chainsaw in her hands. A downed tree lies on the ground before her. Brilliant yellow safety goggles dwarf her small face and the kick of the engine almost throws her off balance. With one foot braced against the trunk, she lowers the whirring chain to the wood, her arms shaking with the effort, her mouth grim as if she were giving medicine to a child.

Evan walks in front of her and waves his arm. "Give me that," he hollers over the scream of the engine.

She turns the machine off. "What?" she yells and pulls out a bright orange ear plug.

He tugs the goggles off her head, takes the chainsaw from her and starts it up. He eases the blade down through the wood, but stops when she pulls at his sleeve.

"That's all wrong," she says, once the noise has died down. "Those are too big for me to carry."

"But you've got Gerald around now."

She rolls her eyes. "And look at him," she says. "Cut them half that size. Try to make the cuts clean. I hate splinters."

"Fine, fine. Whatever you want," he reassures her but she hovers by his elbow and watches the machine's teeth bite into the wood.

When he cuts the engine, he looks at the neat row of logs with satisfaction. "What are you going to do when this batch runs out and I'm not here?"

She sighs with weary tolerance. "I can do it myself, you know, but it's nice to have someone around, even if he's useless with power tools."

They are stacking the wood against the shed when Gerald appears. "Come take a look at the stairs," he announces proudly, so they follow.

With a flourish, he shows them the result: nothing perfect, but a set of stairs at least. Gerald bounces on the lowest step to test it and says, "Hey? Never thought an old guy like me could do it, huh?" Then as an afterthought adds, "With some help, of course."

"Not bad," Evan says, grudgingly.

"Not bad at all," his mother echoes.

HER PARENTS' CAR PULLS UP LATE morning. From where Siobhan sits in the living room, she can hear the engine cut. As she stares at the recliner across the room, the same thoughts run over and over on the tired treadmill of her brain. Evan's furious at her. He has every right to be. What did she do to Kristy? What has she done to Michael?

"Sweet girl!" her mother exclaims then looks her up and down. "You should be dressed, it's nearly lunch time." She holds Siobhan at arm's length and peers at her intently. "What's wrong with your eyes? You really should wear cover-up, sweetheart. A woman's best friend."

"Didn't sleep well."

"Well, it's just me and your father, thank goodness. But what if a stranger had come to the door?"

She takes the bag out of her mother's hand. While her mother updates her on the wonders of their weekend, Siobhan does her best to appear normal, then retreats to the shower with a mumble. Simply dragging the towel across her wet skin feels demanding. As she pulls on her clothes, her mind loops back to thoughts of Mr. Hiller. It's as if some detail is missing, and if she could just put her finger on it . . .

Once she's dressed, she searches for her mother and finds her in the kitchen unpacking what she'd bought on the way home. She holds up a jar of honey in its comb. "You know dear, you really should try — "

Siobhan cuts in. "Evan told me," she says without preamble, "that his cousin was one of Hiller's victims."

Her mother pauses briefly, her hand mid-air, frozen in the act of showing off the honey. "I can't say that I'm completely surprised," she says slowly and turns back to the cupboard. "Yes, what a mess that was."

"Why didn't you tell me?"

"Me?" She is startled, lays a hand against her breastbone. "I don't know if we knew. Not exactly."

"What do you mean, not exactly?" Siobhan presses.

"We didn't know what to believe back then. Albert was such a good man, don't you remember? Such a leader in the community. So respected and loved . . . " Under Siobhan's glare, she falters, as if flustered to find her meek daughter transformed into someone who demands answers. "I mean, there had been rumours going around for *years*. But it sounded like nasty gossip to me."

Siobhan won't let up. "How many years?"

"Oh." Her mother sighs and presses her lips together. She looks more like she's struggling to remember a recipe than anything else. "Since the mid seventies, I suppose. Around the time he started with the youth group." Now Siobhan's mother looks at her, imploring. "You have to understand, it was just too much to believe back then. So, no one thought about it much. The idea was so . . . " She brushes the air with her hand, clears away imaginary dust, a trifling fly, then looks down. "Though I'm sure the bishop must regret that he didn't step in early on."

Siobhan frowns, then turns around and walks back upstairs to her old bedroom. In her mind, she sees a clear image of the white-haired bishop. Livid, she wants to seek him out, indict him, yet at the same time knows she and the doddering clergyman have all too much in common. She wants to be angry at her mother but she is guilty of the same deed. She lies down on the hard mattress and closes her eyes.

Her mind is lost in a half-asleep wander, sad yet vaguely hopeful, when Lea throws open the bedroom door. "Mandy's gone into labour!" she cries.

Siobhan sits bolt upright and stares at her friend in alarm. "Get outta here," she exclaims. She'd half-expected this, but can't believe it's actually happening. Her thoughts spin like a top. Part of her still worries over the conversation with her mother, while the other part struggles to catch up to this new revelation. Waves of excitement, fear, and relief wash over her as she stumbles around the room. "What should I wear?" She looks down at her wrinkled T-shirt in dismay.

Lea grabs her arm. "Who cares? Let's go!" She is obviously more prepared for this moment than Siobhan. She opens a large, overstuffed bag. "Anyway, I've got whatever you need." One by one, she pulls out a cell phone, cardigan, night gown, water bottle, reference book, and a day planner.

"Lea!" Siobhan laughs. "What's all that for?"

"Oh I don't know," she says. "It just makes me feel prepared." She slings it back over her shoulder. "It's my security blanket."

As they sprint down the stairs, Siobhan calls out a goodbye to her parents. They climb into Lea's car. "Wait a minute," Siobhan says. "Are we really going to Mandy's house? I mean, she wasn't serious about wanting us there, was she?"

Lea stops fumbling with the key in the ignition and turns to her, stunned. "Of *course*," she says. "She wants us there. This is what you do for friends."

"But Lea, we'll just be in the way. Shouldn't this be, I don't know, private?"

Lea stares at her silently for a moment. "Are you worried for Mandy, or yourself?"

Siobhan scowls and lets out a frustrated grumble. "Daahh . . . We'd better get going then."

Lea's lips turn up into a smug smile. She starts the car.

After they park, Siobhan follows Lea up the back steps and into the kitchen. Mandy's mother stands over a pan of boiling tea. Even from across the room, the dark liquid smells bitter. "I told her this will help with the pains, but you think she listens to her mother?" she says to them before they're through the doorway. Her imposing presence instantly makes Siobhan feel like she's a child again. She smiles politely and listens for Mandy's voice, but hears nothing.

"Hello Mrs. Sweet," Lea says.

"Marion, please. And I went back to my maiden name years ago." With her mouth wide, she leans towards them conspiratorially. "I'm not Sweet anymore!"

Lea gives her a strained smile then glances sideways at Siobhan. "How's Mandy?"

Marion waves her arm towards the bedroom. "Go ask her yourself. She won't bite." As they sprint down the hallway she calls after them, "Well, in her state, she might!" and laughs heartily.

Mandy paces the narrow strip between her bed and the wall, both hands planted against the small of her back. Dark curls cling to her damp forehead. When Lea tries to coax her to lie down, Mandy brushes her aside irritably. "It helps to walk," she grumbles. "I *told* my mother not to be here," she says through gritted teeth. "She never, *ever* . . . " She doubles over and braces herself against the bed. "Oh God!"

Lea rushes to her side to rub her back. "Breathe," she says. "Just breathe through it."

"I can't," Mandy gasps. " . . . remember how."

"In through the nose, slowly now . . . "

"Where are the the midwives?" Mandy whimpers. "Where's Mick?"

Siobhan wrestles the bag off Lea's shoulder and steps back, helpless. Dread and panic settle deep in her guts, that awful sensation of being the wrong person in the wrong place.

"And why the fuck is my mother here?" Mandy eases up slowly, her face momentarily drawn until relief seeps back into her eyes.

As she watches her friend's face transform, something clicks in Siobhan. This is so *real*, immediate. This requires action. She is only useless if she chooses to be useless. She drops Lea's bag to the floor and says, "Don't worry about your mum."

"What . . . " Mandy is interrupted when two woman enter. "Oh Lisa! Ellie!" she cries. "I'm so glad you're here."

"Mandy!" Lisa sets two cases down in the doorway and gives Mandy a firm hug. Ellie's eyes sweep over the room, assessing the situation "Have the contractions progressed?" Lisa says. She ties her mane of caramel-brown dreadlocks back with a multi-coloured band.

"Oh shit," Mandy says. "I haven't been timing them. I've been . . . too panicked."

Lisa continues to ask Mandy questions while Ellie, with calm efficiency opens a case and unpacks it. Thermometer, baby- and mother-sized face masks, a blood-pressure kit, something that looks like an old-fashioned walkie-talkie, and surgical gloves are arranged top of the dresser. Once she's done, she looks up at Mandy and says, "How are you finding the pain?"

"Okay, maybe I'll go," Siobhan says and frantically waves Lea over. "Do you need anything?" she asks Mandy.

"Your camera," Mandy snaps.

Of course. She forgot it at her parent's house. "Come on, Lea," Siobhan says. "You heard her, she doesn't need us around right now."

Lea looks from Mandy to Lisa to Ellie, who sets up a lamp on Mandy's bedside table. Lisa smiles at them distractedly. "We won't be long," Lea assures Mandy.

Back in the kitchen, Mrs. Sweet — *Marion* — decants the dark, bitter tea into a canning jar. "I suppose with *those* woman taking charge," she says and gestures down the hall with a jerk of her head, "Mandy won't want this after all."

"You know, Mrs . . . Marion." Siobhan tries to make her tone as light as possible. "Mandy needs it quiet so she can concentrate. So we're leaving and . . . maybe we could give you a lift home too?"

"Mandy? Quiet?" Marion peers at her over the top of her glasses. "Mandy's never wanted quiet. Is she trying to get rid of me?"

"Not at all." Siobhan opens her eyes wide.

"No, no," Lea echoes. "We'll call you as soon as things . . . progress."

Marion wipes her hands on a tea towel and glances around the spotless kitchen. "Well, if I'm no use here . . . " She sighs heavily.

Lea gives Siobhan a sideways glance. "Mandy did ask . . . if you could wash all the baby's clothes. She didn't have a chance to clean them herself."

Before Marion can answer, Siobhan scurries over to the baby's play room, gathers up an armload of clothes, and carries them towards the back door. "We'd better get moving."

They drive Marion the few blocks home before she can protest. With cheerful waves, they say goodbye and back up the driveway. "Mission accomplished," Siobhan says.

"How do we stop her from coming back?" Lea asks.

"Good question. Barricade the door?" They stifle their giggles as they park by Mandy's house again. "Ack!" Siobhan slaps her hand against the dashboard. "My camera! Let's walk back to my house to get it," she says impulsively. "It's not that far, really."

"But . . . " Lea sighs. "Oh, all right." She chews her lip, obviously torn between loyalties to two friends. "I guess Lisa and Ellie know what they're doing," she reassures herself.

"Of course they do."

Together, they start down the hill. Siobhan's mind flashes back to the memory of walking with Evan, only two days earlier. How different it was back then. Her shoulders slump. What if Evan shows up at Mandy's, like she'd asked him to? How can she possibly face him? Then her mother's words from this morning echo in her mind, *We didn't know what to believe back then.* The sense of direction she'd felt at Mandy's evaporates and is quickly replaced with dread.

Lea searches Siobhan's face, then wrinkles her brow. "You look terrible," she says as if she's just seen her for the first time. "Have you been crying?"

"No," Siobhan says vaguely, then, "Mmmm, I talked to my mum."

"About?"

"Mr. Hiller, actually." She tries to say it in an offhanded way, but fails to keep the nervous edge out of her voice. She hesitates, but there's something she has to pry open. "You know when you want to pretend something isn't happening? But then you see someone else doing the same thing, and you get angry with them?"

"What are you pretending?" Lea asks cautiously.

"Oh," Siobhan says and kicks a stone down the hill. "Where do I start? I . . . " At this, she falters. Her heart hammers against her chest and she gulps at the air. "I'll tell you later," she says with a shaky laugh.

LANCE: THE ORIGIN OF THE UNIVERSE

BY THE TIME LANCE GETS THE message that Mandy is in labour, his new-found purpose has staggered to a halt. The efforts of the day before — when he'd followed Jason Lashinski through the store and chatted with him like a normal person — had left him exhausted. He sleeps in.

So it's early afternoon when he wanders into the living room and sees the light on his answering machine blink. For a change, he presses the button and listens to the message. The edge of panic in Lea's voice sends Lance into a downward spiral. Then he thinks of Mandy, and with her in mind, musters the strength to get into the van. *It's not like I'm actually doing anything*, he reassures himself. *I'll just hang out there.* He repeats this new mantra as he drives across town.

When Lance knocks, Mick opens the door looking slightly queasy. "It's going to be okay," he mutters, then holds out a beer. Instead of taking it, Lance slips over the threshold and tiptoes down the hallway. He hears voices coming from the bathroom, hesitates in the open doorway, draws in a deep breath, and wills himself to be brave. Armed with this thought, he steps inside.

A woman with a magnificent head of dreadlocks sits on the toilet seat, her legs crossed. On her arm, the lower half of a tattoo of the blue-skinned Vishnu peaks out from under the sleeve of her flowered sundress. A round-faced woman in jeans stands by the sink. Mandy sits in the full bathtub in her bikini top, her elbows propped up on the sides. Her curly hair is swept up in an untidy bun on the top of her head. When she spots him, she raises the mug in her hand in greeting. "Hey Lance!" she says cheerfully. "You made it! This is Lisa," she gestures to the woman on the toilet seat. "and Ellie," she waves a hand towards the woman leaning against the sink. Lisa twiddles her fingers and smiles. Ellie says hello, then turns to massage Mandy's shoulders.

"How . . ." He hesitates. "How are you?" Such an inadequate thing to say, but his mind has gone blank.

"Great! Now that my mother's gone." She sighs and eases herself back against a blown-up cushion. "You should go join the others . . . Oh!" She sits up suddenly and grabs Lisa's hand. Water splashes over the side of the tub.

He watches them for a few minutes. The three women concentrate on the strenuous work taking place in Mandy's body. Lance feels himself momentarily swept up in the almost palpable energy. Then, without a noise, he leaves them.

Back in the living room, Evan and Mick stand at the fireplace. They each rest an elbow on the mantel and grasp a beer in their free hand. "Hey," Evan says in Lance's direction.

"Hey," he replies and spies his beer stranded on the coffee table. He hasn't had a drink for years, not counting the wine down at the beach the night before. Right now, he needs one. For a few minutes, they sip and listen to the moans from down the hallway, until Mick slides a CD into the stereo and turns it up.

"So, like, you guys into percussion? I'm thinking of taking up the congas," Mick hollers over the throb of the African-Indian beat that fills the room. He and Evan fall into a discussion about the album. "This guy," Mick says and gestures to the speakers, "Trilok Gurtu, he's, like, amazing. He plays with Salif, you know."

Before Evan can answer, the front door bangs open. They all look up expectantly. Lea walks in first and calls out Mandy's name. She wanders into the living room with a questioning look. Siobhan follows and Evan grumbles as soon as he sees her. By the way Siobhan's gaze flickers over him, then darts away, Lance can tell something has happened, but their faces betray nothing.

"You want a beer?" Mick offers.

Lea continues down the hall towards the bathroom and Siobhan mumbles, "No thanks."

Evan turns away and picks up the liner notes. "Yeah, it's got a good groove," he says.

"How's she doing?" Siobhan asks as she perches on the arm of the furthest chair. She jerks her head towards the bathroom.

"Not bad," says Mick with forced calm. "We've got plenty of time yet."

"Well I'm just glad the traffic wasn't bad coming into town," Evan continues as if Mick had spoken to him. "Sometimes that stretch between Taghum and the bridge . . . "

Lance catches Siobhan's eye and she gives him a weak smile. While Mick and Evan discuss local traffic, he crosses the room and sits on the couch next to her, but can't think of anything to say. Instead, they exchange unconvincing smiles once again. Lea returns, takes in the circle of anxious faces, and perches on the edge of the couch.

"Ah, you're the teacher, right?" Mick says to her.

"That's right," she replies with a polite smile.

"Cool," he says and nods. With the determination of youth, he struggles to keep a conversation afloat. Lance finds the tension unbearable, especially since he can't place where exactly it comes from. Eventually, they loosen up enough for small talk. The tenuous peace is broken when Mick says, "So yeah, the baby's due on the twenty-seventh. That's what the midwife said. What day is it, anyway?"

Before anyone can answer, Lisa appears in the doorway and startles them all. "Could you turn the music down?" she says. "We're trying to have a baby here." Mick silently obeys. In the restored quiet, they hear Mandy cry out.

"It's the twenty-fifth," Lance says and they all turn to him. In two days, it'll be exactly ten years since Kristy died.

"Hey, a week early," Mick says into the still room, but no one answers.

After a few breaths, Lea presses her hands together and says, "Well, at least we'll have a happier occasion to commemorate."

"The trees have grown up by the side of the road," Lance says. "At her spot, you know, on the North Shore."

"Oh, not this again," Evan mutters.

"Well, we *are* here for both of them," Lea chides him. "Not just Mandy, but Kristy too. You can't avoid it."

Evan glances at Siobhan, whose mouth hangs half open. "We've talked enough about my cousin," he says.

Siobhan sits up with the look of a woman about to leap. "Ev, I — " she ventures, but he cuts her off.

"I've heard your excuses." The words hang in the air.

She persists, her voice quiet and determined. "I didn't *approve* of what he did, Evan," she says. Her mouth turns down at the corners to still her lips. "I wrote to him because I thought it was the right thing."

Evan turns to the wall and rests his elbows on the mantelpiece. "I know," he says heavily. Beside him, Mick scans the room as if he doesn't know where to look, then turns bright red. Careful not to catch anyone's eye, he slips out of the room.

Evan pays no attention, but continues to talk to the wall, "That's the problem. Hiller was a complete asshole, but you still felt sorry for him."

Lea lets out a small "oh," and falls back in her seat.

"Yes, he probably was an . . ." Siobhan hesitates, " . . . asshole. But well, I am too, because God knows, I've screwed up. Haven't we all?"

Evan turns to her, incredulous. "No! What he did was completely different."

She leans forward with her arms outstretched, palms up. "Well, that's just it." She searches his face. "That's what I don't know."

"I can't believe you!" He slams his bottle down on the mantel. "What's to question?"

"I'm just saying . . ." She slides down onto the couch, defeated, and rests her head against the back. "I'm not so sure."

"So," Lea says slowly. "You think he was innocent?"

Siobhan twirls a piece of her hair and stares at the ceiling. "No, I think *he* thought he was innocent. Or . . . " She screws up her face in concentration. " . . . he thought being a good Catholic absolved him."

"Why do we *care* what he thought?" Evan says bitterly.

Siobhan pries her gaze from the ceiling to stare at him. She furrows her brow, but has no answer. Finally Lance says, "Because we have to."

For a long time, no one says anything, except for Mandy, far down the hall. In the living room, they stare at the expanse that divides them while the afternoon sunlight creeps across the carpet.

Over a dinner of take-out pizza, Ellie and Mick teach them how to coach Mandy with her breathing. As first, Evan ignores them, but Mick jostles him in the shoulder and orders him to practice. Startled, Evan half-rises out of his chair, says, "What the . . . ?" and glares at Mick. The younger man's face fills with an earnest intensity. The others puff out their cheeks and exhale across the table, as if they were blowing out a giant birthday cake together. Evan settles down in his seat and tries it once himself.

"Not like that," Mick says, "or you'll hyperventilate."

As the hours tick by, they take turns breathing with Mandy. When Evan's turn comes up, he is terrified. The way Mandy grasps his hand so tightly reminds him too much of Kristy, years ago on the schoolbus. Mandy looks him straight in the eye for long minutes without blinking. The look in her eyes is far too intimate and otherworldly, as if she were a balloon and his arm the tenuous string that held her to the earth. He starts to wonder if she would completely forget to breathe if he weren't there. He's grateful when Lance takes over from him.

It turns out that Lance is the best coach. He never tires, never gets bored of the monotony of inhaling, exhaling, on and on, and can hold Mandy's gaze without a flicker of the eyelids. Night approaches and Evan wonders if they will be stuck together in this house forever, in a Kootenay version of *Groundhog Day*.

Then, suddenly, Mandy's mother arrives, the moans from the bedroom turn into screams, and everyone else runs around and tries to be useful. Evan retreats to the back step and stares up into the evening sky. The stars wink on, one by one.

The door behind him bangs open and nearly knocks him over. "Hurry up," Mick says, nervous and excited. "It's over already!" Evan stands so quickly the blood drains from his head and the backyard dissolves into bright points of light. He staggers after Mick sightlessly, bumps into someone's shoulder, guided by instinct.

In Mandy's room, a lamp sheds light on her face. Her mother and the midwives flank her, their heads bent low to the small bundle on her chest. They all squeeze around the bed. Evan has the urge to bolt, but can't take his tired eyes off the baby.

Lea is the first to speak. "A boy or a girl?" she says in a croaky voice.

"A boy," Lisa answers. "A big healthy boy."

Oblivious to the attention on him, the baby roots around with his tiny mouth until Mandy fills it with her breast. "That's it," she murmurs. His puffy eyes are squeezed shut and a smear of blood still clings to his soot-black hair. After a few minutes, his cheeks relax and he lets go of Mandy's nipple.

"I think he's asleep," Ellie says.

Mandy pulls the swaddling around him tightly, then lifts the baby to Lea, who willingly cradles him. "Oh," Lea breathes, delighted. "Oh wow."

Evan takes a step backward, hits the wall, and realizes he's inched away from the bed. Before he can slip away, Lea thrusts the baby into his arms and moves his hands into the correct position behind its tiny head. "Uh," he stutters, then looks down. The baby's face is relaxed, peaceful, unaware that he is being passed from stranger to stranger. He hardly weighs a thing, but Evan holds his arms rigid, fearful that the bundle will tumble to the ground and shatter into a thousand pieces.

When the baby's chest is still for a few seconds, Evan panics and lifts him closer. He feels a tiny puff of air against his nose and exhales in relief.

He lifts his head to see that they're all waiting for him. With a faint smile in Mandy's direction, he turns to Siobhan, and passes the baby to her. She lifts her arms to accept the weight.

TWO DAYS LATER, LANCE CALLS SIOBHAN'S parents' house — Lance actually picks up the phone and dials! — and tells her he'll pick her up in a bit. She doesn't have to ask why. She simply stands on the sidewalk and waits for his van to pull up. Lea sits in the passenger seat, so she clambers into the back. They don't say anything. Siobhan isn't at all surprised when Lance drives east, towards the orange bridge and the opposite shore of Kootenay Lake.

The road twists and turns as it follows the ragged shoreline of the lake. Driveways dart to the right and left of the road, and lead to tree-shrouded homes. With each curve of the highway, Siobhan's stomach knots tighter, but at the same time, she inches towards the edge of the seat in anticipation. They need to do this. She almost looks forward to it.

Lance pulls off the road at a spot just before a straight stretch and parks. Siobhan slides the van door aside and hops out onto the verge. She stares across the lake to the blue-green mountain that rises out of the far shore. The morning light shines in her eyes and tips the waves with white.

Lance gestures back at the road. "The skid marks faded after a couple of years, but they crossed the centre line around there . . . " He points to the right, then with his hand traces an arc in the air, through the grass by his side and the trees just down the bank, then out into the water. Siobhan remembers how the nubbly residue from the tires clung to the asphalt. They stare down into the lake, at the imagined entry spot on the water's surface. "Her car lopped off a couple of trees. There was a big hole here for a while. But they're pretty tall now, aren't they?"

Lance sits down in the grass and gravel that lines the highway. His legs dangle over the bank. First Siobhan then Lea join him. They look out at the cottonwood saplings before them, their leaves sticky with sap, and at the lake that glitters beyond. Siobhan tugs at a stalk of knap weed and rubs the purple flower between her fingers. Cars whoosh by and birds call out to each other. A slight breeze ruffles Siobhan's hair. They sit quietly until their breathing synchronizes.

"I guess we'd better go now," Lea says eventually. Lance stands up reluctantly and offers his hand to Siobhan.

Late that afternoon, Lea picks up Siobhan and they drive west out of town, towards Bonnington. Cars line the dirt road, parked in ditches and half way up the bank. Three women she recognizes as older versions of high school basketball players climb out of a car ahead. She waves at them weakly and struggles to remember their names.

"Let's see if Hannah needs help," Lea says as she balances a tray of homemade brownies in one arm and a plate of sandwiches in the other.

"Don't be ridiculous, give one to me," Siobhan says, and yanks the tray from her grasp. One after another, they walk through the open back door and encounter the few women crowded around the table.

"Oh wow, what a feast!" Hannah's familiar face emerges as she crosses the room. After she clears a space on the table and relieves them of their offerings, she gives them each a hug.

Siobhan holds her tightly for a long moment before she remembers to let go. "Ahh," she says into the awkward silence. "I like your dress."

Hannah looks down at the orange and blue rayon. "Isn't it fabulous? It's from that stall by the Balfour ferry." She laughs and pats Siobhan on the arm, as if to reassure her.

They wander outside, where a ring of chairs has been set up behind the house. For what seems like forever, they stand around and make small talk. "So what are you up to these days?" Siobhan asks one of the former basketball stars, who she finally remembers is Jennifer. She wishes she could go back to the empty spot by the highway, where they'd sat earlier.

She breathes a sigh of relief when Hannah appears. "We're just about to start, come on." She herds them towards the forest behind the house and calls out over her shoulder, "Ev! Gerald! Time to start!"

Jennifer joins her friends, who stand in a cluster and glance around nervously, as if they expect naked hippies and crystal-waving new-agers to leap out of the bushes. Siobhan spies a few familiar faces: a guy who used to smoke pot behind the school gym, a couple of Evan's cousins — she thinks their names are Jack and Sarah, though she only met them once, so she's not sure — and their old high school counsellor. Lance stands behind Evan, while Gerald joins Hannah. Evan holds a cedar box carefully against his chest. His gaze darts around, nervous, awkward, until it rests on the ground before him.

Though shorter than them all, Evan's mother is obviously the leader. In one hand, she holds a tall stick with a scarlet scarf tied to the top. "Okay!" she calls to be heard above the other voices. "There's a path, but if you get lost, just look for me." She shakes the stick and smiles to encourage them.

Siobhan pulls up the rear and follows the others up the path. As she picks her way through the underbrush, she remembers the many times she'd hiked up there with Evan, Lance, and Kristy. She feels much older now, old enough for regrets. She listens to the crunch of their footsteps. Twigs snap and trees rustle as the procession winds its way up the slope. After a while, the ground levels. Even in the afternoon heat, she can feel the cool air from the creek as they approach a clearing.

Hannah gestures for them to come closer. At her feet, hydrangeas and roses stand in glass jars around a small, square hole in the ground and a mound of dark earth. Beside it lies a granite headstone. Dirt clings to its sides and Siobhan wonders if it was the original marker they'd placed here ten years ago. When they are all assembled in a circle, Evan moves forward to stand near the hole in the ground. He hands the cedar box to Hannah. She holds it in her hands briefly, kisses the top, then eases it into the ground. She and Evan each take a handful of dirt and sprinkle them on top. With the back of her wrist, Hannah wipes her eye then looks up towards Gerald and Jack and Sarah and gestures for them to come over. One by one, they scoop up a fistful of dirt and let it fall through their fingers onto the cedar box below.

"Goodbye," whispers Sarah.

Hannah rests her hand on Sarah's shoulder and gives it a squeeze. She looks around at the small crowd. "Anyone else? There's dirt to spare." She laughs faintly through sniffles.

A few step forward. Lea tugs on her arm, but Siobhan hangs back. "Come on," Lea hisses in her ear.

Siobhan is embarrassed that tears fill her eyes. She can barely see. "I can't," she says.

"You have to," Lea insists.

Reluctantly, she lets Lea drag her forward. She bends down, takes a pinch of dirt and holds it over the soft mound that has formed. The soil is cool against her fingertips. "I'm . . . " she mutters under her breath. " . . . so sorry."

When they are all done, Evan pats the earth down with his hands. His head low, he presses his fingers into the soil until it's packed. Then he steps back to join the circle.

"I'm so pleased you could all make it," Hannah says and takes Evan's hand. "What a special day this is. I don't want this to be formal or anything, so I thought we could all just say what we want to say to Kristy, whenever the moment is right. So go ahead!" The former basketball stars exchange worried glances and shuffle backwards. They listen to the wind in the trees for a minute as Hannah searches the crowd for a volunteer. "Well, okay," she says, "I guess I'll get it rolling," but before she can, Gerald interrupts her.

"I'd like to say something." He takes a step forward, then turns to face the others.

"Oh." She hesitates, frowns slightly, then waves him on. "Oh, all right."

He nods and looks around with an air of authority, a grin on his face. "I first met Kristy when she was only six months old . . . or, maybe five months . . . no, it was definitely six, when Hannah and I went to visit Sally and Stan in Invermere." He pauses to pull on his beard. "Back then, they lived in a tin shack by the highway, and I'll never forget the sound of the rain on the roof. That little baby . . . well, she could have been seven months, now that I think about it . . . " He pauses until he sees Hannah frown at him. "Well, and that little baby had the loudest cry I've ever heard." He holds his hands against his ears and pulls a face of mock horror. "It reverberated between those walls until I thought I'd scream." He laughs at himself. Siobhan hears someone heave a sigh. "But I guess that was a sign that she was a fighter. Hmmm. Well now. We don't like thinking about the dead, not until we're looking into the void ourselves. You know, that face of Kali, the one who gives us life and yanks it from our grasp. No one wants to look at that. But," he looks up at the sky. "When a young life is extinguished, like a flame that's just been lit . . . " He scratches his head as he searches for the right word. "No, a match, you know, a spark . . . "

Evan steps forward and lays a hand firmly on his father's shoulder. "Thanks Gerald," he says loudly. Once their attention is turned to him, Evan hesitates. He looks to his mother, then stares hard at the ground. Siobhan's shoulders slump and she looks down at her feet. There is a long pause and Siobhan expects him to quietly step back. Then she hears his gruff voice. "Kristy was . . . ". Siobhan looks up, but Evan's eyes are lowered. "Kristy was the closest I had to a sister. And she annoyed me like sisters do," A few people chuckle quietly at this. "And . . . I, well, I ignored her." He takes a breath before he adds, "Because she was inconvenient." He bites his lip. "I've never forgiven myself for that." Everyone's quiet. Hannah squeezes his hand. The wind picks up and brushes past Siobhan's cheek. Hydrangea petals scatter across the carpet of pine needles, a constellation of blue dots against the dry brown earth.

On the walk down, Lance falls into step with Siobhan. "I've got an idea for tomorrow," he says. He takes her hand and tucks it into the crook of his elbow.

She holds on tightly to his arm. "Yeah?"

LANCE: PREFLIGHT

LANCE SCANS THE SKY AT DAWN. He notes cloud formations and the direction of the wind, but he waits until late morning before he calls Evan, Lea, and Siobhan. Then he loads the rocket and launch pad into the van. Still lightheaded from the events of the past week, he whistles while he packs a picnic lunch. *The world is a different place now*, he repeats to himself. Overnight, a tiny sliver of some new emotion has worked its way into his brain. He does not want to threaten its existence by naming it, so he simply goes about the morning rituals and hopes that the indirect light of activity and routine will give this new thing room to grow.

Last night, he'd finally decided on a launch site, an open field at the end of Blewett Road, on the other side of the highway. At a certain spot by the unpaved road, a path cuts up through the brush, up a slight slope and along to the field. It's not marked, except maybe by a cluster of chickory or knap weed, but Evan knew exactly where he'd meant when he'd described the place. The area is sparsely-populated, the field away from houses, so there will be few prying eyes. Or so he hopes.

As he pulls up, he recognizes Evan's mother's rusty hatchback by the side of the dirt road. Evan leans against it, arms folded over his chest. In his usual cool way, he makes no sign of acknowledgement apart from a nod then straightens as the van approaches.

"Good timing," he says as Lance opens the back doors. They reach in to pull out the launch pad.

Just then, Lea and Siobhan pull up. Lea bounces out of the car and waves her hand gaily. Today, she looks like she actually belongs on a dusty backroad, with faded blue jeans and hair wind-tousled from the drive. "So," she says. "What's my job?"

Behind her, Siobhan climbs out of the car slowly. She gives him and Evan an uncertain flicker of a smile. Lance catches her eye for a brief moment before he turns back to matters of the launch.

They decide that Lea will be in charge of recovering the rocket. This means that she must keep an unblinking eye on its ascent, then track its flight until it lands. They agree Lance should be the one to turn the ignition key.

Evan leads them along the path, the launcher balanced on one shoulder. Lance hoists the rocket, which is surprisingly light, out of the van. Lea and Siobhan carry the food, and Lea exclaims over the contents. "What's this?" she says as she lifts the lid of the basket.

"Pakoras, it looks like," Siobhan replies.

"Oh," Lea says with an undecided lilt to the syllable. "That's different."

As they walk, Lance explains to Siobhan how to test the rocket for balance. If it is properly balanced, when you swing it over your head, it doesn't wobble in its path. "Oh," she says vaguely. "I think you made me do that once."

Lance nods. After they walk for a few minutes, all he can hear is the swish of brush and crickets chirp, a high pitch like the whir of tiny machinery. It reminds him of the many times he and Evan hiked through the bush. In silence, they reach the edge of the field. The grass here is high and already dried by the sun. Only a slight breeze blows from the southwest. He and Evan stamp down a patch of grass, then set up the rocket. They run through the checklist with a calm, steady focus. Lance folds the parachute and carefully tucks it into the nose cone. Deep inside, the scrap of paper with the hastily scrawled equations lies tightly wadded, to adjust the centre of gravity. The rocket should fly straight this time.

SIOBHAN

LANCE INSISTS THAT SIOBHAN TEST THE rocket for balance. "You know what to do," he says. She protests, holds up her camera and says, "Let me photograph you doing it instead."

Lance shakes his head firmly and takes the camera away from her. "No," he says. "We all have our positions. This is yours."

"Oh, all right," she mumbles. She trudges out to the middle of the field with the rocket balanced across her forearms. Back in town, Mandy might be balancing the new baby in her arms right now, to test his weight. Or maybe she will tuck his scrunched-up face under her chin.

When Siobhan is a safe distance away, she stops and turns to face them. They line up in a row. She watches them carefully. All morning she has mulled over whether she is meant to stand apart and witness, just like she is now.

Then with a deep breath she lifts the rocket. Then with a deep breath she lifts the rocket. Dutifully, she swings it over her head, lasso-style. Sure in its path, the rocket whirls through the air above her. Lea claps.

LANCE: LIFT OFF

LANCE WATCHES SIOBHAN HAND THE ROCKET over to Evan, whose job is to mount it on the launch pad. Once everything is in place, the four friends stand far back along the edge of the field. The rocket stands straight as a yoga master, poised and ready. Lance holds his breath and bites his lip.

"Ready." Evan glances sideways at him. "Set . . . go."

With a barely audible click, the ignition key turns and the rocket disappears. In its place, a puff of smoke lingers. The smoke shifts in the breeze before Lance even registers that the rocket has lifted off. He joins the others who peer into the blue atmosphere. They all strain to locate a clear dot among the hazy cloud of particles. They hold their breath for a few moments and listen for it.

"I can't see it," Lea says finally as she looks this way and that. "Where'd it go?" Her voice rises, anxious.

His head tilted even further back, Evan squints. "You put a pretty powerful engine in there, buddy. Maybe too powerful for that little baby."

Lance holds his hand up to shade his eyes. "Yeah," he says.

THE MORNING THEY DRIVE BACK TO Vancouver, Siobhan wakes early and knows what she has to do.

Slung over a chair, her backpack hangs by one strap. After she scoops up the figurine of St Teresa and the letters, she shoves them in the pack, then slips out of the house without a word.

The Nelson cemetery borders the top-most corner of town, high above the glittering west arm of Kootenay Lake. Directly across, Elephant Mountain seems to rest quietly on its haunches. The walk is uphill all the way, but she welcomes the exertion. Rain begins, spatters her face as she climbs, and releases a dusty cement smell.

She has to admit, the cemetery is picturesque, surrounded by trees and dissected by curving roads. The setting offsets its morbid purpose. It's the kind of place she'd be happy to lie down in and rest a while. "Maybe not just yet," she whispers aloud, momentarily superstitious.

At first she wanders aimlessly and stops out of curiousity to read inscriptions or seek out the largest tombstones. Some are adorned with photographs printed on porcelain and covered with a hinged metal flap, hiding coyly. She lifts the flaps to find faces from the 20s, 30s or 40s, still fresh and wide-eyed.

What was so important about this person that they need such a great pillar after death? she wonders and rests a hand against the cool surface of a granite obelisk. Off to her left, a large cement promontory juts out of one slope and she hikes up to see which dignitary lies there. The monument is to a Catholic priest, but even she doesn't recognize the name.

When she walks back down the slope, she nearly stumbles over a small, flat plaque. Only when she glances down does she realize it's what she came for. It simply says, "A.T. Hiller, 1945 – 1999" but it brings her up short. She stares at the rain bouncing off the cement surface, hands useless at her sides. Finally, she hunkers down to trace a finger across the cast-metal slab. Her finger comes away smudged and she looks at it dumbly. Raindrops, persistent now, scatter the dirt and leave rivulets down her palm.

One of Mr. Hiller's favourite sayings was, "If I don't learn something new every day, then I'll know I'm dead." When she'd first heard him say that, it had sounded so profound. For a few weeks, she'd read an entry in the encyclopedia every night before she went to sleep, with the unspoken fear that if she didn't, she wouldn't wake the next day. She was so earnest back then, so literal.

She pulls the plastic figurine out of the backpack. In the mushy overcast light, its colours are duller than usual. St Teresa looks positively exhausted. With a firm shove, Siobhan presses the base of the statue into the dirt. Mud will splash it and mildew will bloom across its surface, but the plastic itself has a half life that will outlast the surrounding trees. Then she pulls out the letters and lays them down on the wet grass, but almost immediately picks them up again, worried they might get wet. Mentally, she scolds herself. She chews her lip and hesitates. Water runs down the trunk of a nearby pine tree and a squirrel in its branches flicks his tail indignantly. Off in the distance, a garbage truck gears down noisily and the sound bounces between the two mountains, across the lake.

What she most hates is that she has lost her childhood impression of Albert Hiller, her conviction that he was a man who could be easily defined. She craves the assurance of clear boundaries: black, white, good, bad.She hates to be proved wrong. For all these years, the small fist of her mind has hung onto that first impression as tightly as possible.

Reluctantly, she drops the letters back onto the grass, then stands quickly and lifts her eyes again to the trees around her.

Though the rain continues and water squishes between her toes, she wanders around and around the gravestones and plastic flower shrines. She wonders if Kristy would have preferred to rest here, but now that she's seen the clearing by the creek, she can't imagine she would. She peers through wet eyelashes at the rain drops until, with a start, she glances at her watch. Shit, she'll be late.

Vancouver, BC
October, 1999

SIOBHAN

SIOBHAN TAPS THE PEN AGAINST HER teeth as she contemplates
the envelope on the table before her. In addition to the stack
of promo packages that need to be mailed, black and white
photos lie scattered around, wanting only to be slipped into
the envelope. She has to admit, there are a couple of good ones.
Some are no better than snapshots but she's going to swallow
her pride and send them anyway because Mandy would want
them. They are the photographic equivalents of log-book
entries: who was there, what happened. All data, nothing
else. The artist in her shudders, but oh well. The handful of
photos that say more, that capture the really important things,
mollifies her. The mixture of awe and humility on Mick's face
as he holds the baby, who Mandy named Sebastian. Lance at
the back of the room, a shy smile on his face. Lea as she holds
the baby up high, gazing at him. She wants to be a midwife
now. And finally, Evan looking at her sideways, his expression
not exactly welcoming but not pushing her away either.

She slips the photographs inside the envelope and smiles
absentmindedly. The card itself is short. She's never been able

to say the appropriate thing at the appropriate time. The only phrases that come to mind are the boring, typical ones. So she starts off with, *Hey Mandy*, and hopes that sounds suitably non-specific and jaunty, like she just dashed off the note, and hasn't sat here for ages agonizing over what to say. *Here are some photos of the birth and the rocket launch.* That doesn't exactly cover it, in fact, it's pretty lame. She purses her lips and stares hard at the paper.

At first, Michael had been shocked when she'd broken up with him, but she sensed a tiny measure of relief, too. She had heaped the blame on herself, mumbled something about not being ready for a commitment, though that wasn't entirely true. One day, she'd figure it out.

They'd both been very good about it, as reasonable as possible given the circumstances. She'd helped him pack his bags and had carefully wedged foam chips around his still-shiny appliances so they would survive their eastward journey. All the while, she'd pondered whether it was really love they'd had, or simply an affection borne out of familiarity. Already, she could feel him slip out of her life, fade painlessly from her visions for the future.

Yesterday, she had driven him to the airport. She'd said goodbye with a kiss and best wishes for the success she knew he'd receive. He was doing the right thing, she could tell. If she were more ambitious, she would have boarded the plane with him. Instead, she'd smiled bravely and waved him off.

Now, she listens to the stillness of the apartment. With a sigh, she gives up all hope of writing a wittier note. If she doesn't get this into the mail today, it'll never get there. So she scrawls her name along the bottom and throws everything into the envelope before she can change her mind. Her tongue swipes the gummy seal when the phone rings.

"Hello," she says, the receiver pressed between her ear and shoulder. Into the silence, she repeats, "Hello?"

"Oh." The voice sounds stunned, uncertain. "I must have the wrong number — "

She drops the envelope in surprise. "Evan!" she cries and wills him not to hang up. "Evan, is that you?" A long silence answers her, punctuated by the distant sounds of traffic and the insistent beep of a walk signal.

"I thought I'd dialed someone else," he says, then adds in a defensive tone, "Your number's programmed into my phone."

She sighs. "I know. But hang on, please." She squirms in her seat, awkward, but wants to keep him on the line. "I, uh . . . " Damn, what was she going to say?

"I really should go."

"Thank you," she finally says.

This stops him. "For what?"

"For waking me up, I guess."

He takes a while to respond. "No problem," he mumbles. "Wait — it *is* a problem. *You* are. A big one." She bites her lip and listens. "It'll never the same again, Siobhan."

"I know. Just don't . . . please don't erase my number, yet. Okay?"

The line hums as he contemplates this. Passersby holler in the background. "I'll think about it," he says grudgingly. "I gotta go now. I'm meeting someone."

She breathes deeply. Well, it's enough for now. "Thanks, Ev. Bye."

"Bye." Then she's holding a silent phone against her ear. She stares at it for a while before she sets it down on the table.

She sighs, then, with brisk, definite movements, pushes her chair back from the table and grabs her wallet and keys. The sun casts a warm yellow light over her table, but it's that time of year when sunny days are precious for being numbered.

It's her first day of being single again and she suddenly has to get outside. She wants to know what it feels like, every minute of it, before it's all over.

LANCE FINDS SIOBHAN'S LETTER WHEN HE goes to Mandy's old house to pick up the last of her things. There it sits propped against the front door, one corner almost ripped through. Lance peers inside and glimpses some photos wedged between two pieces of cardboard. More manic recording, he muses, but can't wait to see them in spite of himself. Then again, ever since he invited Mandy to live in his house, he's thought very un-Lance-like thoughts. Like how yellow curtains would work better in Sebastian's play room than blue ones would, or how he's pretty good at renovations once he gets down to them, or how he could organize a baby shower. Okay, forget the baby shower. His swamiji would never approve.

With the envelope tucked under his arm, he opens the door. In the living room, lines of dust mark the edges of where the furniture had once sat. Tomorrow, he and Mick will clean while Mandy instructs them, and then they'll be done. He checks the list in his hand and squints at the confident loops and crosses of her handwriting. "Pans in the drawer under the stove," she wrote, and he heads for the kitchen. His hands are calloused from all the work he's done in the past couple of months, He hums under his breath as he stacks the pans.

He wasn't sure what Mandy would say when he'd first offered her the top floor of his house. He'd expected her to politely refuse, but once she'd wrapped her head around the logistics, she threw her arms around him and told him he was a doll. A doll . . . *Well, why confine ourselves to narrow definitions?* he asks himself. *I can be a doll. I can be a clown, a peanut, a superstar.*

Mick stays over whenever he can, and even does the laundry now and then, though Mandy complains about it. "He just jams as many clothes, diapers, and receiving blankets into the machine as can possibly fit," she said to Lance. "So my nice clothes come out smelling like vinegar and wrinkled all to hell." Meanwhile, Mick thinks he's done them all a great favour and lugs the laundry basket up the stairs with loud, virtuous sighs. "He's so eighteen," Mandy says, but smiles to herself.

Mandy and Sebastian — and Mick, when he's there — live upstairs. Lance wonders if he should build an upper deck to open it up. In quiet moments, as he lies in bed and listens to the floorboards creak overhead, he wonders whether there'll be room for Kristy. He knows it's ridiculous to worry, but he wants her to know there's a space for her. He thinks he'll build a guest room downstairs, next to his room, and install lots of windows to face the trees in the backyard. He bought a huge colour print of Kepler's supernova, one of those super saturated bursts of colour, and he'll hang it on the wall. Well technically, it's not a supernova at all, just a remnant, but he thinks she'll understand.

ACKNOWLEDGEMENTS

I would like to thank Keinan Chapman, Sara Graefe, Rick Maddocks, and Rita Moir who read previous drafts and offered invaluable feedback. David Morton answered my questions about model rockets and Sheryl Mair is my home birth expert. The Seven Sisters Writing Group have offered support and friendship over the years. I'm lucky enough to have my Australian comrades, Isabel D'Avila Winter, Michelle Dicinoski, Katherine Howell, Victor Marsh, Helena Pastor, Edwina Shore, and Anna Zagala, who keep me going. West Coast Smoke by Drew Edwards, Entanglement, by Amir Aczel, The Rocket Book by Robert Cannon, and A Handbook of Model Rocketry by G. Harry Stine and Bill Stine were useful resources. Fellow writers have offered support and recommendations at key moments for which I am truly grateful: Don Bailey, Lorna Crozier, Jack Hodgins, Billie Livingston, and Mary-Rose MacColl. Thank you to everyone in the MPhil CW department at the University of Queensland for making my time there so enjoyable and life-changing.

Many thanks to Morty Mint and Verna Relkoff of Mint Agency for sticking by me, and to the team at Thistledown Press for taking the risk. Thank you also to Harriet Richards. Jakob Dulisse kindly helped me out with the author photograph. I'm grateful to the community of Nelson for being so eclectic and eternally inspiring.

Without two people, this book would not exist. Amanda Lohrey, friend and mentor, waded through hundreds of pages of drivel and found the nugget of a story, then helped me to shape it into a novel. Clinton Swanson has read more drafts and has discussed the finer details of this story for more hours than a husband should ever have to. I can't thank either of you enough.

All errors are my own. If I have forgotten anyone, I sincerely apologise. It's been a long journey but well worth it.

ANTONIA BANYARD emigrated from
Zambia to Canada as a young child and
grew up in Nelson, British Columbia. She
has been published in literary magazines
and anthologies in Canada, the US,
England, and Australia. Her children's
non-fiction book, *Dangerous Crossings!* was
published in 2007 and received award
nominations from the Canadian Children's
Book Centre and the Ontario Library
Association's Red Maple Award. She has
degrees in writing from the University of
Victoria and the University of Queensland.
With her writer's group, the Seven Sisters,
she published two anthologies and
performed readings at festivals, schools,
and bookstores across BC. *Never Going
Back* is her first novel.